Marti Talbott's

Highlander Series

Book 3

(Taral, Ralin, Steppen, Edana, & Slava)

By

Marti Talbott

-

Editor: *Frankie Sutton*

Author's note: All of Marti Talbott's Books are clean.

TARAL

CHAPTER I

Laird MacGreagor's ancestor gathered his people, fought for a strip of land, built a village near a loch, and surrounded it with a wall and a moat to keep them safe. It was a pleasant place to live, with ample forests, good hunting, and plenty of grazing lands for their livestock. A wide, wooden drawbridge over the moat was raised at night and lowered each morning. The adjoining road led south with the loch on one side and a meadow on the other. A path from the meadow through the trees led to the MacGreagor cemetery, which had a fence around it to keep the animals out, and logs for visitors to sit on.

Beyond the meadow was a hill and beyond that, the land of the Camerons. On the other side of the loch lived the Fergusons. The very large and sometimes dangerous MacDonalds lived in the north, and the southern part of MacGreagor land touched the imaginary border with England.

Even with the deaths of women in childbirth, injuries that would not heal and various illnesses, year after year their numbers increased until they counted more than two thousand men, women and children. Through the generations, they had to fight to hold their land, and for that reason, the MacGreagor men kept themselves well trained and physically strong. Their rules were simple: every man looked to his laird for direction and each laird looked to his followers for support.

Yet the MacGreagors had a decree other clans did not have. No one knew which ancestor first spoke the edict or what happened to bring it about, but it was a good rule -- the penalty for viciously hurting a woman or a child was death, and Neil MacGreagor was prepared to impose that penalty without hesitation.

Nevertheless, not all dangers were the result of wars or men who could not control their rage, and not all destroyers could be conquered with swords and brute strength. The most terrifying killers came without warning and struck at all hours of the day and night.

*

What Taral MacGreagor loved most was the sunrise. Often it was cloudy and a misty fog covered the land, but on the mornings when the first shades of yellow began to light the world, it never failed to take her breath away. Careful not to wake her parents or her little brother, she dressed, slipped out the door of the small cottage they shared inside the wall, and looked up. The sunrise, she believed, was the face of God and it made her smile.

Dan got up early every morning too, but not to watch the sunrise -- to watch Taral. He discovered her habit quite by accident. As commander of the guards who watched over the MacGreagor Clan day and night, Dan normally stayed up late and did not wake until the bridge went down just after sunrise. Yet on that morning, something made him open his eyes and he could not go back to sleep. So he dressed, stepped outside his cottage and saw her.

Behind the stone and sod two-story keep, several paths led from a wide courtyard to a collection of cottages. His home was on the northern most path and Taral's was at the very end, near the shared vegetable and herb garden. At first, he thought something might be wrong, but then she looked up at the multicolor clouds that stretched all the way across the sky and smiled. Slowly, she turned to examine every inch, as though she had never seen a sunrise before, and her smile seemed to widen with each turn.

After that first morning, Dan never looked at a sunrise or at her the same way again. She had the most beautiful blonde curls hanging down her back and he wondered why he never noticed before, but then she usually wore it braided. Mostly, he liked her smile. The sunrise warmed her heart and her smile warmed his.

*

"'Tis not a question of who loves Taral, 'tis a question of who she loves. A woman has the final say." Neil kissed his wife's forehead and then sat down beside her at the head of the table.

The great hall had changed. Large colorful pillows were scattered about the room with more on order as soon as there were feathers available to stuff them. Fresh flowers decorated the small tables along the walls, and a large bowl of water with floating petals was centered on the long table in the middle of the room. Some of the tall-backed chairs had cushions for comfort and some did not. The same tapestries as before hung on one wall, but the collection of weapons on the other walls had grown considerably. Neil even managed to collect a three-pronged spear some said was owned by a Viking.

Glenna took an apple out of the bowl and offered it to her husband. She took the utmost care to be well dressed in her pleated blue plaid and long white shirt. The clan's mistress was just as becoming as any other woman, with blue eyes that often sparkled, and light brown hair that curled around her face when it was down. Glenna came from a very different clan in the far north, but loved her new home. "I doubt Taral knows how many lads desire her."

Neil took the apple and withdrew his dagger. He wore the MacGreagor colors of blue and white too, except his kilt only came down to his knees, and he had a patch of plaid over one shoulder. "How many do you think there are?"

The blue in his kilt served to bring out the blue in his eyes and Glenna always noticed, especially first thing in the mornings. She loved his dark hair, his large stature, and the kindness he always showed his followers. Matchmaking was Glenna's favorite form of entertainment, and she knew Neil enjoyed it too. "Six or seven, at least. She is pleasing, you know."

"'Tis not her appearance they find so appealing, 'tis her good humor. She smiles constantly and has a talent for making people laugh." Neil cut the apple into fourths. Then, he began to cut one fourth into tiny pieces for his daughter. Sitting on the edge of the table as usual, Leesil put out her hand, giggled when he kissed it instead, and waited for him to feed her. At almost a year old, she was learning to walk and looked more like her grandmother, Anna, every day. Someday, Neil would have to tell her who her real parents were and he dreaded the day.

"Aye and 'tis for that reason, Taral needs our help. If the wrong lad marries her, he will kill her laughter."

Neil stopped cutting and wrinkled his brow. "Kill her laughter? I do not understand."

"In our clan, a lad married a lass like Taral, but once she was his wife, he became jealous when her humor was admired by other lads."

"Did he hurt her?"

"Not the way you think. He told her he hated the sound of her laughter and said her jests were stupid. She believed him and became so distraught, grew quiet and rarely said a word. Everyone missed her humor and hated him for taking it away."

"He was the stupid one."

"Aye and it got worse. When she stopped talking and became glum, he no longer loved her. He could not see that his unhappiness was his own doing, and began to find fault with everything she did. Soon they were both miserable."

Neil went back to cutting little apple pieces for Leesil. "Was there no way to end their misery?"

"Not until he fell off a cliff and died. Some said she pushed him and no one would have blamed her if she did, but I doubt it. He may have been killing her with his words, but she would never have killed him. She truly loved him."

"Did she get her laughter back?"

"Aye, but it took a long time. My father made sure her next husband was a better lad. So you see, we must watch out for Taral. Making others laugh is a gift and 'tis up to us to make sure no one takes it from her."

Neil nodded and put another little piece of apple in Leesil's hand. He had a lot to think about, but most of it did not include Taral. Something was wrong with his marriage and he did not know what to do about it. Glenna was responsive when he held her at night. She smiled often and she loved their daughter, but not since their first kiss, had she reached out to touch him of her own accord.

He, on the other hand, could hardly keep his hands off her at first. He was completely in love with his wife and wanted to hold her and kiss her constantly. Yet it did not take long to see she did not feel the same way about him. Therefore, except for his morning kiss and having her in his bed at night, he kept his desires in check. He reminded himself she was forced to marry him, and maybe she just needed more time. Still, it had been months and more time did not appear to be the answer. To keep from dwelling on it and driving himself daft, he filled his day as full as possible, so night would come sooner and he could hold her again.

Glenna was very wise and taught him something new each day. Like every other man, he wanted children, but so far she was not with child and he was glad. The number one killer of women was childbirth, and the brave men who loved them were not so brave when the labor started. He wondered if it was the fear of childbirth that made her unfriendly. Or perhaps her parents did not openly show affection for each other, and the lack of it was normal for her. Perhaps there were a thousand reasons for her behavior and if he had the courage, he would simply ask her. Yet Laird Neil MacGreagor, leader of men and protector of women and children, was petrified his wife would say she did not love him, and that there was no hope she ever would.

CHAPTER II

It was Taral's habit to watch the sunrise, when there was one, and then help her mother with the morning meal. She was the weaver in the family and spent most of her day making cloth, but after the morning meal, it was her custom to go outside to wait for Patrick's sister, Steppen. As soon as Steppen arrived and Kindel came down the path using her blind stick to find her way, each young woman took a position on opposite sides to make sure Kindel did not get hurt.

From the time Neil first became the MacGreagor laird, he surrounded himself with his most trusted men. All of them were very young, very strong and very unmarried. Now, only Dan and Lorne were still without wives. Walrick married Kindel, Kessan was finally allowed to marry Walrick's twin sister, Donnel, Patrick married Jessup and Neil was married to Glenna.

Daily, the six men gathered on the landing outside the Keep so Walrick could watch Kindel, just in case she took a wrong turn off the bridge again. At least that was their excuse. There was little danger to Kindel as long as Taral and Steppen walked beside her. Lorne had his eye on a woman from the Ferguson Clan and Dan doubted anyone noticed it was Taral he liked to watch.

He was wrong.

Little got past his laird and a curious Neil couldn't help but ask as soon as the women were safely across the bridge, "Do you prefer her?"

Steppen was not yet old enough to marry, so it wasn't hard to guess who Neil meant. His question was unexpected, but Dan quickly recovered. "Nay, she is already married to Walrick."

Neil laughed. Of all his loyal advisors, he thought Dan was probably the most sensible. He was certainly too smart to let Neil pin him down in front of the other men. Dan was also the oldest and had a remarkable memory, which enabled him to keep track of hundreds of men at all times. It was no easy task considering the number sent out each morning to watch the dozens of paths and alert the clan to visitors, intruders, or danger. Indeed, Dan was a valuable member of the clan and he deserved a good wife. Yet, was he the right husband for Taral?

*

Taral did not know exactly when she put away the things of a little girl and began to think about a husband, but it had happened and she found it both perplexing and exciting. Mothers tried to teach their daughters how to choose wisely, but few daughters listened or truly understood the importance. Taral thought she understood and tried to be prudent.

Armitage lived outside the wall. She had not known him before and was surprised when he came one day to ask her to walk with him. He was friendly and polite, so she accepted and on that first occasion, he asked if she would walk with him on Thursday and Friday evenings, weather permitting. She agreed.

He certainly was not shy and always took her hand as soon as she stepped outside her door. His hair was as blond as hers and his eyes were nearly the same shade of brown. He was a good man, she thought, but he certainly liked to talk.

"As you know," Armitage began, "when Neil decided to build the towers, it was I he asked for guidance. I was greatly honored...and he liked the design and so I set about...and, of course, when I am not doing that...so I made sure everything was in good repair."

"I see." Taral nodded. It was true, she did see. After all, it was the third time he told her that story. He was proud of his work, but she wanted to talk of other things. "In this world, what do you love?"

"What?"

He seemed so completely confounded, she felt sorry for him. "I mean what pleases you?"

"You please me very much."

Taral managed to embarrass herself with that question and tried not to show it. "I do not mean that." She wanted to know what was in his heart, not what he could accomplish with his skills and therefore sought another way to ask her question. "When you wake in the morning, what things about this world delight you?"

"Well, I must say my cottage is very well built. I built it myself, as you know, and began it two years...then I put in the bed and after that I added places to..."

By the time they completed their walk, she was back home and exhausted by his answer. He was a good man, she supposed, but he was boring and when she thought he was about to kiss her, she said goodnight and went inside. The day would come when she would have to reject him, but her father wanted her to marry a man with good work habits and Armitage met that requirement.

Olson was the youngest of Taral's admirers and the most fun. He had no schedule and was prone to show up whenever the mood struck him. His looks were pleasing and he got so nervous around her, that he tripped over things, stuttered and once he almost knocked himself out on the low branch of a tree. Taral enjoyed walking with him very much just to see what he would fall over next. He made her laugh and to Taral, laughter was very important.

Still, it was unkind to let him linger when she was not truly interested in him. For most of the day prior, she sought the good wisdom of her mother on how not to hurt Olson's feelings. By the time he arrived, she desperately wanted to get it over with. She took his hand when he offered and walked with him down the path. "How old are you?"

Olson tried to make his voice sounded deep and manly. "I will be eighteen in the spring."

"You are not much older than I. Are you certain you want a wife?"

"I am certain I want you."

"But do you have a cottage?"

The young man blinked repeatedly. "I will build you one."

"How long will that take, precisely? Do you hope I will wait or do you hope I will sleep outside with you even when it rains?"

Olson looked deeply distressed. "Taral, I would never let you sleep outside in the rain. I love you."

His words softened her heart and made it even harder to reject him. Still, it had to be done. "Olson, you are a fine lad and someday you will make a good husband. But the lad I marry must already have a home for me. Wives often give their husbands a child in the first year and how will you shelter a wife and a child? 'Tis not just a cottage, 'tis all that goes inside, and then with a child…"

Olson stopped walking and took a long, labored breath. "You are trying to say you do not love me."

She looked into his eyes, lowered hers, and gave him one quick nod.

He was a man about it and smiled. "Perhaps if you are not yet married and I am older with a cottage, I will be back for you."

"Perhaps by then I will be pleased to have you back." He kissed the back of her hand, bowed and walked away. She was about to go back home when she noticed Armitage near the bridge frowning and watching her. She quickly tried to remember what day it was, but it was only Tuesday and she had no commitment with him for Tuesdays. She dismissed his frown and went home.

Other men smiled at Taral or watched her, she noticed, but she did not find them desirable enough to consider. Dan was the most mysterious and Taral was not completely sure he was interested. He did not ask her to take a walk, go riding or even go for a swim on a warm day, but sometimes when she stepped out to see the sunrise, he was there watching her. After the first few times she noticed him watching her, she began to think of the sunrise as her private time with God and with Dan. She liked that thought very much.

*

In a clan full of people, Glenna MacGreagor was lonely. After their morning meal, she normally left Neil to his duties and played with Leesil upstairs or went for a walk. At her request, Neil cut the number of her guards back to one and the guard spoke only when she asked him a question. It allowed her plenty of time to think.

She was the MacGreagor Mistress, and in the afternoon, she visited the women and tried to make friends, but she was an outsider. Her ways were different and the women seemed tense and worried that she would disapprove of them. She understood it was because they greatly loved her husband, but she was, after all, not just an extension of Neil. It seemed the harder she tried, the worse it got until she almost hated going out in the afternoons. She told herself it would take time, but it had been months and not one of the women had come to visit her or to invite her to take a walk.

She wanted to go with the women in the mornings to bathe. She wanted to talk about having children, gossip about husbands, laugh, cry, and do all the things friends do. She wanted to know why the other wives were with child and she was not, but she could not ask such an intimate question of just anyone. So she walked…spent too much time alone and thought too much…just to fill the long hours of her day.

Neil was no help. Every time she wanted to be with him, he was surrounded by people. Their home was an open door with men, women, and children constantly coming in and out. When she wanted to touch him, she worried someone would come in and he would be embarrassed. Men often stayed into the night and on those rare occasions when they were alone, Neil seemed distant somehow, as though he didn't really want her to touch him. So she kept her distance until she could lie down beside him and be in his arms.

Yet, when she was in his arms, he did not say he loved her -- so he must not.

CHAPTER III

The day began like any other day. Dan watched Taral walk with Steppen and Kindel over the bridge to the loch and waited with the other men until they came back. The men talked of battles, building things, fixing things and the tidbits of gossip the guards brought from other clans. Then they talked about women, which was always their favorite subject.

When Taral did not come back with Steppen and Kindel, Neil noticed and so did Dan. Usually, the fears of the men were unfounded, but there were always wild animals, accidents and MacDonalds to worry about. So when Neil leaned close and told Dan to find her, he did not hesitate.

He hurried across the bridge and turned down the path. Dan slowed as he neared the loch and cautiously looked through the trees for her. Taral was not still bathing and he was relieved. Instead, she was dressed and sitting on a large rock examining her shoe.

He carefully scanned the area to make sure they were safe and then walked closer, but she did not seem to hear him. Worried he would frighten her, he stopped several feet away, spread his legs apart, and put his hands behind his back. Even with wet hair, she was so pleasing he would have been happy watching her for hours. She sometimes wrinkled her brow and at other times bit her lip as though the problem with her shoe was the greatest in the world.

Finally, he cleared his throat. She quickly looked up and the sparkle in her eyes made his heart beat faster. "Neil sent me to check on you. Is your strap broken?"

His eyes matched the blue in his MacGreagor kilt, his skin was tan and the contrast with the white of his shirt was so striking, Taral almost forgot the question. "Not broken, but there is a tear. I was looking to see if I can sew it myself or if I will have to ask someone to take me to the cobbler."

"Neil does not like the lasses to be outside the wall alone."

Taral quickly looked around. A multitude of rocks, both large and small, bordered the jagged edge of water that reflected the crystal blue of the sky. A forest surrounded it and not far from the other side of the loch was the land that belonged to the Ferguson Clan. At one time, the MacGreagors were at war with the Fergusons, but that was many years ago and more often than not, the two clans intermarried and met at gatherings to enjoy each other's company. Even so, there was always a chance one clan would do something stupid and start another war with their neighbor.

There were no Fergusons, nor were any of the MacGreagor women still there and it surprised Taral. "I did not realize I was alone. Tell Neil it will not happen again." It was the perfect opportunity to ask Dan if he loved the sunrise too, but she asked something else instead. "You used to talk to me when we were younger. Why did you stop?"

"I believe I was seventeen and you were twelve. We had harsh words, you swore you would never speak to me again and kept your vow."

"How awful. What did we argue about?"

"I do not remember, but it must have been something very important."

Taral smiled. "Was I a horrible pest?"

"Aye, you were."

"I cannot promise I have changed."

That made Dan smile. "May I see your shoe? Perhaps I can fix it."

She nodded and when he came closer, she handed it to him. Then she felt an odd kind of excitement and quickly looked away.

"I can fix this."

"That is good news indeed." She took the shoe back, put it on and carefully tied the leather straps. Then she stood up and straightened the pleats in her plaid. "I do not ride well and hoped to avoid going to the cobbler."

"You do not ride well? How did you manage to grow up a MacGreagor without learning to ride well?"

"I perhaps ride well enough, but the truth is, I am afraid of horses. They are somewhat larger than I am." She started to walk down the path toward home and was pleased when he joined her, instead of following behind as the guards normally did. She couldn't remember being this close to him, at least not since she was much younger and his nearness was as exciting as his eyes. She took a chance and glanced at his face. It was oval shaped; he had a neatly trimmed beard and a nose that had not yet been broken in the warrior training. For that alone, she admired him.

"I did not think you were afraid of anything."

"What? Oh horses. Everyone is afraid of something. What are you afraid of?"

Dan grinned. "I am afraid of being stupid enough to answer that question."

She laughed and then looked down her nose at him. "You can trust me."

"With my life perhaps, but not with all my secrets."

She liked his quick wit and wanted to keep him talking. "May I ask you a question?"

"Aye."

"Are lasses allowed in the towers? I long to see the world from up high."

"I do not know. I will ask Neil and if he says 'tis all right, I will take you up. But you can see the world just as well from the top of the hill."

"Aye, but that is outside the wall. May I ask you another question?" This time she did not wait for him to answer. "Why does a lad desire sons more than daughters?"

Dan stopped walking and carefully considered his answer. "'Tis not because they love sons more, 'tis because they honor their father's blood. A lad's name is lost when his daughter marries, but his son carries both the name and the blood. 'Tis proof that we lived. 'Tis proof that the clan lived."

If he had asked her, Taral would have agreed to marry him on the spot. Finally, a man who could give a direct and sensible answer to a direct question.

*

His name was Gerald and he was the issue of a marriage between an Englishman and a woman from the Highlands. He therefore knew how to speak both languages proficiently, which was a good thing since his talent took him all over England and Scotland. He was tall, had sandy hair and light brown eyes. More importantly, he was a juggler, wore funny hats and made his living going from festival to festival. He especially loved delighting the children and usually got a hug or two from a little one in each village. To Gerald, who had no wife and no children to love him, a hug was better payment than a good meal, gold, silver or something of value to trade at the next festival.

It was in a port in the south of England that he became ill. As illnesses go, his symptoms were few and not severe. His skin turned a little blue, his throat hurt some, he had a bit of a fever, but no chills, vomiting or diarrhea. A couple of days later, he felt fine. However, he did seem to sneeze a lot more often than before.

Gerald moved on to the next festival, displayed his juggling, enjoyed a hug from a little boy and then packed up to move on again. Two days after Gerald left, the four-year-old boy woke his mother in the night complaining of a sore throat. The day after, the child's neck began to swell and the skin turned a bluish color. He suffered vomiting, fever, chills, diarrhea and still the worst was not yet.

The little boy barked his cough, began to drool and in the end, expended his last ounce of energy fighting desperately for a breath of air that would not come. The swelling in his throat cut off the airway to his lungs and his untimely death came just a short five days after his first symptoms. He was buried next to his little sister who had not survived birth.

Then in the night, his older brother woke their mother complaining of a sore throat.

*

She had only been walking in the meadow for a few minutes when Glenna spotted Jessup heading straight for her. She quickly put her hand up to stop her guard from interfering and let the woman come closer.

Jessup was not happy and it was easy to tell by the look on her face. "Do you speak English?"

"English? Nay."

"Therein lies the problem. I have no one to talk to, you see."

Glenna didn't understand a word, so she tried to understand what was wrong by reading the expression on the other woman's face. When she couldn't, she took Jessup's hand and tried to comfort her. "What is wrong?" she asked in Gaelic.

"Gaelic? Nay." Jessup had not been shy a whole day in her life and living with a Highlander husband like Patrick had not changed that. "We are in the same fix, I see." She looped her arm through Glenna's and started to walk with her. "I am so lonely, I feel like crying most of the time."

At last, a woman was talking to her and touching her like a friend. Glenna didn't know her language and it didn't matter. She wanted to smile, but Jessup was not smiling and she was worried about offending her. "I would like to help, but I do not understand..."

"I have a mother to think of, so I do not get out much, but I saw you here and thought, why not? You are a lass just like me and..."

As they drew closer to her guard, Glenna turned them in the opposite direction. He probably couldn't understand what Jessup was saying in English, but he sure could understand her Gaelic. She had a few things she wanted to get off her chest too, now that she had someone to talk to. "I am so lonely, I could..."

They walked and talked; Jessup in English and Glenna in Gaelic, neither one noticing that their husbands were watching them from the second floor window of the Keep.

CHAPTER IV

As was the custom, each time their mistress went outside the wall, the guards kept Neil aware of where she was at all times. So when he heard she and Patrick's wife were walking in the meadow, the men went upstairs to the window to watch. "I would give anything to know what they are talking about," Neil mumbled more to himself than to Patrick.

"Glenna keeps her voice down so no one can hear, but I can understand Jessup well enough. She has been complaining for days."

"About what?"

"She is lonely. The lasses do not understand her, she has no one to talk to, save me, and my English is not that good."

"Glenna does not understand English at all."

"I know, but neither of them seem to care."

"We should spend more time with them," said Neil.

Patrick nodded. He let the drape fall back down to cover the window and followed Neil out of the room. They were headed down the stairs, when an out of breath guard burst through the door.

*

The women didn't even notice them. Jessup and Glenna were both talking at once, laughing at times and nearly crying at other times, until their husbands suddenly appeared right in front of them. "How long have you been here?" Each asked in her own language.

Neil put his hands behind his back. "Wife, Jessup needs someone to teach her Gaelic. Would you be willing?"

Patrick put his hands behind his back too, but Jessup was not about to put up with that. She walked to him, planted herself at his side and wrapped her arms around him. "What is he saying about me?"

Patrick could never resist her and wrapped his arms around her too. Then they both noticed that Neil moved to stand by his wife, but they did not touch and in fact, did not even look at each other. "Neil is asking her if she will teach you how to speak our language."

Jessup smiled and reached out to take Glenna's hand. "Would you? I would be forever grateful if I could yell at my husband in more than one language."

Patrick smiled and as he interpreted, Glenna began to smile too. "Tell her I like her very much and I will be pleased to teach her."

Jessup let go of Glenna's hand and leaned a little closer to her husband, "Why do they not touch? Does he not love her?"

Horrified, Patrick clamped a hand over her mouth. "Neil speaks English very well, you know."

"Oh, I forgot."

Neil would have liked nothing better than to answer her, but with the nod of his head, his guards came out of the trees to surround their laird, his mistress, his second in command and Patrick's wife.

Glenna was instantly frightened and moved a step closer to her husband, "What is it?"

"Three MacDonalds crossed into MacGreagor land this morning." Neil paused while Patrick interpreted for Jessup. It was Laird MacDonald, Patrick explained, whom once had Neil kidnapped and meant to kill him before he escaped. After that, the MacDonalds were told not to enter MacGreagor land."

"Will you fight them?" Glenna asked.

"Not if we can prevent it. We will wait to see if they do it again."

"And if they do, then will you fight them?" She noticed the look of fear growing on Jessup's face as Patrick whispered in her ear and instead of her own alarm, she touched Jessup's arm to comfort her. Then she turned to hear her husband's answer.

"They out number us. We are better trained, but they are many more. If we go to war with the MacDonalds, we will need the help of the Fergusons and the Camerons, neither of which want a war. On the other hand, if we do not fight, they will see us as weak and attack."

"Why would they attack?"

"They lust after our land and our loch. For years, Laird MacDonald has tried to divert the water into his own loch, but we will not allow it. We need it, as do the English south of us. If the water dries up, the English will come to see why."

"Then we must fight either the MacDonalds or the English?"

Glenna asked.

Jessup straightened her shoulders. "The English will not fight us as long as I am here. I will go to the King and stop them."

Neil studied the look of determination in her eyes and then decided to interpret for Glenna. As he expected, Glenna looked thoroughly confused.

"She knows the King of England?" Glenna asked.

"Aye. 'Tis a long story and I will tell you, but inside. 'Tis not safe for you to be outside the wall just now." Neil held out his hand and wondered if his wife would take it. When she did, he was pleased. Patrick and Jessup were practically wrapped around each other and Neil wanted to do the same, but for now, his wife was holding his hand. It was not enough, but it would have to do.

Glenna was surprised he would touch her in front of his men. Her hand felt so good in his and she couldn't help but be jealous of the way Patrick had his arms around Jessup. What she would give for Neil to love her like that.

*

In London, Gerald attended four different festivals and three family gatherings. He heard there was a terrible illness sweeping across the south of England and he was grateful he was no longer there. Going steadily north, he decided, would be a good thing.

*

Dan walked Taral inside the wall, and then went to the Keep to find a needle and some strong thread. A few minutes later, he went to her cottage and it took him all of three minutes to sew the tear in Taral's shoe strap firmly enough to keep it from breaking.

"I remembered why we argued."

She sat on a chair outside her door with one shoe on waiting for him to finish. "I have been trying to remember too. Do tell me."

He tested the strength of the strap one more time and then handed the shoe to her. "We argued over your sister, Maree. You said she would never leave the clan no matter how much she loved Yule and I said she would."

"You were right."

"Aye, but being wrong was not what upset you. It was what I said after."

"Which was?" she asked, closely examining her shoe strap.

"I said a wife must always do what her husband says."

Taral giggled. "I hope you do not still believe that. If you do, I will be upset all over again."

He waited for her to finish tying her shoe and then offered his hand to help her stand up. When she took it, he thought his heart had stopped completely. No woman's touch ever made him feel that way, and for a second he had a hard time remembering what they were talking about. "I do not still believe that in all instances."

She narrowed her eyes and dropped his hand. Then she began to walk down the path hoping he would walk with her. He did and it pleased her greatly. "Let me guess. A lass must obey her husband when what he says is in her best interest."

"Exactly."

"And the husband is the one who decides what is or is not in her best interest."

"You are wise beyond your years."

She rolled her eyes, "I am curious, what sort of things would you not allow your wife to do?"

He was not sure how it happened, but she was walking with him, smiling and seemed to be enjoying his company as much as he was enjoying hers. The courtyard was filled with returning hunters, men carrying water in from the moat and horses being put in the stable for the night. When Neil and Glenna walked over the bridge from outside the wall, everyone stopped. It was not that Neil was holding Glenna's hand; it was the number of guards surrounding them that concerned the clan.

One of the guards walked to him and began to whisper in Dan's ear. Dan listened intently and then smiled at Taral to reassure her.

CHAPTER V

He began to walk with Taral again, but instead of crossing the bridge, he turned them up another path. It was then he noticed Armitage watching them. Dan was well aware of his competition and it was far from unusual for a woman to have more than one suitor. Men just normally expected it and tried to think of ways to outwit their opponents. Sometimes they challenged each other to a physical fight, but it rarely impressed the women. More often than not, the woman chose the loser over the winner anyway.

Armitage was a different sort of opponent. Dan did not care for the man's frown, and the way it was directed at Taral and not at him. He believed Armitage meant for his glare to intimidate her and it made Dan wary.

Taral wasn't thinking about Armitage, she was considering what just happened and it changed the way she thought about Dan. He was commander of the guards and she had forgotten that. Officially, there was no fourth in command, but if anything happened to their laird, Patrick or Kessan, Dan would probably move up. Being the wife of their laird's advisor was a worthy and coveted station.

It also meant that he would be on the front line of any battle and possibly the first to die. Marriage to Dan would not be the same as marriage to Olson or Armitage. If she were as anxious as some women were, she would stay clear of a man like Dan. Yet, how could a woman be practical when a man's nearness and his touch thrilled her heart so? Taral finally remembered to ask him, "Is something wrong?"

Dan stopped walking to study her searching eyes. Some men tried to hide the truth from their wives, but in his position, Dan needed a woman he could be honest with and talk to. This would be a good test to see how she would handle it. "Three MacDonald's crossed into MacGreagor land this morning."

"I see." She knew what that meant and there was no need to discuss it, but she could see the concern in his eyes. For his sake, she resumed walking and decided to get their discussion back where it was. Dan would have plenty of time to worry about the MacDonalds later. "I believe you were about to tell me what sort of things you would not allow your wife to do?"

He was greatly relieved. Taral did not panic. In fact, she didn't even flinch and he admired her for it. Not that it really mattered, he admitted, he was already madly in love with her. "Naturally, I would not like my wife to do anything dangerous."

"Oh, of course. What do you consider dangerous?"

"Everything she does when I am not with her."

Taral playfully smacked his arm. "I intend to marry a lad who will let me do just as I please."

"Even if it is dangerous?"

"Well, he will let me ride a horse and I can think of nothing more perilous. He will let me swim, walk in the forest and have his children. Then, if we are at war, he will let me fight right beside him. What could be more dangerous than that?"

Dan stopped walking again, turned to face her and looked deep into her eyes. "Good heavens, you are right. You have suddenly changed my whole way of thinking."

She rolled her eyes again. "Then you agree a wife is not required to always do what her husband says?"

"I did not say that." He started to walk again and turned away to hide his smile. The more they talked, the more he was sure Taral would be the right wife for him. Now all he had to do was convince her to marry him. He turned back, offered his hand, and his heart leapt when she took it.

"What exactly did you say?"

He was thinking about kissing her and having a hard time even remembering what subject they were on. "It will take a very long time to explain why a wife should do as her husband says. A lad is a very complicated creature."

"Not according to my mother. She says she can always tell what my father is thinking."

"She sounds very wise. Do they talk occasionally or does she just know?"

Without even realizing it, they had walked all the way up one path and started down another. She liked being with him and she liked trying to out-think him. Just now, he managed to change the subject completely. Taral decided to do the same. "When you went to the Keep just now, did you ask Neil if I could go up in the tower?"

"I did, but he is against it. He fears all the lasses will want to go and they will distract the guards. However, if you like I will walk with you to the top of the hill tomorrow."

"I would like that very much, but I cannot tomorrow. Armitage asked me to walk with him and I already promised."

"I see, another time then."

Taral felt a jab of regret and tried to think of a way to get out of her promise to Armitage, but it was a question of honor and she would never shame her parents by breaking a promise.

Dan was not happy to hear she would be seeing Armitage the next day, but he dismissed it as normal jealousy. He was hardly in a position to ask her not to see him. "How is your sister?"

"I have not seen Maree in months, but I am sure she is well. We would have heard if she were not."

"Perhaps I could take you to see her."

Taral was both surprised and pleased. "I would love to go. Can we take my mother and brother with us?"

"We can take as many as you like. 'Tis only a three hour ride to the Cameron hold and I promise to protect you from your horse."

She giggled and glanced up at the position of the sun in the sky. It was nearing the evening meal, so she made her excuses and hurried home to help her mother. She left so fast, she forgot to ask when they might go see Maree, but then she remembered she would see him in the morning when she watched the sunrise -- if it was not raining.

*

As soon as they were inside, Neil dropped his wife's hand. He answered Dan's question about letting Taral go up in the tower, and then took his seat at the head of the table to answer more questions and to hear what his advisors had to say about the MacDonald problem.

Jessup noticed the disappointment on Glenna's face and went to stand by her. She stared at Neil hoping he would see that he was ignoring his wife, but he didn't look her direction and the longer he kept his eyes away, the madder Jessup got.

Finally noticing, Patrick saw the look on his wife's face and rushed over to silence her before it was too late, "He is our laird, you must not..."

Jessup had fury in her eyes when she reached up on tiptoe and whispered her reply in his ear. "For your sake, I will be still. But know this -- even the King of England would not treat a wife this badly -- even one he did not love." She grabbed Glenna's hand and practically dragged her up the stairs. She waited for Glenna to open a door and turned to glare once more at Neil before she went in. He did not notice.

Glenna held back her tears. She had a friend finally and for that, she was thrilled. She watched Jessup examine the room and smiled at her muttering and her nods of approval. Then Glenna walked to the window that faced the loch and pulled back the drape.

The view excited Jessup and increased the size of her smile. She pointed, said the word "lake," and taught Glenna to say it. In return, Glenna taught her the word "loch" in Gaelic. At the other window, they taught each other the words for meadow and before long, they were touching items and exchanging the words. They laughed at Jessup's lack of an accent and Glenna's inability to speak without rolling the words. They were both laughing and having such a good time they did not care that their husbands and the other men downstairs had grown silent to listen.

"I could do with a touch of wine," whispered Glenna. She pretended to hold an imaginary flask to her lips and drink. Jessup enthusiastically nodded and that was all it took for Glenna to decide to go back down stairs and get some.

When she opened the door, she realized everything was quiet, so she slowly crept out to look around the corner and down into the great hall. Every eye was on her. She stood tall, straightened her skirt and held her head high as she descended the stairs. Then she walked across the room, grabbed two goblets, and the biggest flask of wine she could find, and headed back up. She only briefly glanced at her husband when she neared the top. "We are thirsty."

CHAPTER VI

Like the waters of the tide, the epidemic spread northward taking life from the young, the old, the infirm and then the men and women who tended them. Yet all did not die and some did not even get sick. It was a puzzle with no sufficient answer. Had Gerald, and others like him, known they were spreading the destroyer from place to place, each would have gladly plunged a dagger through their own heart. They did not know...no one did.

In the days that followed, Glenna learned two very important English words from Jessup. The words were "bloody" and "awful." The subject came up when Jessup arrived one morning to ask if Glenna wanted to go to the loch to bathe. It had become Jessup's habit to ignore the men in the great hall when she arrived and simply head up the stairs where she usually found Glenna playing with Leesil.

She opened the door to Leesil's room and closed it behind her. "Good Morning, Duchess." In English, Mistress was not such a good name for a woman, so Jessup nicknamed Glenna, duchess. And to you too, princess." She kissed the baby on the cheek and took a seat on the bed.

"Good Morning." Glenna wondered sometimes who was teaching whom. It seemed she was learning far more English than

Jessup was Gaelic.

"Do you want to go to the loch to bathe this morning?"

Glenna understood two words -- loch and bathe. She wanted to very much, but doubted Neil would let her. She lifted Leesil into her arms and went out on the balcony to ask. "Neil, I want to go to the loch to bathe with Jessup."

The men got quiet and waited for Neil to consider her request. There really was no way to keep her safe at the loch without sending guards, and that would be uncomfortable for both the men and the women. "Nay, 'tis too dangerous."

"Glenna turned to Jessup and shook her head."

Jessup rolled her eyes. "I thought my life was difficult, but yours is bloody awful."

Glenna didn't need to know what the words meant, she could tell by the look of disgust on her only friend's face. So she nodded to her husband and repeated them. "Bloody awful." She followed Jessup back inside Leesil's room and closed the door.

Jessup's words stung Neil. He thought their life could be better, but 'bloody awful' was the last phrase he would use to describe it. If this was any indication of how his wife felt, he had better do something fast or Glenna would make him keep his promise, take her back home and set aside their marriage.

"We could take them to the loch ourselves," said Patrick.

"Nay, we cannot chance it. Unhappy wives or not, the MacDonald would love nothing better than to get his hands on Glenna. I have seen this lad and he forces lasses. I will not let that happen to her, not as long as I draw breath."

*

War plans were a necessary evil and being prepared in case the MacDonalds were up to something was imperative. Where was the best place to fight them, how many lines of defense did they need and how quickly could they get word to Laird Ferguson and Laird Cameron if they were under attack?

It was midmorning before the words crept into Neil's mind again. 'Your life is bloody awful.' He looked up, but Glenna was not on the balcony and he realized he didn't know where she was. If she had gone outside the wall, he would have heard and inside there was little danger. Still, he had not noticed her leave. For a moment, he thought about going upstairs to look for her, but dismissed the idea. There was too much to do and a whole clan to worry about. She would just have to understand. He shared his noon meal with the men and briefly saw Glenna put Leesil down for her nap. Then, as soon as the meal was over he and his men went back to work.

*

Jessup's mother, who had no idea who or where she was, loved sitting naked on a rock in the water. She let Jessup wash her, while she splashed in the water like a child. The women loved watching her too. She had pure white hair, beautiful eyes and pink cheeks that made her look like an angel. She was never unhappy and at seventy-one, lived far longer than anyone in the clan ever had.

Dressing her in a plaid after her bath was something else again and Jessup was always grateful when someone offered to help. Yet this day, Jessup was very upset with Neil and could think of little else. She had half a mind to tell him what she thought, but then Patrick would be mad and she loved him too much to embarrass her husband. On the other hand, Glenna needed help and who else could do it?

There had to be a way to wake Neil up, before he slowly killed his wife for lack of attention. It was clear she loved him, but after days of visiting Glenna at the Keep, Jessup had no idea if Neil loved her. What a nightmare that would be -- married to a man who did not love you. She decided to wrap her arms around Patrick as soon as she saw him and never let go.

There was one thing she could do. As soon as she had her elderly mother down for a nap, she headed to the Keep to rescue Glenna. She slipped in the back door, walked right past all the men in the great hall, went up the stairs and found the duchess. Then she took her hand and slipped them both down the stairs and out the back door.

Neil, Glenna noticed, had no idea she was leaving.

They walked the paths for a while and then went to Jessup's cottage. They tried to learn more of each other's language and because it was taking such a long time, both became frustrated. So they just sipped wine and spent the rest of the afternoon together. It was, at least, somewhere for them to be and someone for them to be with. Glenna wondered how long it would be before Neil discovered she was gone.

*

It was difficult for Kessan to keep quiet. He grew up with Neil and thought he knew the man, but his actions toward Glenna were so far out of character, Kessan didn't know what to think. He believed they were perfect for each other and still thought so, but there was no affection between them. Something terrible must have happened.

When they were boys, Kessan would have simply asked what was wrong, but Neil was his laird now and a warrior did not pry into his commander's personal life. Everyone in the clan was concerned too and when they saw him holding her hand outside that day, the gossip spread that maybe they had solved their problems. Since then, however, the tension and restraint between their laird and their mistress seemed worse.

Glenna often walked out the door and Neil did not even look at her. Every other man in the room did and Kessan even exchanged glances with Patrick when Neil did not notice. A man in love always knew where his wife was, didn't he? Maybe he was wrong. Maybe Neil just did not love her or maybe she did not love him. On any other occasion, it would be prudent to just let them work out their own problems, but in times of war, a leader needed to be thinking with a clear head. It was for this reason Kessan planned to talk to Patrick, once Neil dismissed them for the day.

*

It was not unusual for guards to come in and out of the Keep to let Dan know the status on different issues, nor was it unusual for him to leave and come back. So when one came to whisper in his ear that Armitage was headed for Taral's cottage, Dan excused himself, hurried down the steps, around the corner of the Keep and across the paths to the wall. Then he climbed the ladder to the guard tower nearest her home to watch.

CHAPTER VII

Right on time, Armitage arrived to take Taral for a walk. The sky had been overcast all day and he decided they would sit on a log in the garden and talk rather than walk, just in case it started to rain.

She, on the other hand, wanted to walk the stiffness out after sitting most of the afternoon at her weaving loom. When he insisted they sit, she was not pleased, and when he offered his hand, she refused to take it. She failed to notice the flicker of rage in his eye.

"Why do you come to see me only on Thursdays and Fridays?"

Taral's bold question was so unexpected, he was taken aback. He waited until she was comfortably seated on the log and then sat down beside her. "I bring my wares inside the wall to barter on those days."

"I see, so you are saved the trouble of making a special effort to see me." She was trying hard not to let her irritation get the best of her. "Do you believe a wife must do everything her husband says?"

Armitage was having a hard time concealing his anger and shot her a warning glare. "'Tis best if she does."

"Why is it best?"

"Because a lad carries the responsibility for the family. 'Tis up to him to keep his family safe and well."

She did not like his answer. It was not sensible the way Dan's was. Instead, Armitage seemed stern and demanding, although the tone in his voice betrayed neither. "Aye, but what if the wife does not agree?"

"To keep harmony in her marriage, she…"

"Is she allowed to say she does not agree?"

"Of course she is, a lad does not own a lass."

Taral sighed her relief. Maybe she was judging him too harshly.

*

Dan was becoming more and more alarmed. He couldn't see the look in Armitage's eyes, but he could see the man's clenched fist. He quickly descended the ladder and started up the path. Behind him, the regular guard took up a position to watch and got ready to whistle the alarm if there was trouble.

*

Taral was not deterred. She really wanted an answer to her question. "Suppose a lass wishes to do the wash on Monday and her husband wants it done on Tuesday. Should she do as he wishes?"

"Taral, I do not understand why you are asking all these questions. Everyone knows the wash is to be done on Tuesday." If he saw the disdain in her eyes, he ignored it and instead grabbed hold of her hand. "I do not want you to walk with Olson or Dan. You are to walk only with me."

She should have felt some sort of warning, but she grew up in a world where women did not fear the men in their own clan. Besides, she was furious. It would be a cold day before a man told her whom she could and could not walk with. "What did you say?"

"I said, you are mine now and you will not walk with other lads."

Her first hint of danger came from the tight grip he had on her hand. "I wish to go home now."

"A wife must always obey her husband. You will stay until I take you home."

"I am not your wife."

He finally saw the fury in her eyes and looked suddenly ashamed of himself. "I am so sorry. I did not mean to upset you. I love you and I want you to be my wife. I should not have spoken so harshly and it will never happen again."

She looked down at his hold on her hand and when she did, he let go. She looked into his sad eyes and had mixed emotions. She might have loved him someday and she believed he was sorry for his actions. She was also relieved to learn the truth before she formed a more permanent attachment. "We will not make a good match." She stood up and was about to leave when he grabbed her arm.

"Why not?"

"Because I plan to do the wash on Monday. In fact, the day I do the wash will be up to me, not my husband."

"But we are betrothed."

"I have not agreed to marry you."

Her arm hurt and his grip was too tight. She looked from the anger in his eyes to the pain he was causing in her arm and back again, but he did not release her. "Let go of me."

"You will not walk with anyone but me."

"I will walk with whomever I please." She vaguely heard the guard's whistle and tried desperately to pull her arm away, but his fingernails were sharp and digging deep into the artery on the inside of her elbow. Blood began to drip on the ground.

From out of nowhere, Dan suddenly appeared by her side. "Let go of her!" Dan's eyes were fierce and his glare complete enough to make the man release his grip.

Armitage's face turned a ghastly color. "I did not mean to hurt her."

Dan's rage continued to build and his voice grew louder. "You meant to hurt her, do not deny it!" He put his hand on his sword and pushed Taral behind him where he could protect her if Armitage lashed out.

"I swear, I did not mean to hurt her."

"You lie! We are taught to cause great pain to another lad's arm just that way so he cannot draw his sword. We are also taught *not* to hurt a lass from the time we learn to walk." Dan was shouting now and having a hard time controlling himself. "I will kill you myself!"

"It will not happen again, I swear it." Other men were pouring out of cottages with their swords drawn and Armitage could see both Patrick and Neil running up the path toward him. Terrified, he started to back into the garden.

The veins in Dan's neck were huge, the muscles in his chest and arms were flexed and it was all he could do to keep from pulling his sword. "A lad who hurts a lass must die. 'Tis the way of the MacGreagors."

Taral was so shocked, she wasn't sure if she was seriously hurt or if the argument between the two men was upsetting her. Tears began to run down her cheeks, she grabbed hold of the back of Dan's shirt and leaned her head against him to steady herself. The next thing she knew, Neil had her in his arms and was carrying her away. Only he wasn't walking, he was running toward the Keep and yelling at the same time. When she looked down, her injured arm was in her lap and there was blood everywhere.

Neil raced down the path and then up the steps to the landing. He carried her through the door, across the room, sat her on the top of the table and quickly cleared everything off with his arm. Then he gently helped her lay down.

To Taral, it seemed like everyone was moving too fast. Glenna and Jessup were standing back with their hands covering their mouths. Soon, the motions of all the people hovering around her began to slow. Mayze was there handing cloths to Patrick, who was wrapping her arm too tight. She was oddly feeling tired and having trouble focusing. When she looked up, Dan was holding her other hand, smiling and saying something she didn't understand. She heard her mother cry out and then everything went black.

*

Dan carried the unconscious Taral to her home where she could die in her own bed. There was little hope she would live after losing so much blood, and it took forever to get it stopped.

Glenna and Jessup cried together, and then Jessup went home to take care of her mother, and Glenna went up to bed. She knew what Neil was about to do and she wanted to tell him she approved, but he was surrounded by his men. Just as many of the MacGreagor's did that night, she got on her knees and prayed first for Taral and then for the soul of Armitage MacGreagor.

*

Neil had not yet killed a man. Even in the war, the only blood he shed was that of his brother and at his brother's own doing. He waited for hours to see if Taral would live, not that it would make a difference. The sentence for intentionally hurting a woman was the same no matter if she lived or died.

He thought about his father's words and knew it had to be done. A man who has the evil in him does not change, and goes on hurting first his wife and then his children. If a laird loves his followers, he must rid them of the evil when it first comes to light. Hours passed and when he was certain he was not executing the man out of anger, he went to the wall, took down the sword that killed his brother and then went outside.

Waiting for him in the courtyard, Patrick and Kessan were already mounted and after Neil swung up on his horse, the three of them rode across the bridge, through the meadow, into the forest, up to the top of the hill and then down the other side where Armitage was being held.

Neil dismounted, raised the sword and with both hands drove it into the heart of the evil. Then he wiped the blood off on the man's kilt, went home and ordered the bridge raised.

CHAPTER VIII

Taral kept breathing.

When she woke up the next morning, she was in her own bed with her relieved parents, her brother and Dan by her side. Through the small window, she could see the sun was just beginning to spread its magnificent colors across the sky and she smiled.

"Would you like to go out?" Dan asked. When she nodded, he carefully lifted her out of bed and carried her outside to see the rest of the sunrise. He cradled her in his arms, held her close and put his head against hers. "If you will let me, I would like to spend the rest of my life making sure no one ever hurts you again."

She nodded. It was all she had the strength to do. Then he began to slowly turn so they could see the sunrise together.

*

More often than not, friendly clans shared a festival and in the southern part of Scotland near the ocean, Gerald showed off his ability to juggle four apples at the same time. It was then the children of Scotland first came to know the horror of the sore throat and the fever. The infection spread from person to person in as little as two days and killed them in less than six.

Those who lost loved ones felt helpless and confused -- for what sin were they being punished?

Farmers left their plows in the fields to make wooden burial boxes. Priests rode from clan to clan giving last rites, spreading what little comfort they could and hoping not to become ill themselves. Whole families were torn in half, uncontrollable tears ran down cheeks, and the killer in the night moved on.

*

Glenna was thrilled to hear Taral would live. She was ready to comfort Neil if he needed it after the execution, but when he finally came to bed, he just turned his back to her and went to sleep. She did not take offense. Her husband had to deal with the taking of life on his own terms and she had to set her feelings aside and let him.

Yet the next day, and the day after that, and the day after that, she was back to being so bored she wanted to scream. She stared out the second floor window of the Keep in the direction of the loch for an hour more, but there was little new to see. She wanted to walk in the meadow, pick flowers and fill the great hall with their sweet aroma. She wanted to bathe in the loch, she wanted…it was the same old list of desires and she was sick of it. Two women gave Leesil her bath and put her down for a nap. She could do it, but Neil said the women liked to help, so Glenna let them and endured her uselessness for yet another day. She wondered how Neil's mother stood the futility of her duties, and would have gone to the little graveyard where Anna was buried to think about it. She was still not allowed outside the wall. All the other women were, but not her.

Glenna MacGreagor was a prisoner.

She finally let the drape fall back and went down stairs. Then she walked out the door and turned up the northern path. She tried to smile at a group of children, but she didn't feel much like smiling. It would soon be time for the evening meal and most of the women were inside their cottages. The men were home or just getting home and their lives would be happy and fulfilled during the evening hours.

At least she was outside instead of waiting in their bedchamber for Neil to remember he had a wife. They would go to bed, hold each other for a little while and in the morning, it would all start again.

Glenna knocked on Taral's door to ask if they needed anything. Her mother assured her Taral was doing much better and there was nothing they needed. Glenna nodded and went into the garden. She swatted a bee away, smelled some fresh mint and picked a flower. No one came to talk to her.

Then she remembered Kessan showing her a hidden door behind the last cottage on the northern path, which happened to be Taral's cottage. Curious, she stepped behind the bush to see if she could find where to slip her fingers behind the rocks and pull the door out. To her surprise, it was easy to find and the door was not all that heavy. She pulled it away and leaned it against the inside wall.

She entered into the passageway, remembered to hold on to the top strap and pushed the other door out with her foot. At last, she felt like she could breathe again. She stepped out, set the outside door aside, and took a deep cleansing breath. Glenna wondered why she hadn't thought of this before.

On the other side of the moat, and for as far as she could see, the forest stretched out before her with its tall trees and thick foliage. She remembered Kessan telling her the path through the trees was the secret way to the Cameron village and it was that path the women and children used to escape the attacking Fergusons.

It was also the place three women were murdered during their war with Neil's brother. Glenna took a moment to remember them and wondered; if faced with the same danger, she would be brave enough to fight. Hopefully, her courage would never be put to the test.

Neil would probably not approve of her being outside the wall, but she doubted anyone saw her and there wasn't much danger of him finding out. Besides, she would go back in soon. On the other hand, doing something forbidden was probably the only way to remind him she was still alive.

Glenna suddenly scolded herself. When did she become so full of self-pity? Her life wasn't really that bad and could be a whole lot worse. Other women had a child every year, worked hard from morning till night and collapsed into bed hoping their husbands would *not* touch them. How dare she not count her blessings? It was time to do something constructive and stop waiting for the rest of the world to make her happy.

Sufficiently self-chastised, she looked down and noticed flowers growing on the two-foot ledge between the moat and the wall. She leaned over to pick one and the door moved slightly. She giggled and began to worry that she might knock the door into the moat and Neil would be furious.

Then she remembered Kessan saying they were supposed to keep the doors closed so their enemies could not see where they were. He told her to feel the rocks and find the smooth ones, which she did. Glenna laid the flowers down next to the wall to mark the place and put the door back in place. Then she decided to walk a little ways around the outside of the wall and look for more flowers.

*

He was exhausted when the other men left the great hall. Neil picked one up, blew out the other candles on the table and went up the stairs to bed. The MacDonalds had not come on their land for more than a week and Neil was convinced their infraction was just a mistake. Tomorrow he intended to let Glenna resume taking the walks she loved so much.

Careful not to wake her, he set the candle on the table and closed the door. He sat down in the chair and was about to take off his shoe when he realized his wife was not in his bed. Neil stood up, grabbed the candle and raced out the door. He looked in Leesil's bedchamber, then the next one and the next.

In a panic, he practically ran down the stairs. Then he stopped. Kessan and Patrick were sitting at the table watching him.

Patrick shook his head. "She is outside the wall, where she has been since before Leesil woke from her nap. She closed the secret door and could not remember how to get back in."

"And you did not help her?"

It was Kessan who answered. He liked Glenna and hated the way Neil treated her. "Do not blame us, she is your wife. Besides, she will not let us. She wanted to see how long it would be before you noticed she was missing. By now, she is probably plotting how to kill you and I am tempted to help her. 'Tis dark outside and has been for hours. She would not even let us take her something to eat. She said she would wait for you to care if she ate or not."

Neil leaned against the wall and closed his eyes. "Have I been that dreadful?"

Patrick walked to the door and held it open. "The clan is taking wagers on where she will sleep tonight. My bet is in the Cameron hold on her way back to her parents."

Kessan drank the last of his wine and stood up. "And I will take her, although you promised to do it yourself as I recall. Can you think of one good reason for her to stay?"

Neil slowly shook his head. "Which door?"

"The one in the very back." Patrick answered. "Go, I will stay with Leesil."

CHAPTER IX

Neil could have, and probably should have run up the path, but he needed to think of something to say to her. How could he not realize she was gone? When did he stop knowing where she was? Did he really need to plan a war or was it just an excuse to keep from thinking about his failed marriage? Did he stop loving her completely or just give up on wanting her to love him? He had plenty of questions and no answers. How could he find something to say to her when he could not even justify his actions to himself?

When he got to the wall, both doors were open. Neil took a deep breath and stepped through the passageway. It was pitch black outside and he could barely see her silhouette. He held out his hand, but she did not take it. "Glenna, come back inside…please."

She was tired of being outside the wall anyway, so she folded her arms, breezed past him, walked through the passageway and headed down the path. She could hear him put the doors back in the wall. In fact, it was so quiet she could hear his food steps behind her. The rest of the world was sound asleep, or so she thought.

People peeked out of windows and around corners. Glenna was going to let him have it, it was about time, and they all wanted to watch. As soon as Neil walked by, men and women began to ease out of their hiding places. They were ready to jump back out of sight should their laird suddenly decide to turn around. He did not, and as Neil followed Glenna up the steps and into the Keep, they got as close as they could to the doors.

When Kessan and Patrick came out, they too stayed on the steps to listen. Gossip could sometimes be very harmful, but the clans thrived on it, and third or fourth hand gossip, guaranteed the context would be scrambled. Once that happened, no one would be quite sure what she said, and this night, they all wanted to get it firsthand. The clan did not care what Neil had to say. What could he say, after all? Most of them guessed she would not let him say much and they guessed right.

Glenna headed straight for the table, grabbed a goblet and filled it with wine. Then she drank it down and glared at her husband. "I am not happy." Her voice was soft at first.

"I know. Glenna, I…"

"I am tired, I am going to bed."

"Fine."

He held the candle for her and was ready to light her way up the stairs. "I want my own bed." She refilled her goblet and drank it dry. The more she drank, the louder she got.

"Do you intend to get drunk?"

"I might. It has been a very long…and lonely night. Wine is exactly what I need." Glenna was getting so loud, the people outside no longer needed to lean toward the doors.

Patrick and Kessan exchanged hopeful glances. Yelling was a good sign. It is when a woman is silent that a man must worry.

Every man knew that.

Glenna was practically yelling. "At least the wine will keep me warm, which is more than I can say for my husband this night."

"Glenna, the whole clan can hear you."

"Neil, the whole clan knows you left me outside the wall for hours, and the whole clan ignores my existence just like their laird. The only one who will talk to me does not even speak my language! And the whole clan can see you married a woman you do not love. You have embarrassed and humiliated me long enough." She poured another glass full.

"Glenna, you are wrong. I…"

"I am not finished. I will remain your wife because I will not dishonor you, but I will live separately. I will bathe in the loch, I will walk without a guard, I will come and go as I please and I will not warm your bed." She took a moment to empty her glass again.

"Glenna…"

"I am not finished! If you do not like my terms, you can take me home and dissolve this bloody awful marriage." With no evening meal, the wine was having a faster effect than she thought. Glenna set the goblet down and walked to him. "Well, maybe I am finished." She took the candle out of his hand and started up the stairs. "Stay away from me, Neil MacGreagor, you no longer have a wife. You do not deserve me." As soon as she reached the top of the stairs, she turned, walked to the end of the balcony, went inside the bedchamber at the opposite end from his and closed the door.

The people outside should have been delighted. Glenna gave him what for and he deserved it. Yet now they realized they were as guilty as he was. Most of them hung their heads, and then slowly and quietly went home.

Kessan rubbed his forehead. "He will ask for our advice in the morning, what do we tell him?"

"I do not know." Patrick took a deep breath and let it out. "Did you notice the lasses were ignoring her?"

"Nay, did you?"

"Jessup said Glenna was lonely, but I thought it was because of Neil. We are all guilty."

"Aye and we must all make it up to her. I suggest we go home and see if our wives know what to do."

*

She could hear him pacing long into the night and she hardly slept either. Finally, she drifted off and when Glenna got up the next morning, the hour was late. She grabbed her washcloth and soap, and then went down the stairs where her husband and daughter were sharing their morning meal. She walked to the table, ignored him, hugged and kissed Leesil and then headed for the door.

"Glenna, can we…"

"Nay." She opened the door, walked out and let it close behind her. The bridge was down, the women were heading to the loch and she ignored them too. She wondered just how far she could get before Neil had someone stop her. She made it across the courtyard and just before she stepped on the bridge, she looked back. Neil had Leesil in his arms and was on the landing watching her.

Defiantly, she walked across the bridge expecting guards to

surround her at any moment. They did not, so she kept right on walking. When she reached the loch, she walked along the shore until she was well away from the other women. She had nothing to say to them and could not endure their looks of pity.

Again, she looked all around and then back down the path, but there were no guards and Neil was not coming to get her. The only ones at the loch were the other women, in different stages of dress and undress -- and different stages of pregnancy. Most of them were watching her.

She ignored the stares of the other women, stripped down, walked into the water, and submerged. It was so peaceful under the surface of the water she wished she could stay down forever. Then she wondered how long she could stay down before fifty or a hundred guards jumped out of the trees and into the water to save her. The mental image made her laugh and she quickly came to the surface.

Of course, Neil would never let his men see her naked. At least he had that in his favor. She used the soap to wash her hair and cautioned herself not to start listing his good qualities. She would give in to him eventually, but not before he sufficiently suffered. The man needed to be taught a lesson and she only intended to teach him this lesson once.

Her husband had no idea how lucky he was. Her mother would have knocked the wind out of him long before now and maybe that wasn't such a bad idea. However, her mother once broke her father's ribs, so she would probably never do that to Neil.

Glenna shook her head in disgust. There she was again, loving him instead of keeping her resolve. She put her head back to rinse her hair and closed her eyes.

It felt so good to let the water cleanse her whole body. At last, she could feel the sun on her face. At last, there was no Neil, no guards watching her every move and no women ignoring her. At last -- she was in the loch where no one could hurt her and no one could see her tears.

CHAPTER X

"Glenna?"

She didn't know anyone was so close and it startled her. For a moment, she wondered if she fell asleep in the water. When she looked, Taral was next to her smiling. "Should you be in the water with your hurt arm?"

"I do not know. I love the water and today 'tis unusually warm. When Neil is upset, he swims back and forth across the loch until he feels better. When my arm is well, I intend to try that."

"Are you upset still?"

"I can see his face. Armitage was so angry and when I close my eyes, I still see him. Do you think I will ever forget?"

"I hope so." Glenna held up her bar of soap. "Would you like me to wash your hair?"

"I would like that very much. Mother will help me brush it when I get home." Taral turned and leaned her head back. "When I was on the table in the great hall, I saw your face and it comforted me to know you were there. Glenna, please do not leave us. I know we have been cruel, but we did not mean to be."

"I never thought that of you."

"You came to see me last night and I did not go out to walk with you."

"Taral, you were hurt. I did not expect you to."

"Are you going to leave us?"

"Nay, I am just not going to be your mistress anymore." She waited for Taral to submerge and then helped her rinse the soap out of her hair. As soon as Taral came back up, she smiled. "Dan was very worried when you were hurt, do you prefer him?"

"I hope to marry him, but he has not yet asked."

"I like Dan; he will be a good husband for you."

"I should get out now, my arm is aching."

"Do you need help?"

Taral glanced at the other women and started to laugh, "Nay, but Jessup does. Her mother just tore out her pleats again. She does that every morning. Usually, I hold her mother's hands, but Jessup was afraid her mother would hurt me today."

Glenna smiled. "Jessup needs to sew the plaid. I will show her how." She got out of the water, helped Taral out, quickly got dressed and hurried over. She held the elder woman's hands while Jessup pleated her skirt again. Instead of starting to walk her mother back, Jessup threw her arms around Glenna. "I heard what you did, bravo, my dear, bravo!"

Glenna didn't understand the words, but the gesture was clear enough. They helped Taral dress and then the four of them walked back toward the Keep. Yet just before they got to the bridge, Glenna remembered she did not have to go back. She handed her cloth and soap to Jessup.

"I believe I will take a walk now that I am free. Will you keep these and I will come get them later?" She noticed the confused look on Jessup's face and quickly hugged her. Then she pointed, used her fingers on her arm to indicate a walk and turned down the road.

*

"Now where is she going?" Surrounded by his usual number of advisers, Neil was still standing on the landing with Leesil in his arms watching his wife walk down the road. If she keeps going, in a few days she will reach England.

"I doubt she cares." Patrick answered. "'Tis a bit terrifying to know she is out there alone, though."

"Aye, but I hardly have a choice."

"Perhaps I should take some weapons and a horse to her," Kessan suggested.

"Good, do that. Perhaps she will let you ride with her." They watched Kessan go to the stables, bring out two horses and put an extra bow and a flask of arrows over his shoulder. Then they watched him mount and ride out. In a few short minutes, he came back with both the horses and the weapons. Kessan looked at Neil and shook his head.

Glenna was getting farther away.

Dan was more interested in watching Taral than Glenna. He watched her come back over the bridge and thought she went up the path with Jessup. Then she reappeared, gave him a perturbed look, and walked over the bridge. Taral turned down the road and if she kept going, in a few days she would be in England too.

"Uh oh," he muttered. He slapped Neil on the back and went down the steps. "Glenna will let me protect Taral. Taral has agreed to marry me."

"Good." Neil took yet another deep breath and watched Dan run across the bridge and catch up with the women. They exchanged a few words; Dan dropped his head, turned and headed back.

Walrick caught his breath and watched three more women go across the bridge. "Good grief, Jessup, Donnel and Kindel are going too. This is your fault, Neil, do something."

"What do you suggest I do? Name it and I will do it." He watched Dan come back across the courtyard and take the steps two at a time to reach the landing. "I thought we were betrothed, but Taral says I did not ask her properly."

"How did you ask her?" Neil wanted to know.

"I said, 'If you will let me, I will spend my life protecting you,' but it appears that is not sufficient."

"It sounds sufficient to me," Neil said, and the other men nodded their agreement.

Patrick's wife was holding her head high and had not even looked his direction, "I wonder if I am still married?"

"So do I," grumbled Walrick. He could do little but watch Glenna and Taral wait for Jessup, Donnel and Kindel to catch up.

Neil was surprised. "I knew Jessup was unhappy, but why would Kindel and Donnel join them?"

Walrick rolled his eyes. "Kindel says I love you more than her."

"Donnel says the same," added Kessan. "They are right, you know, we do neglect them. I have not taken Donnel for a walk since I married her. Come to think of it, I have not taken her anywhere since I married her."

When Lorne, the shyest of them spoke up, all the men turned to listen, "I will marry a Ferguson soon. I was with her last night and she has agreed."

They congratulated him, but their hearts were not in it. Finally, Walrick said, "Before this is over, you may be the only one with a wife."

Neil waited to see if the rest of the women in the clan would go with Glenna. Yet they did not and he realized the unhappiness of the five wives really was his doing. His marriage was so unusual, he did not have to court Glenna at all or think about how to ask her to marry him. He supposed if it had been any other woman, he would have taken her for walks and tried to get her to fall in love with him. He spent time with his horse nearly every day, but not his wife and if she accused him of loving his horse more, he would have no way to deny it. No wonder she did not yet love him. He gave her very little to love him for.

*

Taral took Glenna's hand. "Where are we going?"

"I have no idea. I have never been down this road."

Taral wrinkled her brow. "You have not? Not even once?"

"Nay, not even once. Where does it go?"

"Well, it goes to some cottages and then it stops. At the end, there are three paths. The one to the west goes to the sea and the one to the right goes to another sea, although I have never seen either."

"Where does the one in the middle go?"

"England."

Jessup smiled, "Are we going to England?" She asked in English.

"England, Nay," answered Glenna. She decided they should start back and turned. Then she reached over and patted Donnel's arm. "You do not need to come with me, you know."

"I wanted to. I have neglected you more than anyone. 'Tis because of you I have my brother back and a good husband ... although I never see the lad."

Glenna giggled, "I see too much of him." She stopped walking and looked around. "Where should we go?"

"Can we go up on the hill?" Taral asked. "I love seeing the world from up there and no one ever takes me."

"Of course we can. We can go anywhere we want," Glenna answered.

With Jessup holding her arm on one side and Donnel on the other, Kindel felt comfortable walking at their same speed. She could still see some shapes, but nothing was clear any more. "Neil is very protective of us, but 'tis not his fault. His father was the same way."

"Kindel, do not excuse my husband. He has been very bad and he must pay." Glenna turned into the meadow and waited for the other women to stop laughing. "We must think of some way to get our husbands to spend time with us and not each other."

Taral agreed. "Once I am married to Dan, we will be sisters of a kind. We will all have husbands who love each other more than they do us. I have been watching and the husbands do not leave the

Keep until well into the night. If I am to be one of you, I best help you put an end to this before I am miserable with you."

"You are very wise," said Glenna.

"Well, wise may not be accurate, but I know what I want. Dan has not yet kissed me. Is that normal?"

Glenna answered, "You have not been well, you know. Perhaps he is afraid of hurting you. Besides, I hardly know what normal is."

Kindel started to laugh. "I had to tell Walrick to kiss me the first time. Men are so stupid."

"Aye," Donnel said. "They are stupid and too proud to ask us anything. So long as we fill his bed and tend his children, he is happy."

Jessup was catching only a few words, but she didn't care. She was thrilled just to be with women her age. She thought the men were probably watching them, but she refused to look up at the window. Let her husband worry just like the rest of the men. Whatever Glenna was planning, she was all for. Once they made it through the trees and reached the top of the hill, she helped Kindel find a rock to sit on and began to comb the ends of her wet hair with her fingers to dry it.

Said Taral, "'Tis beautiful from up here."

"Aye," Glenna agreed. "'Tis just like the story Ewing used to tell of an imaginary land. I was thrilled when I first came here. That was before I discovered 'tis a prison."

"What if I do not like it when Dan kisses me?"

All the women giggled at Taral's question and it was Kindel

who answered, "If you do not like it, but you love him, then you have to teach him. But you must not tell him, you must show him. It can take a while."

CHAPTER XI

The women were laughing and it made the men in Neil's bedchamber window watching them even more nervous. "They are planning to poison us," Walrick whispered.

Kessan rolled his eyes, "We will be lucky to live through the night. Neil, you have to do something."

Patrick sighed. "Thank goodness Jessup cannot understand them. Do you really believe they are dangerous?"

*

"Dan promised to take me to see Maree," said Taral. "She is my sister and she married a Cameron. 'Tis only three hours away. We should all go and give the lads time to miss us."

Glenna's eyes lit up. "That is a wonderful idea, but Dan can hardly miss you if he takes us."

"Then we should ask someone else to take us," said Taral.

"We should ask Patrick for Jessup's sake. She does not speak Gaelic yet," said Glenna.

"Aye, but Bridget Cameron speaks English. I say we leave them all behind."

Donnel nodded. "I agree. In fact, I say we go in the morning."

"I am hungry," Kindel complained.

"Me too, I have not eaten since yesterday noon." Glenna helped her stand up and then looped her arm through Kindel's. "An apple sounds wonderful."

Taral agreed. "That does sound good. I cannot do my weaving until my arm stops hurting, so if anyone wants to go for a walk later, you know where to find me."

*

Just as they broke through the trees, Glenna pulled Kindel to a stop.

"What is it?" Kindel asked.

"Our husbands are waiting for us in the meadow."

"How far away?" Kindel leaned closer to Glenna.

"Only a few feet."

"Do they look upset?"

"They have their hands behind their backs. I suppose that means they are not going to banish us."

Jessup wrinkled her brow, "What is wrong?"

Patrick tried not to smile when he answered her in English, "Kindel wants to know if we look angry."

"Oh." She did not mean to break ranks with the women, but if she wasn't close to Patrick soon, she would burst into tears. Besides, she needed him to interpret. As she hoped, he welcomed her into his arms.

"Glenna," Neil began. "You once bragged you could out drink me. Are you willing to place a wager on it?"

His wife narrowed her eyes, "What sort of wager?"

"If I win, you will try to love me."

"What?" She was so surprised by his challenge, she did not know what to say. "You want me to *try* to love you?"

"Aye, you have been my wife these many months and only once have you kissed me of your own choosing. And then it was only on the cheek."

"That cannot be true…can it?"

"Aye, 'tis true. You are afraid to touch me."

She glanced around at the others watching her and then sharply straightened her shoulders. "I am not afraid to touch you!"

"Then what stops you?"

"You are constantly surrounded by people. Do you expect me to get in line behind the children so you will hold me?" She studied the shocked expression on his face and then turned away. "You do not have time for a wife." She walked around him and headed for the bridge.

"Do you accept my challenge or not?" he asked, watching her walk away.

"I accept…you will lose."

"And what do you want if I lose?"

Glenna stopped and turned back to look at him. "I already have what I want. You are just too stupid to know it."

"She actually told him he was stupid?" whispered Jessup as soon as Patrick finished interpreting.

Neil nodded, "Aye and she is right, I have no idea what she is talking about."

*

He was unusually fatigued.

A warrior in the Forbes Clan, he planned this visit for weeks and looked forward to it. His sister was a Ferguson elder and the only family he had left. His wife had passed, his children lived far away, and he enjoyed seeing his sister, her children and her grandchild occasionally. Yet during the noon meal, he felt hot and asked if he could lie in her bed for a while.

In three days, he was dead and the Fergusons feared they were facing the dreadful plague they had heard rumors about.

*

Dan smiled and offered Taral his hand. "I thought you might like to see a sunset for a change."

"I would like that very much." She wrapped a folded plaid around her shoulders, stepped out and closed the door of her parent's cottage behind her. The sky was already beginning to darken in the east and the light, fluffy clouds had a tinge of purple and pink.

He guided her toward the back wall and leaned against it. "When I was a child, my father taught me all sorts of things. However, he neglected to teach me how to ask a woman to marry me." Slowly, he pulled her to him until he could take her in his arms. "You are very pleasing."

"Am I?"

"Aye. You are even more pleasing when you watch the sunrise. I want to see the sunrise and your beauty every morning. I want you in my arms at night and I want you to love me as much as I love you." He lightly kissed her lips and when she put her head on his chest, he languished in the feel of her in his arms. "How am I doing so far?"

Taral giggled. "Not so bad. You will be pleased to learn you must only do this once in your life."

"I am so relieved. Should I continue?"

"Please do."

"Will you marry me?"

"Aye, but you must promise to teach our sons how to do it."

"I promise." He kissed her lovingly and was about to kiss her again when he spotted Lorne coming up the path holding hands with a woman from the Ferguson Clan. She was a pleasant looking woman with a warm smile and a yellow Ferguson plaid. He stood up straight and waited until they approached. "Ah, this must be Dolak. We are pleased to meet you." His friendliness was rewarded by a light kiss on the cheek -- a kiss from an infected Ferguson.

*

Glenna sat at the end of the long table in the great hall with her goblet in one hand and a flask of wine in the other. She glared at her husband who was seated at the other end. "Shall we?"

Patrick, Kessan and Walrick sat on one side of the table with Jessup, Donnel and Kindel on the other side facing them. Patrick interpreted everything for Jessup in English, while Walrick described everything for his blind wife.

"You will sleep in my bed this night," Neil vowed through gritted teeth.

Glenna narrowed her eyes. "Not if I am still able to walk to my own without falling over the railing."

He filled his goblet, waited for her to fill hers and then drank it down. "You need not fear falling over the rail; I will carry you to my bed."

Glenna filled her goblet again. "'Tis I who will have to drag you up to bed."

Their guests switched from watching Glenna at one end to watching Neil at the other -- just to make sure he was keeping up with her. While they watched, Kessan made sure each of them had a full goblet of wine and they were happy to drink up as well.

It was the first time their wives had been invited to the Keep and when life was mellow again, Kessan thought he might suggest they all share a meal and an evening once or twice a week in the future -- when life mellowed out again.

"If you win, you have my permission to let me sleep where I fall." Neil saluted his wife with his goblet and then downed it.

"Thank you. I would grant you the same, but 'tis unnecessary. You will find me in my own bed come morning."

Patrick leaned around Kessan toward Walrick. "She will beat him. I have never seen him drink even this much."

"Aye, but he is much bigger. He will win," Walrick said and Kessan nodded.

"Care to make a wager?" whispered Patrick.

Jessup took a sip and then set her goblet down. "Isn't that just like a lad? He wants her in his bed and he has not even kissed her yet."

Neil glared at Jessup for a moment and then looked at his wife. He set his goblet down, stood up and walked down the length of the table to Glenna, while he interpreted what Jessup said. Then he pulled Glenna out of her chair, kissed her breathless, let go and went back to his seat.

As soon as she recovered, Glenna went back to glaring. "Not good enough, MacGreagor. You will not get me into your bed unless you out drink me. And that, we both know, you cannot do."

Kindel was beginning to feel the effects of her wine too. "Bravo, Glenna. Do not let him get away with a thing. Did he kiss her yet?"

Walrick rolled his eyes. "I was so shocked, I forgot to tell you."

Kindel patted her husband's hand. "Why were you shocked? All lads need to practice kissing."

"What?" He stood up, walked around the table, swooped Kindel into his arms and headed for the door. "If it is practice you want, practice you will get."

Glenna watched them leave and then watched Patrick and Kessan make their excuses and take their wives home. "Now see what you have done."

"Me?" Neil shot back. "What did I do?"

"You kissed me and shocked everyone, even me. I did not think you had it in you."

"I did not think you wanted me to."

"Of course I wanted to you to, I love you. 'Tis a pity you do not love me."

'Why do you keep saying that? Of course I love you."

"Do you? When were you planning to tell me?"

"I told you…did I not?" When she shook her head, he was stunned.

"You only want me to satisfy your lust."

The wine was making his head swim but her words cut into his heart. "I meant to say it." He closed his eyes and put his head down on the table. He really couldn't remember telling her. A few moments later, he felt her hand on his shoulder and it took his breath away. Finally, she was touching him. He sat up, pulled her into his lap and kissed her passionately. "I love you more than you will ever know. Promise you will never stop touching me."

"I promise." She got up, took his hand, and tugged until she got him to stand up. "Come with me, I will put you to bed before you pass out."

"Do you promise to be in my bed when I wake up?"

"I promise. I also promise not to tell anyone how easily I won the wager."

He smiled. "You are a good wife."

She put his arm over her shoulder and walked him toward the stairs. "And you love me."

"I do love you."

CHAPTER XII

The oldest died first. She was Jessup's mother and at seventy-one, her frail body kept death away for only three days after her fever started. When they laid her in the wooden box, she still looked like an angel. Then Patrick became ill and there was nothing anyone could do to help him. Just before her beloved husband died, Jessup memorized his face and knew it would have to last her a thousand years. She was devastated and once her mother and Patrick were laid to rest, a guard took her back to England.

When Dan got sick, Taral asked the priest to marry them so she could be in his bed at least once before he died. She did not conceive and therefore, there is no proof he ever lived. Taral did not become ill.

All the men, even the hunters put away their normal occupations to cut wood and build burial boxes. Once the plague did its worst in the eastern clans, more priests came to administer last rites and then move on to the Cameron and MacDonald Clans. Two of the priests unknowingly carried the germ with them.

Walrick buried his blind wife Kindel, his brother-law Kessan and his twin sister Donnel. It was more than he could bear, so he went into the forest to grieve and never came back.

Mayze and Dugan buried their little boy. Neil and Glenna

buried Leesil next to her mother and father, in the little graveyard with the fence around it that needed to be extended once more.

Before the last days of the plague ended, more than half of the MacGreagors were dead.

*

There came a stunned silence in the Highlands. It passed from clan to clan, made them forget about their wars and remember to be grateful for what little they had. Husbands who still had wives held them closer, children were loved a little better, and the people became more mindful of their God, his gifts and his sunrises.

After their grief subsided, another little life was conceived -- a life that would carry the blood of Neil MacGreagor and his father, Kevin MacGreagor, and all the generations before him -- a life that would insure the survival of the MacGreagor Clan. He would one day become a mighty warrior and a laird just like his father. And, somewhere, there would be a wife for him.

-end-

RALIN

CHAPTER I

Walrick wanted to die. His beloved Kindel was gone and there was no way to bring her back. He loved her even before she went blind and he had no doubt he would love her until the day he died -- which he hoped would be soon.

His twin sister Donnel was dead too, and so was her husband, Kessan. Yet losing Kindel hurt the most, so he walked into the forest to grieve that day and somewhere in the midst of his torment, his mind left him.

He sometimes walked, but in no specific direction. He sometimes crawled but to what he knew not, and sometimes he rode an unfamiliar black stallion that seemed to know and love him. Walrick paid little attention to the horse. His mind erased his thoughts almost before he had them, each heartbeat echoed his unbearable emotional pain and when his body hurt, he did not feel it.

He must have eaten for he was not dead of starvation, and he must have quenched his thirst for neither had that consumed him. He wanted to stop breathing just as she had. He wanted her illness, he wanted her in his arms, he wanted her…

And so he mourned until the space of six months passed and he knew not who or where he was.

At last, his heart rested, sleep came from physical instead of emotional exhaustion, and just before he woke, Kindel came to him in a dream. She was not blind and she was just as pleasing as he remembered. She took his hand, walked with him in a field of flowers and his heart filled with love instead of grief.

When he woke up, she was gone. He quickly closed his eyes and tried to get her back, but she would not come back. For a time he decided it was not a dream, it was a memory, but that could not be. He had not walked with her until after she was blind and never in a field of flowers. In his dream, she was happy, she was not suffering and she was alive. He reasoned then, that there had to be another existence -- a life after death he would share with her again someday. He frantically wanted to, so he believed it, and no one would ever be able to convince him otherwise.

He took a deep cleansing breath and, at last, he was at peace. He understood then, that he would not die and in fact, did not want to die. Slowly, he gave up the hope of seeing her again in his dream and opened his eyes.

He was not alone.

They wore kilts of an unfamiliar green and gold color with green shirts. There were five in all and none held their swords. Instead, they each stood with their legs apart and their hands clasped behind their backs. They wore shoes laced up to their knees, their kilts were a little shorter than normal and instead of a separate section of cloth, the strip over their hearts was part of their kilts.

Walrick rolled his eyes, turned over and tried to go back to sleep. "Go away."

"Nay, we cannot." Gelson was a big man at almost six feet, but none of them compared to the size of the giant stretched out on the large, flat rock before them. Both the kilt he wore and the one he slept on were blue. He was dirty, disheveled and probably daft, but they needed a man like him and Gelson was determined to find out just how daft the giant was. "We will have you as our laird."

Walrick did not bother to open his eyes, "You will not."

"Are you daft?"

With his back still to them, he raised a brow. "Aye."

Gelson was pleased and walked around the giant to look at his face. "He is not daft. If he were, he would not admit it." Gelson ran his fingers through his wavy blond hair and with a sparkle in his blue eyes, nodded to the other men. In unison, they started to pick Walrick up.

Yet before they could, he hopped to his feet, spun around and drew his sword. "Dare you touch me?"

None had ever seen such quick movements and certainly did not expect it from a man of his size. They were not afraid of him, however. Instead, the men exchanged glances of approval. As soon as Gelson went back to stand by them, they all knelt down on one knee.

"I am still dreaming," Walrick muttered.

Again, it was Gelson who spoke. "We give you our pledge. You will be our laird and we will be your followers. We will obey you, defend you and all that we have will be yours. Amen." The men rose up, drew their swords, brought them to their foreheads in salute, and then put the swords back in their sheaths.

He was ready to fight and if they killed him, he would not have cared that much, even though he just decided to live. Nevertheless, he had never heard of men drawing their swords without intending to use them and found their salute oddly flattering. "Who are you?"

"We are MacClurgs. We need a leader and you need a home."

"I am not a leader."

"You are leader enough for us. We have watched you for days. You are tormented by the loss of your wife, but you are a good lad. You do not kill except to eat and you do not curse God. You are a very good lad indeed."

Walrick could not believe his ears. "You have been watching me?" How had he allowed that to happen? Had he been so out of his mind he could not feel five men watching him?

"Aye, we have watched you for days. You need a bath. We were picking you up just now to throw you in the river."

He followed the man's gaze to a glistening body of water he did not know was there. Then he tried to think of the last time he had taken a bath. He could not remember. "I will save you the trouble." He put his sword away, walked to the water, sat down on the ground and unlaced his shoes. Then he stood up, let his weapons and his clothes fall way, and walked into the water.

It was cold and it reminded him why he had not chosen to try to drown himself. He caught the block of soap one of the men tossed him, quickly washed his whole body and his hair, and then tossed the soap back. He rinsed, got out and shivered. No wonder he couldn't remember taking a bath, this water was freezing.

The lad, who handed him a clean MacClurg plaid to dry off with, was little more than a boy and when he looked at the rest of them, Walrick could see how young they all were. As soon as he was dry, their leader handed him a clean shirt.

"I am Gelson. I hope it fits. My wife made the shirt for you and 'tis the biggest one she has ever made." He took the wet plaid out of the giant's hand and folded it.

Walrick took the shirt and put it on. It was indeed big enough. "How old are you?"

"I am the oldest and I am nineteen." Gelson pointed to each man as he introduced them: Mark is eighteen, Cobb and Austin are seventeen and Burk is the youngest at fifteen."

"You have been watching me for days?"

"Aye, we have watched you practice your warrior skills and tried to learn your ways, but we need you to teach us. You will be our laird, we will learn from you, and be a great clan someday. You may have your pick of lasses to marry."

Walrick could not comprehend it. They watched him for days and tried to learn his skills? He didn't remember practicing his warrior skills. He was daft ... he had to be! "Save your lasses. I will take no other wife." He put on his belt, pleated the second MacClurg kilt Gelson handed him and then noticed the smile on all their faces. "It means nothing, 'tis clean clothing and that is all."

"You wear our colors. You will be our laird," said Cobb.

"It means nothing," he repeated. Walrick sat down and started to put his shoes back on, but then he noticed his reflection in the water. His beard was straggly, his dark brown hair was far too long and he looked like some sort of lunatic. Even his blue eyes looked darker than he remembered. The MacGreagors, he thought, would have taken a broom to him for coming home looking like that.

Walrick slowly looked around. He was in a beautiful green glen. Forests lined both sides of the river and beyond the narrow meadow was the tallest hill he had ever seen. It was beautiful but it was not home. How far had he come from the MacGreagor hold? How many died after he left, he wondered. He had not meant to desert his clan and now he was ashamed of himself. He should go back. "What day is this?"

"'Tis Friday," Gelson answered.

"And the month?"

"January."

"January?" Walrick was so shocked, his mouth dropped. "Has the plague passed this way?"

"Aye, months ago. We lost many and are only two hundred now. All the clans suffered. Some lost as many as half."

"Half? How many did the MacGreagors lose?"

Cobb hesitated. "Who are they? We have never heard of the MacGreagors."

Walrick MacGreagor was lost. He did not know where he was or how to get home, but he did not feel overly distraught by the knowledge. As long as he believed he would see Kindel again, the rest of life was not worth getting upset over. He looked once more at the reflection of the mad man in the water, slowly withdrew his dagger and began to trim his beard.

CHAPTER II

His clothing was clean, his hair was trimmed and he felt almost human again. Yet when the black stallion walked to him, Walrick felt uncertain. He knew the horse had been with him for some time and remembered glimpses of being nudged awake or made to slide off near water so he would drink, but the horse was not his. Did he steal it? Perhaps not, the horse wore no bridle and as big as Walrick was, he could not have captured the beast without a bridle. Timidly, Walrick raised his hand and patted the animal's nose. To his amazement, the stallion put a front leg back, bowed and then straightened.

It made him smile for the first time in months. He grabbed hold of the horse's mane and swung his body up. Then he patted the horse on the neck to thank him for his loyalty, and smiled again when the horse nodded as though he understood. This had to be a dream. Yet it was a pleasant one and he hoped he would not wake up.

He looked again at the men. Each was now mounted on a horse, yet when he looked around earlier, he had not seen any horses. Again, he surveyed his surroundings, but the glen, the river and the hillside looked the same. There could be no other explanation; some of his mind was not yet clear. Maybe all of it was not clear. Just in case, Walrick charged himself not to make any rash decisions until he could sort things out.

Gelson moved his horse around until he was next to his new laird. "For now, I will be your second in command. Do you have a name?"

"I am Walrick."

"'Tis common, but a worthy name for a Scotsman. You have an accent that is different from ours, but we will get on with it soon enough. You are Walrick MacClurg, laird of our clan."

"If I choose."

"If you choose. But you must choose us, we need you."

MacClurg? What an odd name. Oh well, what did it matter what they called him. "Do you have enemies?"

Gelson nodded and as soon as the rest of the men fell in to surround and protect their new laird, he headed them down the glen floor and then up the side of the hill. "All clans have enemies. We are small, we are untrained and we are easy targets for the MacDuff and the Buchanan."

"You are two hundred? How many lads?"

"I lied, we are one hundred ninety six. One hundred twenty two are lads, forty one are lasses and thirty three are children. The plague took many of our lasses and children."

"Do not lie again," said Walrick.

Gelson MacClurg turned away and hid his smile. His laird gave him an order and he was pleased to hear it. Finally, they would have reliable leadership, not like the on-again off-again guidance Knox doled out. He wondered if he should tell Walrick about Knox and decided not yet. Let him see his new home and his people before they gave him the bad news.

*

He thought the land of the MacGreagors was beautiful, but nothing he had ever seen was as glorious as the basin of the MacClurgs. No wonder they had enemies. From the crest of the largest hill he had ever topped, the landscape below took his breath away. A jagged patchwork of forests and meadows stretched on for as far as the eye could see and there was not just one loch, but several. "How much of this is MacClurg land?"

Gelson threw out his hand expressively. "As much as we can hold. Most of the clans have more than enough land and we are not challenged often. We fight over more important things."

"What could be more important than land?"

"Lasses, cattle, horses and sheep…but mostly lasses. The lads will be happy to know you do not want a wife."

"How do you live?"

"We have small herds of cattle and sheep, and the hunting is good. Our gardens flourish, our children grow and we rarely do without, except when the river floods." Gelson pointed west. "That is our village."

Walrick had to squint to see it, but in the distance, he could make out several cottages surrounding a large stone building. "And where do your enemies live?"

Gelson pointed south and then farther west. "The people to the north and east do not bother us. They are small clans as well and like to farm the land. We often trade our fresh meat for their grain and vegetables."

"They are your friends?"

"They would like to be." He started his horse down the hillside toward home. "We would very much like to join our clans someday, but 'Tis complicated. When you become our laird, you will correct the problems."

"If...I become your laird." If? Was Walrick actually considering their offer? He never envied Neil's position as laird. If anything, he pitied the man his burdens and responsibilities. He admired Neil, yes, he loved him, that too, but did he want to become laird of the MacGreagors? Absolutely not. On the other hand, what else did Walrick have to do? These men were so young and probably did need someone to show them how to fight. At least in that regard he could be useful.

Walrick could not go home, at least not yet and he was not altogether sure Neil would have him back after he deserted the way he did. That was the truth of it finally. Walrick MacGreagor had deserted his laird. What an awful reality that was. Now he wasn't so sure he wanted his mind to clear. Wasn't there any time in the first few hours or even in the first few days after he walked into the forest that he thought about going back? Six months he stayed away. Six whole months and now he was cursed to live with the guilt of doing something he did not even remember doing. What other disastrous reality was out there for him to face? Had he killed anyone?

Suddenly, he was sitting on his horse in the middle of a courtyard. On the ground before him was a woman lying flat on her back with her hands tied to a stake. The stake was above her head, her pain was obvious, and her eyes begged his help.

Walrick's rage was instant. He slid off his horse, pulled his dagger and knelt down on one knee. With swift movements, he cut the woman loose, unbound the rope from around her wrists and surveyed the damage. Then he stood, scooped her up into his arms and turned to face the men. His eyes were cold and his glare was heart stopping. "Have you so many lasses you can foolishly tie them to a stake and let them die?"

None of the five men knew what to say and none of them had ever seen such anger in a man. They feared for their lives and dared not move.

Through gritted teeth, Walrick gave his second command, "Gather your people!" To his amazement, instead of whistling, all five men quickly dismounted and scattered in different directions. They called out names, pounded on cottage doors and begged the people to gather. Several refused to come and slammed doors in the men's faces.

The ones who did come walked cautiously into the courtyard in total awe of his size. Men, women and children gawked as they watched him stand the woman down, hold on until he was sure she would not fall, and then examine her wrists again. The woman did not speak. To her, the giant's eyes were kind and she hoped God had finally sent someone to deliver them from Knox. She hoped it very much and could not take her eyes off the man who saved her.

CHAPTER III

The woman's rope-burned wrists were not as serious as Walrick feared. He put an arm around her and drew her to his side. When he turned to face the small crowd, his fierce glare was back. "For what reason was this lass tied to a stake?"

Pretending to be unafraid, an older man with graying hair came forward and lifted his chin defiantly. "She committed adultery!"

Walrick turned on the man, stared into his eyes and made him take two steps back. "Is that all? She has not hurt a child or killed anyone?"

The elder dropped his eyes. "Nay, she has not."

Walrick looked beyond the elder and studied the people. The women and children, he realized, were too frightened of him and he did not mean to do that. Intentionally, he softened his expression and his voice, and then directed his words to the men. "A lass is the only means by which a lad can have sons, and a clan must have sons to survive. When a lass is harmed, the son she carries inside will also be harmed. As long as I am here, you will cherish your lasses and see that no one hurts them."

Men and women alike nodded their understanding, but the elder was not finished. "What punishment should we give her then?"

Gelson's excitement was growing by the second. That morning when they went to collect the giant, he feared this particular elder would be the hardest to win over. Yet now the elder was not arguing and was instead asking their new laird for direction. It was a better beginning than Gelson could ever have hoped for.

Walrick welcomed the elder's non-combative tone too and answered, "Let her clean up after the horses or do extra wash. Scorn her and do not speak to her if you must, but set a time. and when her penitence is ended, take her back in your arms."

Gelson smiled. "When you become our laird, you can see this does not happen again."

Walrick ignored him. "Where is this lass' home?"

Gelson pointed down a path and when the giant started to take the woman that direction, all the people followed.

"Is a lass more valuable than a lad?" asked Cobb.

"Of course not." Walrick stopped walking and turned to look back at the people. "Who has witnessed this lass' sin?" Just as he thought, no one answered. "Who is her accuser?" Again, no one answered. "She has no accuser?"

A woman's voice came from the back of the crowd. "Knox is her accuser. He is everyone's accuser and enjoys his punishments." The woman slowly made her way through the people until she stood right in front of Walrick. On each side, she held the hand of a twin, a boy and a girl, with curly blond hair and angelic faces.

Walrick could hardly take his eyes off the little girl and when she smiled, he returned it with one of his own. "Who is Knox?"

"He is my husband and believes himself to be laird of this clan. But we did not choose him and wish to be rid of him."

He turned his attention back to their mother. She was a pleasing woman with golden hair, but Walrick was not sure he could trust her. He was not sure he could trust any of them and a wiser man might have mounted his horse and ridden away. "You would turn against your own husband?"

"He is a cruel lad. I was forced to marry him and I owe him nothing. For the sake of my children, you must become our laird and rid this land of Knox."

"He is their father. Children must honor their fathers."

The woman scoffed, "He does not even remember their names. He married me to form an alliance, but he was tricked by my laird and I pay the price."

"If the clan does not wish this lad to lead them, why not cast him out yourselves?"

It was Cobb who answered, "Before our laird died, we promised to let the son live. We have cast him out twice, but he does not stay out and we cannot fight his guards. You could kill him, you have made no vow."

Walrick saw the mother glance behind him and noticed the look of fear on her face. He calmly let go of the woman he held by his side, moved away and turned around.

Knox was half his size and held a sword in his hand. He had bushy hair, a pointed brown beard, narrow eyes and a flat nose. His grip on his sword was feeble and Walrick guessed the man was half, if not completely drunk. His six fearless guards were fearless no longer. They took one look at Walrick's intense glare and began to back away.

"Get off my land," demanded Knox.

"You should put that sword away before you hurt yourself."

"You dare mock me?" said Knox.

"I do."

It was not the answer Knox expected and it took him aback. Slowly, he regained his composure and steadied his resolve. "Do you mean to challenge me?"

Walrick did not waste another glare on the puny man. "Did you tie a lass to a stake?"

"I did."

"Then I am challenging you."

Knox gritted his teeth, "Draw your sword."

"There is no need."

Laird Knox MacClurg could not remember a time when anyone seriously challenged him and he was not sure what to do. He had not killed a man or even fought one. His guards were supposed to do that for him, but ...

While Knox was thinking it over, Walrick grabbed hold of the man's sword and wrenched it out of his hand. Then he put his face just an inch away from his opponent's and smiled. "I won."

Knox blinked. His hands began to tremble and if Walrick had not grabbed his shirt, his knees would have buckled. "Are you going to kill me?"

Walrick let go of the man's shirt and let him fall flat on his back. "Let you and your lads be gone. The people do not want you here and neither do I."

"This is my land and I am not leaving."

"Then I will fight you." Walrick tossed the man's sword on the ground beside him. "Get up. Put your sword back in your sheath and if you draw it again, then I will know you intend to fight."

The heart of Knox MacClurg was already cold, but now he found himself humiliated, cast off, and shunned by his own people. He would fight this giant someday, he silently vowed, but at a time and place of his choosing. He got to his feet and put his sword away. Then he turned, nodded to his men and left by the back path.

The people watched Knox and his men mount their horses, ride across a shallow part of the river and disappear into the forest. "He will be back," the elder said. "He has nowhere else to go." The rest of the people nodded their agreement.

"What does he normally do when he comes back?"

"He normally orders his men to kill someone to scare us. It works, too," Gelson answered.

"It will not work this time." Walrick went back to the scorned woman and took her hand. "I will take you home now."

"Nay, my husband will beat me."

"He will not. A lad may set his wife aside, but if he harms her, he will answer to me."

Again, the people followed the giant and those who refused to come out earlier joined them, until nearly the whole clan was in attendance.

Gelson could hold his question no longer. "Then you will be

our laird?"

"I have not yet decided." When he reached her home, Walrick knocked on the door and as soon as a man answered, Walrick grabbed his shirt and pulled the smaller man up on his toes. "You may cast her out, but if you hurt this lass I will break your neck. Do you understand?"

The terrified man quickly nodded and kept nodding until the giant was pleased enough with his answer to let go. Then he backed into his cottage and kept going, until his back was against a wall and he was sure he was out of reach.

The woman reached up on tiptoe, kissed the giant on the cheek and with a new resolve, followed her husband inside and closed the door. This night he would not beat her and she wanted nothing more than to bathe her wounds, have a meal and go to sleep.

CHAPTER IV

Walrick turned and was about to go back down the path but when he looked, the girl twin had a hold of his hand. That was the very instant Walrick MacGreagor became Laird Walrick MacClurg. The touch of a little girl, who looked a lot like the twin sister he once lost, brought back the rest of his mind and he was whole again.

This time he was all grown up, he was able and he would give his life to keep this twin safe. He lifted the little girl into his arms, kissed her cheek, took hold of her twin brother's hand and smiled.

Right there on the path, the people gave their votes and then their vows to obey and protect this laird of their choosing.

Not long after, rumors began of a giant in the north who was fierce, fair minded, loved children and would kill to protect a woman. Every woman in the MacClurg Clan suddenly held her head just a little bit higher and her shoulders just a little bit straighter. If the rumor was true, and it was true, every woman in Scotland would envy them.

*

From the very beginning, Laird Walrick MacClurg had his work cut out for him. He refused to sleep in the three story main building until every shred of evidence from the cowardly previous owner had been removed. He ordered the walls washed, the ugly brown tapestries removed, new window coverings made and the floors swept. He had all the furnishings, including the long table and chairs, taken outside and then scrubbed top to bottom. The women were more than happy to help and the unmarried ones tried to flirt, but he treated them with kind regard only.

Unlike the MacGreagor keep, each floor was one big room, the staircases were enclosed and there was no balcony from which to look down into the great hall. There was, however, a great view of the land from any one of the four windows on every floor that faced each direction. It was on the top floor Walrick chose to sleep.

Occasionally, he thought about the man lurking in the trees and watching his every move. Someday Walrick would probably have to kill Knox. The MacGreagor way was to execute a man who hurt a woman and the one he found tied to the stake was proof enough of the man's evil. Walrick was not certain it was fair to take a man's life until after he knew the rule, and so far, Knox had not re-offended. Still he was out there somewhere plotting and planning. Walrick was not worried, just annoyed.

So a week into his new position as laird of the MacClurg Clan, Walrick mounted his horse, nodded for his men to follow him and rode to where he heard Knox was encamped. He made his men stay back, walked into the clearing alone, filled his lungs with air, let loose a warrior's cry and drew his sword.

Knox and his men were terrified. They were seven against one, but he was such a big one. The muscles in his arms were nearly bigger than their thighs and because he was so tall, his sword was considerably longer than theirs. Walrick was a very dangerous man and they knew they did not stand a chance against him.

"Fight me or let all of Scotland know you are cowards."

Three of the seven alarmed men tried to square their chests, but acting brave was not the same thing as actually being brave, and they quickly slumped. Thomas MacClurg cautiously spoke up. "If we withdraw our loyalty to Knox, will you let us live?"

"Withdraw your vow and you will live. The MacClurgs need men and your wives need husbands. But know this, if your heart is not good, I will know and you *will* die."

Knox gasped. "You cannot leave me. I am your laird!" His jaw dropped as one after another of his men moved to stand behind Walrick.

Walrick glared at Knox and flexed his muscles once more. "Draw your sword."

"What?" Knox moved back three paces.

"Draw your sword and fight me or all of Scotland will know you are a coward."

The coward took the coward's way out and started to run for his horse. To further his humiliation, the men laughed when Knox tripped over a log and fell on his face. Wearily, he got to his feet and reached for his mount's reins. He seated himself in his saddle, looked back one more time at the giant and all the men who abandoned him, and then vanished behind the trees.

Walrick put his sword away and walked back to his horse. "I will not have him worry us in the night or steal from us in the daytime. Austin, you and Burk take him south for five days and leave him there. Let him keep his weapons but bring his horse back. Give him only enough food for one day and for the sake of his son, we will not say he is a coward. We will only say he went south to find his fortune, agreed?" He waited for all the men to nod and then got back on his horse.

By the time Austin and Cobb started after him, Knox was completely out of sight.

*

Laird MacClurg carefully looked over each of the six men who once guarded Knox. "You will bathe the stink of your former alliance off your bodies before you come home. The MacClurgs are good and honorable people. Do not disappoint me."

As he decreed, the six came home clean and humble.

Still more rumors began about the giant who deposed the former MacClurg laird and sent him off to find his fortune elsewhere. The word "coward" appeared nowhere in all the mumblings.

CHAPTER V

Walrick had a room to sleep in, but then there was the question of building a big enough bed for him. The men measured the number of hands from his feet to the top of his head and built the bed with three hands extra. The women filled it with straw and made extra-large plaids. When it was finished, the MacClurgs told the Grahams, the Grahams told anyone who happened to be passing by, and the huge bed on the top floor of the MacClurg Keep got bigger and bigger with each telling.

*

Walrick began his warrior training almost immediately. At first, all the people gathered to listen and nothing else was getting done. So he appointed five men and five women for the morning sessions, and an equal number to hear him in the afternoon. Those he taught were commanded to teach the others. It was not until he learned all their names that he discovered he was also teaching two Graham warriors and their wives, who wore MacClurg colors so he wouldn't notice. He assured them it was not necessary and they were welcome.

As payment, the Graham laird sent him fresh honey bread and offered the pick of the Graham women for a wife. He ate the bread and gently rejected the offer of a wife.

He taught the whistles, the rules of keeping clean, how to

position their swords correctly, how to get to their feet quickly, and how to sneak up on a man in the forest without being heard. He taught the women how to find the best places to hide themselves and their children, how to shoot well enough to defend themselves, and how to throw a man if they needed to. The women especially liked those lessons, although none of them could throw the giant. The one lesson he stressed most was to set aside time to practice every day.

His exhaustion each night was good and he quickly fell asleep.

*

Someone was watching him. There was nothing on the third floor but his bed...no table, no chairs and no reason for anyone else in the world to be there. Yet when he opened one eye, three women were less than five feet from him.

They wore unfamiliar plaids, sat on the floor with their hands folded in their laps and kept their eyes glued to his. Behind them stood a MacClurg woman he had seen only once or twice before. Her name was Sarah and he remembered her, because right from the beginning she was not afraid of him. He admired bravery in a woman. Not only that, her smile was infectious.

She was not smiling now.

Nor was he pleased to find four women in his bedchamber and needed to have a serious talk with his night guard. He needed to have a lot of serious talks with a lot of different people, and the work ahead made him pull his cover up and roll away from the woman. "What could you possibly want this early in the morning?"

Sarah cleared her throat, "This is my sister, and these are her friends. They came in the night to ask refuge with us."

He was afraid of that. A little more than a week as laird and he was already facing a war over women. Maybe if he went back to sleep they would disappear. Of course, he should have expected this. The marriage customs of the northern clans were perplexing. For generations they apparently married out of duty or necessity, but few chose mates out of love. It was on this subject Walrick was the least prepared to rule. Naturally, he put a stop to forcing a woman to marry, and gave little thought to the customs of the other clans.

Apparently, the women wanted sanctuary because of his ruling, and he shuddered to think how many women would come wanting the same thing. On the other hand, he had plenty of men needing wives and growing a clan required marriages.

Her name was Allie and she was the youngest. "Laird MacClurg, we have talked it over and decided I should be the one to offer myself to you."

"I do not want a wife."

"I do not want a husband. I have already had one and he was not pleasant. I was not sorry to bury him, I promise you that."

Slowly, Walrick turned back over to face them. "You would give yourself to me without benefit of marriage?"

"Only if you agree to let us stay. We will not be a bother. We are good weavers and we eat very little."

He did not think less of her. He thought only of the despair that drove her to make such an offer. He slowly sat up and ran his fingers through his hair. "I would never require such a thing of a woman, and we have more than enough to eat." When he finished rubbing the sleep out of his eyes, he took a better look at them. All four women were smiling and he knew without saying it, he would risk war and let them stay. "From what clan have you come?"

"We used to be Buchanans."

"Until now?"

"Aye."

Gelson's sword did not fit well in its sheath and Walrick could hear a slight clink when the man moved. "Gelson?"

Walrick's second in command sheepishly stepped out from behind the door. He swallowed hard and mustered all his courage. "They are lasses and we need more lasses, you said it yourself just yesterday."

"Aye, but we are not prepared to go to war."

"Then we will hide them until we are ready to fight."

"Hide them where?"

"Here."

Walrick rolled his eyes, "Here? In the Keep?"

"Why not?"

"Because 'tis unseemly for a lad without a wife to sleep in the same place as unmarried lasses."

"Oh, I had not thought of that."

Walrick took a deep breath and let it out. "Who else knows they are here?"

"No one."

"They can stay. See they wear MacClurg plaids and build each a loom. More lasses mean more clothing. I will sleep elsewhere."

*

Austin and Cobb listened to Knox bellyache constantly for five days, and were exceedingly glad when they could pull him down off his horse and leave him there. Just to make sure the vile man would not strike out at them after they turned their backs, they carried all his weapons a good distance away, dropped them on the ground and swiftly rode off.

That night, they hunted, cooked a good meal of roasted grouse, pulled out the flask of wine they refused to give to Knox and celebrated. In the glow of their small campfire, they saw two figures walking toward them and to their surprise; the figures were women.

"We are hungry," said one.

Austin quickly got to his feet. "We will be pleased to share our meal with you. Sit and we will feed you."

The women eagerly sat down near the fire. They were pleasing and both young men were happy for the company.

"I am Julie and this is Clara. We are going to find the giant."

Austin and Cobb quickly exchanged glances. Austin tried to break off a drumstick, but it was still too hot. He pulled the stick that was skewered through the bird away from the fire, held it up and blew on the drumstick. "Why do you wish to find the giant?"

"You have heard of him?" asked Clara.

"Aye."

"We hear he does not force lasses to marry. Have you heard that as well?" Julie reached over, tested the meat, decided it was not too hot and pulled it away from the bird. Then she handed it to Clara and when Austin turned the bird, she pulled the other drumstick off for herself.

"We have heard that. How do you intend to find him?"

Julie shrugged. "We will find him or die trying. We cannot go home now that we have run off. Do you know where he is?"

Austin could see absolutely no reason to deny it. "Aye, we will take you to him." He smiled when both of the women's eyes lit up. It was clear Walrick was going to attract women and Austin wanted a wife. He already had his eye on Julie and with four days to go before they reached home, anything could happen. Perhaps she would fall in love with him.

Clara swallowed her bite of bird and flirtatiously grinned at Cobb. "We want to marry for love."

Already betrothed to Julie and Clara by the time they returned, Austin and Cobb were excited to tell their laird all about them. Walrick, on the other hand, wondered exactly what he had done. These two women were from yet another clan and they too came because of the gossip. He feared a stampede of women, with a dozen clans riding up the glen ready to fight for them.

CHAPTER VI

Laird Ronan Graham favored dark blue for his kilt color, had sandy hair and brown eyes. For two months, he sent his men to learn from the new MacClurg laird, listened to all the gossip and tried to understand what kind of man Walrick MacClurg really was. When he could not quite make it out, he mounted his horse, surrounded himself with guards and rode to the rich, green glen of the MacClurgs. Behind him, he led the largest stallion he could find.

As he expected, as soon as the MacClurgs saw him, they passed a whistle down the glen to alert the others. He could hear them, but he could not see them and he was impressed. The whistles kept their laird apprised of the intruder's exact location and the distance to be traveled before he arrived. The whistle was also two bursts indicating the visitor was friendly, as opposed to a sharper one that would signal danger. Of course, a real intruder would not know that and any kind of whistle would make him consider turning back.

As Laird Graham drew closer, MacClurg guards joined his procession, nodded their welcome and escorted the man they hoped to call friend into the courtyard.

Walrick stood in front of his keep with his legs apart and his hands behind his back. Beside him stood Gelson, his second, and

Mark, his third. He'd heard much about Laird Graham, knew the clan hoped to make an alliance and he was pleased to see him. "Welcome."

To size Walrick up, Graham remained on his horse and frowned. "I sent three lasses from which to choose a wife, but you rejected them. What must a lass be to please you?"

Walrick held the man's eyes. "She must be in love with me."

Slowly, Graham smiled. "If you wait for love, you may die a very lonely lad." He got down off his horse and pulled the unsaddled stallion forward. "I brought you payment for the training you give my lads. I hope he pleases you."

The black stallion with no name had been gone for a week and Graham's timing could not have been better. This horse was a sturdy dapple-gray with a white mane. It was big enough to carry his weight well and Walrick was honored. "I am indeed pleased. Come, you will share my meal and drink my wine."

Graham handed the reins of both horses to one of Walrick's men, and then followed him inside. He looked around, nodded his approval, and then took a seat at the table. "Knox was an unreasonable lad. He bargained from greed instead of need and we often did not trade with him. You appear to be a reasonable lad."

Walrick poured wine in a goblet and handed it to his new friend. "Do you fear the Buchanan and the MacDuff?"

"I see you get right to the point. We sometimes quarrel with them over stray sheep, but not often. We have not gone to war with either for a very long time. However, I do not recommend falling in love with one of their daughters. Their price can be brutal." At

Walrick's bidding, Graham took a seat at the table.

"Do you speak from experience?"

Graham laughed. "My wife was a bonnie lass, but it was nearly my ruination before I met her brother's price. Laird over enough soon became laird over little." His smile dropped for a moment, but he quickly recovered. "I firmly believe a lad must guard his heart with greater care than his property."

"I agree. Tell me, what do you hear of the MacGreagors?"

Graham looked perplexed. "I hear nothing of them. Who are they?"

Walrick poured his own drink, and then sat down next to Graham at the head of the table. "Have you heard of the MacDonalds, the Camerons or the Fergusons?"

"Nay, are they southern clans?"

"Aye, they must be southern clans." He had not actually thought about how big Scotland was. All his life he was content to be a MacGreagor, worry about his neighbors or the English, and let the rest of the world do as it pleased. Yet now he was beginning to believe he was a lot farther from home than he thought. Neil talked about the vastness of Scotland when he came home after marrying Glenna, but it was not something Walrick ever imagined he would see. Now he wished he had paid closer attention.

"They say you harbor three Buchanan lasses, is it true?"

"Aye, how have you heard this?"

"There are few secrets in the Highlands."

Walrick was glad they knew. Now he could get the women out of his home and go back to the comfort of his bed. "We have seen

Buchanan warriors watching from the woods. They hope to capture the lasses and take them back, but they do nothing."

"They do not come to look for the lasses -- they come to watch you train the lads."

"I see. How many Buchanans are there?"

"Perhaps seven hundred, maybe less. The plague took many of their lads and too many of all our children."

"Will they fight us for the lasses?"

"If they wanted them back, Laird Buchanan would have come for them by now. We have another problem, however."

"Which is?"

"There is a thief among us. He steals only food and not a lot at one time, but enough to feed two or three lads. We know you sent Knox away, but 'tis possible he is back?"

Walrick shrugged. "My lads took him five days south and left him with no horse, but he might have made his way back. I will have to kill him someday, I suppose."

Graham reached over and slapped him on the back. "He needs killing and I will gladly do it if he is found on our land."

*

Killing Knox would be easy; finding him in this vast land was something else again. Walrick split up his warriors, and sent them in different directions each morning for three days, but they found nothing. Then on the afternoon of the third day, Walrick and Gelson learned the truth.

From a good distance away, they watched a boy grab a lamb from its herd and carry it off into the woods. The men rode to the place they last saw the boy, tied their horses, and then crept into the forest. They soon heard voices, but the voices were not of grown men…they were the voices of children. The two men quietly slipped from tree to tree until they were close enough to see.

The eldest of the boys never could get it just right and he hated cutting throats, but the lamb was all the food he could find and his followers were hungry. While the other two boys held the lamb still, he pulled his dagger and was about to cut its throat, when one of the girls gasped. The boy quickly turned, discovered the height of the giant, dropped his dagger and yelled, "RUN!"

The boys let go of the lamb and scattered with the rest of the children, but the littlest child was not afraid. She slowly got to her feet, walked to the giant, looked up at him and then hugged his leg.

Walrick's heart instantly melted. He picked up the four-year-old and kissed her cheek. "You need a bath."

It took almost a whole minute before the other children dared peek around the trees to see why everything was so quiet. The man was still standing there, only now he was holding their Carla. A second man was also there, but he was not as big and not nearly as frightening.

The oldest boy finally mustered his courage and boldly stepped away from his hiding place. "Carla is ours, let her go."

Walrick was impressed with the boy's boldness. All of the children were so filthy it was hard to tell their plaids were once yellow. They were also far too thin and it troubled him. He wondered just how long they had lived in the woods. "A warrior must be wise as well as brave. He must choose to fight only those battles he has a chance of winning."

"Then you agree I am brave?" the boy asked.

"You are very brave. How old are you?"

"I am in my ninth year."

"And are you the eldest?" Walrick asked.

"I am." The boy picked up his dagger, put it away, spread his legs apart and folded his arms.

"Where are your parents?"

"Passed."

Walrick cast his eyes down for a moment. "What clan are you?"

"We will be our own clan someday. Carla will be my wife and we will be happy."

"Will you be their laird?" Walrick asked.

"Aye."

"You will make a very find laird. We are MacClurgs and we will be proud to be your neighbors." He waited for the little boy to give his nod. "A clan must be strong to survive. The followers need clean clothing, new shoes and better food. If you agree, you can live with us until you are grown."

The boy had to give that a lot of thought. One by one, the children began to step out and go to Walrick.

Walrick felt sorry for the oldest boy and tried a little harder to convince him. "If you are not happy with us, you may take your followers and leave any time you like." That seemed to be all the encouragement the boy needed and the relief on his face was great.

*

There were seven children in all and once he got them home, cleaned up and fed, they came to live in his home. The children needed women to care for them and once more Walrick was forced to spend his nights in a bed that was too short...in a cottage that was not his. He was beginning to think he would have to take a wife just to get back in his own bed. Instead, he moved the larger bed into the cottage.

Walrick sent word to Laird Graham that the thieves were caught and Knox had not come back. The children needed more than just clean clothing, good food and a warm bed. They needed affection and Walrick had plenty to give. The eldest boy followed him everywhere, and after giving it considerable thought, asked if they could become MacClurgs until they were grown. A few days later, they decided Walrick would be their father...until they were grown.

How could he object?

More women came to live under the protection of the giant, but it was not as many as he first feared. Most clans soon kept a closer eye on their young women. The men built new cottages, married the willing women and the clan slowly began to grow.

Therefore, at the age of twenty-four, Walrick lived among the MacClurgs, became the father of seven, watched his children grow, trained new fighters, avoided wars with their neighbors, and let the memory of a loving wife and his MacGreagor family fade.

He did not consider taking a wife again until almost three

years had passed.

CHAPTER VII

The hierarchy for most of the clans had changed. The plague took away as many lairds and commanders as it did warriors. Wives died, or moved in and out of places of honor according to their husband's health, or lack thereof.

The MacGreagors, the Fergusons, and the Camerons lost more than half of their numbers, but the MacDonalds suffered fewer losses in comparison, and the threat of war intensified. The elder MacDonald, who feared a plague more than anything else, was one of the first to die. Unfortunately, his son survived and soon became an erratic, harsh ruler, who saw MacGreagor land as the paradise he did not have, and would do anything to get.

Only one question remained -- what was taking this new MacDonald laird so long to attack?

*

All his life, Neil MacGreagor heard stories about a black stallion. His mother, Anna, taught the horse to do tricks, spoke of her great love for the beast, and of the odd way she always knew the horse would not let her fall. A similar horse once brought his injured Aunt Rachel home when all hope of recovering her was lost.

Therefore, when a horse fitting the same description appeared in the meadow, Neil walked over the bridge to see this magnificent creature for himself. Laird MacGreagor's dark, wavy hair hung down to his shoulders, he wore the traditional blue kilt, that almost matched the color of his eyes, and new shoes that laced up to his knees.

The stallion kept clear of the other men, but when Neil arrived, the horse walked right to him. Their eyes met and when the horse nodded, Neil smiled. Of course, it was not the same horse his mother spoke of. That horse had to be long gone, but this one could be an offspring. He had the same pure black coat and black mane, without a spot of white or gray on its coat anywhere. That alone made the stallion unique. Neil patted the horse's nose and then stood back to admire his size and strong muscles.

When he again looked into the horse's eye, Neil felt an odd foreboding. It made him look down and after only a moment or two, he suddenly knew what to do. A wash of relief crossed his mind and he could breathe again after months of worry. His decision was made, it was the right one and somehow the horse was confirming it.

*

She had a square face like her brother's and when she was little, Steppen's blonde hair was almost white. Now it was closer to brown, which made her dark brown eyes stand out. Just like many other MacGreagors, she had no one left. When the plague came, she was somewhere between childhood and womanhood. She did not need a constant caretaker, but at fourteen, she was not ready for a husband either. Out of regard for Patrick, Neil and Glenna insisted she move into the Keep with them. Now Steppen was seventeen and very much like a sister to them both.

She poured water into the basin, dipped her cloth and began to wash her face. "They say the giant is thirty hands tall." The air was heavy with the coming rain and even binding back Neil and Glenna's bedchamber drape to let in the fresh air was not helping.

"No one is thirty hands tall, not even Neil." Glenna sat down on the bed, looked out the window and caught her breath. "Steppen come see. My husband is with a beautiful horse in the meadow."

The younger woman walked to the window and then leaned against the frame. "He is very beautiful."

Glenna could not pull her eyes away. "I do not recall ever seeing that horse before."

"Nor do I. How odd, it has no bridle yet he lets Neil hug his neck. Most horses would fear capture, but I believe this one would even let Neil ride."

"So do I. He is a glorious creature."

Steppen forgot all about the humidity. She watched the stallion walk into the forest and kept watching to see where it would go. A few minutes later, she spotted it climbing to the top of the hill. The stallion's black coat glistened as it caught the sunshine, and when it turned to look back, she believed the horse was looking right at her.

*

Neil was happier than he had been in a long time. He walked into his bedchamber and lovingly touched his sleeping son's head. At two, Justin MacGreagor had his great grandfather's name and his grandfather Kevin's traditional blond hair that could, and probably would, turn dark like Neil's someday.

Neil smiled and took hold of his wife's hand. "Come with me, I have something to show you." He helped her up and then nodded to Steppen. "You too, come."

He opened the door to the bedchamber where Leesil once slept, moved the bed and used his dagger to pry up a slat in the floor. Carefully, he removed the MacGreagor sword and pulled it out of the sheath. Then he held it straight up and let the gold blade glisten as it caught the light.

Steppen's jaw dropped. "You have it? But 'tis just a legend."

"'Tis not a legend. An Englishman made this for my grandfather years ago."

Mesmerized by its shine, Glenna gently touched the gold with her finger. "What legend?"

It was Steppen who answered, "The legend holds that the sword is lost, and any MacGreagor who hears where it is must recover it for the clan. But 'tis not lost."

"Nay, 'tis not lost," Neil said. "Few know where it is and those who do will keep the secret to their deaths. Now the two of you know."

Steppen's shock slowly turned to a grin. "You trust me to keep the secret. I am so honored."

"You may not be so pleased when you hear the rest of it. I am depending on you to save yourselves and the sword if anything happens to me."

Steppen quickly moved away. "I will not hear this."

"You must, Steppen. If we are attacked, you must take the

sword, find a new place to hide it and keep it safe for my son."

Her eyes searched her laird's for a long moment. "You will stay to fight if the MacDonald attacks us?"

"I will do everything in my power to save all the MacGreagors, you know that. Give me your vow, Steppen. Promise you will guard the MacGreagor sword and give it to Justin when he is grown."

Neil put the sword back in its sheath and held it against her to measure the height. Just as he hoped, Steppen had grown tall enough to wear the sword without it dragging on the ground. It was too long for a woman and not easily drawn, but she could manage to carry it. After being hidden for so many years, Neil tested the strength of the sheath strings and then examined the sheath with the MacGreagor markings. He decided replacing both would not be a bad idea. "Your vow, Steppen, I must have it."

She rolled her eyes. What choice did she have? She was a MacGreagor; she loved her laird and would do whatever he wanted no matter the cost. She would even haul a sword all over creation and turn over every rock until she found a place to hide it. Finally, she let out an exasperated breath. "I am not happy, but I give you my pledge." She held still, let Neil kiss the top of her head, huffed and left the room.

Neil watched her go, set the sword on the table and then took Glenna in his arms. "I have something unthinkable to ask of you."

"What?"

He lovingly kissed her lips and then tightened his arms around her. "When the attack comes, we must let Steppen take Justin." He felt her try to pull away, but he held her close until she relaxed against him. "If all of us are caught together we will all die. But if we are separated, then at least two of us will have a chance to survive. No one loves the boy more and Steppen will take good care of him." He let Glenna pull away then and looked into her eyes. "I will not demand it. I love you too much to break your heart, but I truly believe 'tis best for our son."

"But..."

"Do not give your answer now. Think about it and we will talk tonight when I can show you how much I love you."

"If they do not attack tonight."

"Aye."

"Perhaps you should show me now." Glenna giggled when he closed the door, picked her up and carried her to the bed.

"Perhaps I will."

*

The rain came, went away and threatened to come again. The MacDonalds did not attack that night, nor the next or the next. Neil had the leather worker make a new sheath and strings for the sword, and then put it back under the slat. Everything else was normal, even the meal he and Glenna shared with Steppen at the beginning of each day. Yet the tension was always there.

Seated at the table, Steppen bit into her apple, chewed and swallowed. "Do you think Walrick will ever come back?"

Neil raised an eyebrow. "I am pained to say it, but I believe he is dead."

"Do you believe it, Glenna?"

"I believe he would have come back if he could."

"Sometimes I think of him and when I do, I do not think of him as dead. Before he married Kindel, he used to take me riding. Patrick would have had his head if he knew, but Walrick liked answering all my questions. He said it made him think of things he had not considered before."

Neil grinned. "You do have a talent for that."

Steppen turned up her nose and pretended to be whispering to Glenna, "Do not tell Neil, but I sometimes watch the bridge expecting to see Walrick come back." She paused to eat another bite of her apple. "I suppose a wild beast might have gotten him, but of all the MacGreagor lads, a beast would have to be daft to try to defeat Walrick."

Glenna patted Steppen's hand. "Perhaps you are right and he will come back someday."

"I hope so. Should I take a husband?"

CHAPTER VIII

If Neil was used to anything these days, it was Steppen's ability to change subjects without warning. "Do you want a husband?"

"Not yet, but I should have one. I mean 'tis the responsibility of every lass to have children for the sake of the clan, especially now that our numbers are so few."

Neil frowned. "Aye, but the clan would not have you marry a lad you do not love simply for the sake of bearing children. It would be unthinkable."

"I know the clan would not ask it, but if I love the clan I should do it without them asking," Steppen argued.

Glenna rubbed her brow thoughtfully. Sometimes Steppen was still a little girl in search of a great and profound reason to exist. "Marriage is for a very long time and 'tis not always easy. At the end of the day, 'tis important to be in the arms of a lad who loves you."

"I could never hope to have a love like yours."

Glenna frowned. "Why not? Every lass is entitled to love."

"Then why is every lass not happy?" Steppen asked.

"Because she does not wait for the right lad." Glenna watched Steppen set her apple core in the bowl and handed her a cloth to wipe her face and hands. "Come, we will see if we can find the right lad for you in the courtyard."

Steppen stood up and crossed her eyes at Neil, "As if there will be a lad out there I have not already decided against."

Neil chuckled, watched them walk away and the big wooden door close behind them. Steppen was right, there were fewer men to choose from, and they had to be inside the wall for her to meet them. He asked all the women to bathe inside more often now, and did not encourage them to go riding or even for a walk outside the wall. The women and children were becoming more like prisoners and everyone hated it. He sighed. Soon it would all be over and they could taste freedom again…at least those who survived could.

*

Gill MacGreagor was an average looking man with a light shade of blond hair and blue eyes. He was as smart as any man and would have liked being a more important member of Neil's new command. Soon after the plague ended, Neil chose not to have so many advisors and instead, asked his men to take on extra duty by keeping a closer eye on the MacDonalds. It was indeed their most important duty, but it kept Gill away from home more than he liked.

He met her during one of those restful times when he could let his guard down a little and enjoy the tranquility of the loch. More often than not these days the loch was deserted, but two little boys jumped from rock to rock along the shore and Gill was remembering when he was that age. How simple life was then, with little to worry about, except having to face Kevin when they did something forbidden.

Suddenly, she walked right into him. He was so startled, he turned and reached for his sword. A moment later, he realized she was crying and had been paying even less attention to their surroundings than he had. One look at him and the woman's tears turned to sobs.

They were nearly strangers, but they both wore MacGreagor colors, which meant she could trust him. When he opened his arms, she gladly went into them.

He held her for a very long time and let her cry. There was plenty for MacGreagor women to cry about and if he were not a man, he might have given into the impulse occasionally himself. Yet men with clouded vision cost lives. They did cry, of course, when someone died, but crying for any other reason was an appalling sign of weakness, and such a man would not survive long among the MacGreagor warriors. Even the littlest boys were not allowed to cry.

Gill dared to close his eyes for a moment. She too was a blonde with blue eyes, he noticed, although he had not seen much of her eyes before she burst into sobs. The top of her head came up to the bottom of his chin, her hair smelled like flowers and she felt perfect in his arms.

She suddenly realized what she was doing, pulled back and looked up. His smile was kind and his eyes were sympathetic. "I…"

"What makes you cry?" To his relief, she did not move away. He wanted to stroke her hair but decided against it. Maybe if he didn't move, neither would she.

"I do not know, everything I guess."

"My mother often did not know what made her cry, so my father simply held her until it passed. When she would let him, that is. There were times when he feared for his life."

The woman in his arms giggled and he continued, "My father was quite good at ducking too. He found an old shoe and when he came to the cottage at night, he tossed the shoe in the door. If it came back out and made him duck, he stayed away a little longer. But if it did not come back out, it was safe to go in."

"And she did not know what upset her?"

"Not that I recall. It must have been little annoying things or I would remember. What about your mother?"

"Mine died when I was very young." The woman moved away and dried her tears on a cloth she pulled out of her belt. "Thank you for holding me. I am better now."

He was about to ask her name when he heard the anguished cry of one of the boys. Gill ran over, quickly pulled the boy out of the water, set him on a rock and examined his foot. It did not appear to be broken and he meant to smile his reassurance at the woman, but when he looked, she was gone. He stood up and looked in all directions, but he did not see her anywhere. The woman had simply vanished.

For the rest of the day he walked the paths, checked the loch often and looked everywhere for her, but she was nowhere to be found. He thought he knew most everyone, but women had a way of growing up while a man was away or distracted by more important matters. The next day, he was forced to go back out on

MacDonald watch, but he did not forget her. He remembered the feel of her in his arms, the smell of her hair, the glint in her blue eyes and the wet spot her tears made on his chest. Sometimes when he thought about her, he touched that place on his chest.

He spent his time trying to think of ways to find her. He also worried about her safety and where to hide her when the attack came. There would be an attack -- everyone knew it, and everyone was making plans. The men would stand and fight, but they could only hold out long enough for the women and children to escape. How could he protect her and help her escape if he could not find her? What was life all about if he could not save the woman in his heart? The days turned into weeks, the weeks into a couple of months…and then at last, he found her.

*

Ralin was the daughter of a good MacGreagor man who died in the plague. She thought the world was ending when the vile illness ravaged her people. Milk cows had no one to milk them, sheep lost herders, and vegetables went unpicked and undelivered. Farmers demanded their warrior sons be returned to help in the fields, children needed new parents, and when none were easily found on the outside, several were brought inside the wall.

Therefore, Ralin, who lived all her life outside the wall, now shared a cottage with Taral inside and they became the best of friends. They worked their weaving looms from morning until evening and kept the secret of what they were making well hidden. The yarn came to them in the night and they did not know who brought it, but each morning a bolt or two sat just inside the door.

Likewise, the finished goods were gone. The work gave them plenty to do and keeping busy was a privilege. However, it kept Ralin indoors.

As she loved to do, Taral began each day by watching the sunrise, even when it was not filled with brilliant colors. It was still her special time with God and Dan. She was still very attractive to the men, but she was in no hurry to remarry, so neither of the young women went out much.

Ralin was interested in a man she met once by the loch. She did not know his name, but she remembered him very well, and on the rare occasions she and Taral went for a walk, she secretly looked for him. She could not find him, however, and began to believe he was more of a daydream than a real man. Yet when she thought about him, she could still feel his arms around her.

CHAPTER IX

Taral sat beside Ralin at the outside edge of the moat and touched the water with her hand. "Do not talk of it anymore."

"Not talking of it will not make it go away. Our mothers would want us to make a firm plan of escape."

"We have fretted over an attack for years and it does not come. If the MacDonalds mean to take our land, why do they wait? They could have had us much easier months ago?"

"Who understands why Laird MacDonald waits? He dams the water and then releases it for no reason at all. He sends lads on our land to provoke us, yet instead of fighting, they run away and he allows it. The old laird was bad, but I am convinced his son was born out of his wits."

"Then they are just as likely not to attack. I say we stop fretting over something we cannot prevent, and enjoy our day. Let Neil and the men fret. That is their job."

Ralin did not want to be the wise one. She would rather be stupid and let the rest of the world make all the decisions. Still, someone had to think of these things and with neither of them having family, she supposed it was up to her. "All I want is for us to have a firm plan just in case."

Taral rolled her eyes. "What good will a plan do? We cannot go to the Camerons. The laird they have now fears the

MacDonalds will attack him if he gives us refuge. South is England, north leads right into the hands of the attackers, and the MacDonalds will track us down and kill us if we run to the Fergusons."

"You make it sound as if there is no hope."

"Do I?" Taral closed her eyes and bowed her head. "I do not mean to sound hopeless." She leaned forward and hugged Ralin. "Do you forgive me? I do not know what is wrong with me lately."

"I forgive you." Ralin retuned her hug and then relaxed. There really wasn't a good answer. Wars were an unavoidable part of life, it seemed. In a clan war, the women were not normally killed, but they sometimes suffered a worse fate, such as marriage to a disgusting man. The thought made Ralin shudder. "Perhaps we should go south to England."

"We do not even speak the language. We should have asked Jessup to teach us. We should have done a lot of things differently. Now all we can do is pray there will be no war."

Ralin took a deep breath and let it out. "But if there is a war and if we do not escape together, we will meet somewhere and then decide where to go. We will meet where the road to the south becomes three paths, agreed?"

"Agreed." Taral hugged the woman she sometimes called sister again, got to her feet and headed back inside the wall. She was starting to let all this talk of war upset her, and when she got upset, she lost her good humor. "There will not be a war, I will not let there be."

*

He wasn't actually looking when Gill MacGreagor finally found Ralin. He was just walking along the outside curve of the moat, thinking about filling his empty stomach, when he spotted her sitting in the grass beside the water. He stopped. For the rest of his life he would remember the vision of her at this very moment. This time she would not get away.

Instead of racing to her, which was his first impulse, he pulled a flower out of the ground and set it in water. He hoped to get her attention when she floated by. He thought one flower might not do, so he floated two more behind the first.

She was deep in thought when the first flower passed her outstretched hand. She thought about war, about love and about how the water on her hand soothed her. The second flower touched her finger and she smiled. Then she saw the third flower, looked up and there he was -- the man who held her at the loch. Her stomach suddenly felt as though someone was twisting it and she feared she would not catch her next breath. She soon forgot about that breath and held the next one as he came closer.

"May I sit with you?" As soon as she nodded, he crossed his feet at the ankle and sat down in front of her. Then he gave her three more little flowers. "Neil does not want the lasses outside the wall, you know."

"I know, but this day I could not resist touching the water."

"I have been looking everywhere for you."

"Have you?"

"Where did you go that day?" When she lowered her beautiful eyes, he guessed it was a personal matter and he should not have asked. "I could have found you, but I did not know your name. What is it?"

"Ralin."

"Ralin is a pleasant name." He tried not to look in her eyes too often, but he was charmed and could not help himself. "Ralin, there is a gathering with the Fergusons tomorrow, will you go with me?"

She liked the way he said her name. It sounded different somehow. "Do you have Ferguson relatives?"

"Nay, but I do not let that keep me from a gathering. There is always plenty of good food and I like making new friends. Do you have relatives there?"

"I suppose we all have Ferguson relatives. Our people have married theirs for years."

"True. My name is Gill, will you walk with me?" When she nodded, he stood up.

She took his hand and let him pull her to her feet, but then she saw his smile and a wave of nausea passed over her. Taral told her what it was like to be in love, but Taral failed to mention all of these strange symptoms. Ralin felt giddy, scared and desperate for his arms all at the same time. If he let go of her hand, she would probably drop like a leaf.

"Do you have a special place you like to go?"

"Nay."

"I have looked everywhere for you." He knew he already said that and tried to remember all those glorious things he intended to say, if he ever saw her again.

Ralin dropped her eyes to his chest. "I left because I was embarrassed. I let a stranger hold me and I should not have."

"I am not truly a stranger; you just grew up without my knowing."

She smiled, realized her hand was still in his, and started to walk with the man she had imagined walking with in so many of her daydreams. "Shall I make a confession?"

"Please do."

"I looked for you too."

He was overjoyed and his smile told her so. "I am a warrior and have been away far more than I care to be." When they got to the bridge, Gill turned them so they could walk back around the moat. As they strolled, he constantly searched the trees for possible attackers. He was, after all, finally able to protect her, and it made him feel more like a man than he ever had before.

"Does Neil send you to watch the MacDonalds?"

"He does. The border is long and it takes several of us."

"Do you think they will attack?"

He stopped walking to look at the concern in her eyes. "I think their laird drinks too much, and he will attack when the mood strikes him. Do you still have family?"

"Nay, do you?"

He began to walk again and delighted in the sensation of having her so close. "I have a brother. He is married and they have one child. They live outside the wall and I would like you to go there. My brother can keep you safe."

"Do you really believe we will be safe outside the wall?"

"I am counting on it. If they attack, I will meet you there when I can."

She took hold of his arm with her other hand and made him stop walking. "May I take Taral with me?"

"You may take anyone you want. The families on the outside will do all they can to hide the lasses and the children."

"How can the ones on the outside possibly hide themselves and another three or four hundred people? Neil is our laird and he should tell us what we are to do, but all we have are rumors. Why does he keep silent?"

"We must trust Neil. If he tells us his plan now, he risks letting the MacDonalds know what it is."

"Do you believe he has a plan?"

He saw the doubt in her eyes, followed his impulse and drew her into his arms. "I know he does. I do not know what it is, but Neil will not let us down. Do not judge him so harshly."

"I am frightened."

"I know, many are frightened. I have watched Neil struggle with his decisions, and he does not make them until he has thought of every outcome. Sometimes I think he would rather not be laird, but he stays with us and for that I am grateful." Gill lifted her chin with his finger tips and kissed her forehead. "Try not to fret, we are together now and I will not let anything happen to you."

She did feel safe in his arms. All the butterflies and the awkwardness went away when he held her and she was amazed at how right it felt. He gave her warmth, comfort, a place for her to take Taral if they were attacked, and a very important reason to live. Then he gave her one more thing -- a fear that something would   happen   to   him.

CHAPTER X

They met in the darkness of night at the southern edge of the loch, and Laird Neil MacGreagor was all wet from swimming the moat when he arrived. He came with little moonlight to light the way and only two guards, which he kept well back while he spoke to Laird Shaw Ferguson. "We have no choice."

Ferguson looked old and completely worn out. The threat of war took its toll on everyone, even those not directly involved. Friends for many years, both men knew this was probably the last time they would ever see each other. "I understand and I do not blame you. What can we do to help?" Ferguson asked.

"After I am dead, tell the people to leave and burn the place -- burn it for my sake."

A saddened Shaw Ferguson put a hand on Neil's shoulder. "I will miss you, my friend."

"And I you." Neil grasped the man's arm in farewell, let go, joined his guards and started back into the darkness. Ferguson's lack of a pledge to give sanctuary to MacGreagors did not go unnoticed, and Neil could hardly blame the man. An alliance with Laird MacDonald was Ferguson's only chance to keep his people alive and stay in power. How long that would last was anyone's guess.

One thing was abundantly clear -- the MacGreagors could not

flee to the Fergusons.

The MacGreagors had been on Walrick's mind a lot lately and he could find no specific cause for it. His world held little out of the ordinary, except for a woman who sometimes wanted to marry him, or a squabble between two of his adopted children. Life was easy and sometimes just as boring as it had been for the MacGreagors. He liked to go fishing or to a loch to swim on days like that.

Yet today he was inside his great hall considering where to build new cottages. Having thrown all the old wall hanging out the door, the women had made new ones, and the place was looking much better. Weapons were never discarded, no matter whom they once belonged to, and they too hung on the walls. A very large hearth kept the three floors warm enough and offered a place for the women to cook.

Building cottages closer to the river was out of the question in case the heavy rains came, and building into the forest meant more risk of fire. On the other hand, building down the glen made them more vulnerable to attack, should they one day have a problem with another clan. So far, the MacClurgs minded their own business and the other clans left them alone.

*

At twenty, Ayson was still unmarried. He was a pleasant looking young man, but painfully shy and Walrick doubted he had ever spoken to a young woman, let alone kissed one. Therefore, when Ayson came to ask for a wife, Walrick did not take his request lightly. "You know I do not force lasses to marry. How precisely do you think I can get you a wife?"

"You must know some way to do it, you had a wife once."

He remained seated at the end of the table and tried to remember exactly how he convinced Kindel to marry him. He quickly gave up on that. "Having a wife hardly makes me an expert on getting one. Do you prefer a particular lass?"

"Aye."

"Who?"

"She is Effie."

"Effie had a Buchanan husband she did not like. It will not be easy to convince her."

"I know, but I do not know where to begin." Ayson stared at the floor, interlaced his fingers and put his hands under his chin as if in prayer. "You could ask her for me."

"You want me to ask her to marry you."

He looked up with hopeful eyes. "She would do it if you ask her."

Walrick frowned. "She would marry you to please me? That would be the same as forcing her."

"But you do agree a lad should have a wife, I have heard you say it."

"Aye, 'tis good for a lad to have a wife." Walrick did think that, and with the passing of so much time since Kindel died, he sometimes thought about one for himself. The MacClurg women were pleasing, but they were not bonnie like MacGreagor women. Of course, he probably elevated their beauty in his mind because he missed them. When did he start missing them? He shook the thought out of his mind and made himself concentrate on Ayson's problem. "I will see her. Bring Effie to me."

Ayson was so happy he nearly fell over his own feet trying to get out the door. A few minutes later, both Ayson and Effie were standing in front of him.

Walrick stood, tenderly touched Effie's arm to reassure her and then motioned for her to sit down. "Ayson has something to say to you." The young man went ghostly pale, his eyes bulged and he gulped hard. "Just say it, Ayson. Men do not die from this sort of thing."

A pretty woman by most standards with dark hair and dark eyes, Effie looked from Ayson to Walrick and then back to Ayson. She was starting to get upset. "Have I done something wrong?"

"Nay," Ayson quickly said. "You could never do anything wrong. I…"

"What then? You asked me to make you a new fishing net, but that was only two days ago. Did you expect it so soon?"

"Nay, Effie, you misunderstand." He looked to Walrick for help, but his laird was suddenly gone. Ayson was stuck now, and the only thing left to do was to sit down and blurt it out. He pulled a chair closer and took her hand. "I want you to marry me."

"Is that all? Good grief, I thought I was being sent back to the Buchanans." She pulled her hand away, stood up and headed for the door.

"Wait."

"For what?" she asked.

"You have not given me your answer."

"Oh. My answer is...I will think about it."

"Think about it? How long will that take?" He followed her out, spotted Walrick leaning against the wall, rolled his eyes at him, and hurried after her.

Walrick laughed. He enjoyed watching the love chase and maybe he really was ready to fall in love again...if the right woman came along.

*

The Ferguson gatherings were always fun and usually held in a clearing on the other side of the loch. Gill took Ralin's hand, helped her step over logs and moved branches out of her way as they walked through the forest. He wanted to kiss her and tried to think of ways to get her alone, but they were in the midst of several MacGreagors and he would not likely have the chance until much later.

The best of any gathering was the gossip and as soon as they reached the clearing, they were quickly joined by two Ferguson women, who had plenty of stories to tell. None paid attention to the women spreading plaids on the grass and setting out bowls of special delights brought by both clans.

"...they cannot find a horse big enough and it takes all of two plaids to cover the giant sufficiently," said one of the Ferguson women.

Ralin doubted that, but she did not argue. She loved the feel of her hand in Gill's and what she really wanted was to be alone with him. It was not fitting, she knew, but to be in his arms again was all she seemed able to think about.

"…three babies?" the other Ferguson woman was saying.

"Three babies? All in the same birth? Did they live?" Gill asked.

"Aye, they are well, though their mother vows she has been cursed. No lass has the milk for three babies and…"

He moved closer to her and it pleased him when Ralin leaned against him. Her arm was against his strong shoulder and it was the greatest feeling in the world. It was not enough, however. He wanted to let go of her hand and put his arm around her waist, but he was not at all sure how she would react to such a public display of affection. He already loved her and had for weeks, so touching her was the most natural thing in the world. Yet he should at least see if she felt the same before he became too bold.

The first Ferguson woman couldn't seem to stop talking, "…so when she caught her husband in the woods with that other lass, she took her broom and began to hit him over the head. Then…"

Ralin had already heard that story, but as long as she was touching Gill, she could hear it over and over again. She kept thinking of the way he kissed her forehead the day before, and wondered if he would kiss her lips any time soon. The last time a boy kissed her lips, she was only twelve and she wanted to kill him. Women often told stories about kissing and she wanted to know if any of that was true. Some of it sounded down right awful, but Taral said kissing was exciting.

The woman was now telling a different story and Ralin hadn't been paying attention. She was ashamed of herself, but only for a moment. What she wanted to do was look at Gill's lips, but there was no chance she was brave enough to do that.

"...and got a cat to follow her home just by dropping little bits of meat along the way. Now the cat is not shy and comes to see the whole clan. We must be careful, you know, for the cat has sharp claws, but..."

The two Ferguson women had to be running out of gossip soon, Ralin thought, and when she spotted Taral talking to a Ferguson warrior, she smiled. It would warm her heart to see Taral fall in love again. Maybe she and Gill could help that new friendship along a little. She stood up straight, made her excuses and then took Gill to meet Taral.

The Ferguson warrior was a pleasing man and Ralin approved of him immediately. His name was William. He warmly smiled and nodded his greeting first to her and then to Gill. The men talked of their various warrior positions and as always, the conversation turned to the impending war with the MacDonalds.

Ralin did not want to talk of war. She wanted Gill to be close again and when he was not and seemed more interested in William than in her, she began to think of all sorts of evil things to do to get his attention. Then, as if he read her mind, he ran his thumb gently across the back of her hand and the sensation sent her heart racing. He had not forgotten her.

"'Tis your wall," William was saying. "The MacDonald knows about all your hidden doors and the wall will trap the MacGreagors inside. You should tear it down."

Gill frowned, "Believe me, we have thought of that. You are no safer, burning and pulling down your wooden wall would be easy. At least with a stone wall and a moat, we will be harder to kill."

"How many warriors do the MacDonalds have?" William asked.

"My guess would be eleven hundred," said Gill.

The Ferguson bowed his head. "You are three hundred and we are not quite three. They are nearly double our number."

"Aye, but we are better fighters. If we stood together, we might kill enough to send them home."

William Ferguson lowered his voice and leaned toward Gill, "I do not think our laird will fight with you."

Gill took a deep breath and let it out. "I do not think Neil expects him to. As for me, I would prefer you save all the lasses and children you can."

"I have a suggestion." When she had the attention of both men, Ralin grinned. "After we are gone, the Fergusons should spread a rumor that the MacGreagor hold is haunted. Everyone knows the MacDonalds are superstitious. Perhaps we should say there is a curse on the place."

William smiled and then bowed to Ralin. "I will be happy to tell my sister that. You were talking to her just now, and once she hears something, there is not a soul in all of Scotland she is unwilling to tell."

Taral rolled her eyes, "War, war, war, is there nothing else to talk of?"

Ralin laughed. "Food. I am starving."

CHAPTER XI

The land Gill's brother farmed was a few miles from the MacGreagor hold, but not such a long ride by horse. The countryside was peaceful and after leaving the gathering, he and Ralin took their time admiring the forests, the hillsides and the herds of sheep and cattle along the way.

The cottage was small, but comfortable with colorful hangings on one wall and an assortment of weapons on the other, just like most homes. Gill pulled a chair away from the table for Ralin to sit on. "My brother has always loved farming. He likes to watch things grow and be a part of it. He is happiest when the new plants sprout out of the ground."

Ralin nodded and then accepted the goblet of wine Gill's brother handed her. "You have a good life here."

"Aye, my wife and I love it. In fact, we have decided if war comes, we will not fight. We will hide until it is safe to come out and then become MacDonalds."

"Truly? You would give up the MacGreagor Clan?"

"Not in our hearts, but we love the land and want to stay for the sake of our children," Gill's brother answered.

"But you will tell your children they are MacGreagors?" Ralin asked.

"Aye and we will teach them the MacGreagor ways."

Ralin paused to choose her words. "I have been thinking about that a lot. Glenna says they will not kill the lasses, but they might make them marry MacDonalds. I would hate that and even if I did love a MacDonald, my heart would break if I could not wear a MacGreagor plaid on my wedding day. I wish, at least, to be buried in one."

Gill was going to ask her anyway and they had just arrived at his brothers home, but now seemed the perfect time. "If you were married to me, you would not have to fear being forced to marry a MacDonald."

"Are you asking?"

"Aye."

Ralin glanced at Gill's smiling brother, at his sister-in-law, and then at the face of the child sitting across the table waiting for her answer. She looked back at him. "Do you intend to fight this war or hide like your brother?"

He knew the question was coming but not quite this soon. He also knew if she cared for him, she was not going to like his answer. "I am a warrior, fighting is what I am trained to do and if Neil says we fight, then I will fight."

"If you fight, you will die and then I will be forced to marry a MacDonald anyway."

"Are you asking me not to fight?"

Ralin dropped her eyes. "I do not know what I am asking. War against so many sounds so hopeless and I do not want you to die." She hardly noticed when Gill's brother took his family outside and left them alone. Why wasn't life more simple? She would marry him in any case, but was she to love for just a little while and then lose him like Taral lost Dan? She did not think she could bear it, but then he was taking her in his arms. A tear rolled down her cheek and she put her head on his chest.

Gill held her tight. "Marriage does not come with the promise of a long life together. 'Tis only for a moment at a time and I want to spend all those moments just like this." He kissed her hair. "I have waited a long time to get you back in my arms."

"But I am frightened of losing you."

"I am frightened of losing you too. Promise me, if we are attacked, you will escape and come here to the safety of my brother's home. Then if I am able, I will come to you when the war is over."

"Will you promise to bury me in a MacGreagor plaid?"

"I promise. Try not to die before you are very old, for my sake."

Ralin giggled. "I will try." She lifted her lips and when he kissed her at last, his lips were warm and gentle. She slipped both her arms around him and when he kissed her again with more passion, she knew she was in the arms of the man she would love the rest of her life - no matter how long or short that was to be.

*

There was a sense of urgency in the air. Gill and Ralin married the next day to make sure she could be wed in a MacGreagor plaid. They were not the only ones with that same idea. The priest said the words over six other couples and although they met only the day before, Taral and William Ferguson gave their pledges to each other as well.

Neil was pleased and urged all the men to settle their wives outside the wall for an easier escape. None of the men argued.

The night was clear and the moon nearly full when Gill spread his plaid under a tree and made a bed for his bride on his brother's farm. They spent two days together, talking, laughing and doing what all young married couples do. Yet there came a time when they both knew Gill had to go back to his border duty.

Gill sat with his back against the tree and his arms around his wife. "I am comforted you are already here and I do not have to fret you will be trapped inside the wall."

"Where exactly am I to hide when they attack?"

He kissed her forehead, leaned his head against hers, and closed his eyes. "A few days ago, you were upset because Neil did not tell us his plan."

"I remember."

"For months, we on the outside have been preparing hiding places. My brother and I dug a cave in the side of the hill. 'Tis well concealed and as soon as he gets the word, he will take in enough provisions for a few days."

"How long does Neil want us to hide?"

"Until it is safe to come out. The MacDonalds cannot patrol all this land and still protect their own. They will chase us in the beginning, but eventually they will have to go home and leave only a small patrol along the main paths."

"And then where will we go?"

Gill held her just a little bit tighter. "I do not know."

She felt his strong shoulders slump. "If we are together, it will not matter where we go."

"Aye, as long as we are together."

*

For the second time, Gill snuck inside the MacDonald hold. Their keep and collection of cottages sat on a hill, and the only way to see what was happening was to put on a MacDonald kilt, walk up the embankment and pray no one discovered him. Like any other clan, the MacDonalds had crying children, elderly people seated around small fires to keep themselves warm in the evening air, and young couples holding hands while they walked the paths.

His mission was to see if the MacDonalds were preparing for war and if so, how soon it would come. To find that out, a spy had to listen for the sharpening of swords, the weeping of women and the making of arrows. A hunter carried only about ten, but a warrior carried at least twenty arrows in his sheath, and a week ago when he was here, the sheaths looked to be only half-full. Now they were full and men were making extras.

So also, were torches prepared and horses gathered and waiting. The last signs would include the saddling of horses and the weeping of women, but he was not about to wait that long. As nonchalantly as he could, Gill walked down the hill. He followed the path and when it was safe, he diverted off to find his horse, change his clothes and notify the others watching the border.

It was finally time -- the war would begin tonight just as Neil predicted. The full moon was the key. There was a full moon every month, but for months it was hidden behind misty rain or fog. Each time, Laird MacDonald called his war off for another month. Tonight the sky was crystal clear and the moon would be at its brightest.

Gill's heart was racing, but causing a panic was the last thing the clan needed. Therefore, when he drew near, he slowed his horse and pretended nothing was wrong. Casually, he guided it over the bridge into the courtyard, remembered to smile at a passing woman, and nod to the boy who took his horse to the stable. The boy would soon see the horse's excess sweat, know it had been ridden hard and the rumors would begin. Gill could not help that.

He took his time walking up the steps and even paused on the landing of the Keep to admire the beauty of the meadow in the moonlight. Then he opened the large wooden door and walked into the great hall. He found Neil with Glenna, Steppen, and little Justin, nodded to Neil and then smiled at the women.

Steppen had no idea what his nod meant and returned Gill's smile as she got up, poured a goblet of wine and handed it to him. She thought nothing of both Glenna and Neil going up the stairs and instead, urged Gill to sit and help himself to an apple. Gill declined, but it didn't bother her. None of the guards ever sat at the table and most didn't drink the wine. She would help herself to it later.

Suddenly Gill went outside to guard the door and Neil had a hold of her shoulders. "Do you hear me, Steppen? You must go and now!" He untied her belt and let her MacGreagor plaid fall away. Glenna quickly picked it up and put it together with a

Cameron plaid. Then Neil put her belt back on and helped his wife pleat both plaids together with the MacGreagor plaid on the outside.

While Glenna did the same with the boy's little kilt, Neil hung the arrow sheath over Steppen's shoulder and added her bow. "Take the boy into the meadow as though you mean to play with him, and then ease him into the forest and up the hillside."

Steppen was finally coming to her senses and realizing what it all meant. "What will you do?"

"We will be fine." Next, he tied the MacGreagor sword with its new strings and ordinary sheath around her waist. "We are counting on you to save both him and the sword." The last thing Neil added was the strings to her dagger sheath. "Soon there will be MacDonalds in the forest watching us, so get away as quickly as you can. When you get over the hill, turn south. You will find a tree with a red cloth tied around it. At the back of the tree is a sack of food and more provisions. Go deeper into the forest and stay the night. Change your clothing and put the Cameron plaid on the outside, but keep both together to use for warmth and to hide the MacGreagor colors. Once you are on Cameron land, go south."

"South?" Steppen asked.

Neil drew her into his arms. "Aye, go to Jessup and we will meet you there."

"Go to England?"

"Do you remember how Jessup said to find her?"

Steppen tried extra hard to concentrate. It was all too much and her first concern was for her laird and mistress. "I remember.

Do you promise to meet me there?"

He held her fiercely one more time and then stood her back. "I swear it." Neil scooped his son into his arms and made his kiss quick. He let Glenna kiss him, set the boy down and put Justin's hand in Steppen's. "God will watch over you." He turned Steppen around and practically shoved her out the door.

There, the hardest part was over and making the separation quickly kept them all from losing their composure. Neil trusted his own emotions least of all, but he had far too much to do and could not afford the slightest weakness. He took Glenna's hand and walked with her up the stairs to the bedchamber window, so they could watch. The window covering had been closed for days, just in case an overexcited MacDonald decided to take a shot at them. He moved the curtain aside just enough so they could watch. Steppen did exactly what she was told -- she let the two-year-old run and play, pretended to laugh at him and took her time, as though there was nothing in the world to hurry them. Then they saw both of their loved ones go into the forest and disappear.

CHAPTER XII

"I am pleased you are not crying, wife."

Glenna turned in his arms and nuzzled his neck. "I have decided to cry later. Besides, 'tis only for a few days and I have a gift for you."

"What might that be?"

"You are to have another son."

"Am I?" He let the curtain close, kissed her passionately and then held her close. "Or a daughter."

"Aye or a daughter."

"Shall I tell you I suspected?" he asked.

"I suspected you suspected. Will you be sending me away as well?"

"I will not let the MacDonalds have my wife or any of my children. You will go with Gill. He will make only one stop to get his wife and then take both of you into England."

"Why Gill?"

"All lairds have a traitor and I do not know who ours is. I trust Gill and no one will suspect he has you."

"And what will my husband be doing?" Glenna asked.

"Praying, mostly."

*

It had not been easy digging a tunnel under the moat without anyone being the wiser, and it had taken two of the three years since the plague. It looked a lot like the one he saw at Jessup's house. Few knew about it and he trusted the ones who did, but before this night was over, they would all know about the tunnel -- all except Steppen.

He could not chance telling her. She was the first to go and if Steppen got captured, Laird MacDonald would not hesitate to torture her. She could not tell what she did not know and a lot of lives depended on the tunnel.

Giving his son to Steppen was the decision that weighed heaviest on Neil's mind. He wanted to send the boy with a hundred guards, but a hundred or even ten men encamped together with a little boy would draw the attention of more than one hostile clan.

It was also what Laird MacDonald expected Neil to do. Sending a child out alone with only a woman was the last thing Laird MacDonald would expect. Neil saw the truth of it that day in the horse's eye. He would make himself the decoy, he would be blatant about it with a ten man guard, and make Laird MacDonald's men chase him instead of his wife or his son.

*

Laird MacDonald was not the only one who waited for the full moon. Neil needed it so he could send the people out into the night and give them a head start. He only had a few hours left at best, and he carefully examined the faces of all the men gathered in the great hall before he began. They were good men and he owed them a great deal of honor and respect. Now, however, he was about to ask them to do the unthinkable -- carry on without him.

He told them about the tunnel and then said, "Tonight, we will set aside the MacGreagor name and go our separate ways." He paused to wait for their grumbling to stop. "I do not want this, you know that. But if we stay and fight we will lose our lives as well as the land. If we let them kill us, we will have no more MacGreagor sons with which to honor our fathers. You must find other clans to take you in."

"We could find more land," said one of the men.

At that, Neil nodded. "I intend to do just that. I have seen vast lands where no one lives."

"We will go with you," a man in the back said.

"I would like nothing better, but eight hundred of us going north together would be an easy target for the MacDonalds. It would also frighten other clans. We would likely have to fight our way to a new land and fighting is what we must avoid." He picked up his goblet and drank half a glass of water. "I will find the land and send for you."

"How will you send for us if you do not know where we are?"

Neil smiled to reassure them. "I will send my guards back to spread the word. If you come to me a few at a time, we will not raise suspicion or attract undo attention. Agreed?"

Their nods came slowly, and for a time each man was lost in thoughts of taking his family to unknown parts of the world, and finding new clans to live with. If it was frightening to them, their wives were not going to take it well at all. Yet there was no other way and they soon came to that realization.

"You will each take ten with you. The MacDonalds will

expect you to run to the Ferguson, but 'tis a trap. Cross their land either north or south of their hold, and go to the Kerr or the Forbes. If they cannot take but a few of you, send the strongest on. Do the same if you cross the other direction into Cameron land."

He paused to let them absorb his instructions. Then he went on, "The weavers made as many unfamiliar plaids as possible and they wait for you at the end of the tunnel. There are not enough, so barter if you can and steal if you must. The sooner you put aside your MacGreagor plaids the safer you will be."

As soon as a man began to speak, Neil raised his hand. "I have bargained with the King of England, and he will not accost you if you need to cross into their land. However, I recommend you hide for a few days first. The MacDonalds will give up chasing us soon enough and then you can travel with less fear."

"What about horses?"

"Some will be waiting for you. Some you can get from the outside families. There are MacGreagors who will likely stay and I have no quarrel with that. A lad must consider his family when he decides what to do."

Neil touched the shoulder of the man nearest him. "Let not your family see your sorrow. Go, collect your ten and come back. Tonight we begin a short separation and then a new life."

*

Steppen was already exhausted. She found the cloth bag of provisions right where Neil said it would be, and hung it on her already overburdened shoulder. Justin thought walking deeper into the forest was a game, but he was being very good and keeping his chatter to a whisper. They saw no one and she was convinced no one saw them.

It got darker and the moonlight was good, but it did not shine through the trees well enough. By the time Justin stumbled over tree limbs twice and she nearly fell once, Steppen was ready to give up. She reasoned anyone looking for her would have the same trouble and she would hear them.

She unloaded her shoulders, took off her plaids, put the Cameron plaid back on and spread the MacGreagor cloth on the forest floor for them to sit on. She hoped she would find another in the bag and was delighted when she did. At least they would be warm enough. There was nothing to do then, but lie down, wrap the plaids around them and try to sleep.

For Steppen, sleep would not come.

*

Neil lovingly kissed Glenna. "'Tis only for a few days."

"I believe you. Tarry if you must, but come to me unharmed," she said.

"I love you." He hugged and kissed her one more time, and then moved a wooden box off the trap door under the stairs. Gill took a candle and was the first to go down the ladder, with Glenna right behind him. His duty was to light other candles in the cubbyholes along the way so it would not be so frightening for the women and children. When he was ready to climb up the ladder on the other side, he glanced back at Glenna. She was prepared, so he blew out the candle to keep it from being seen on the outside.

Carefully, Gill pushed on the wooden plank hidden deep in the forest. It opened not far from the clearing on the south side of the loch, where Neil once held his counsel during the war with his brother. Gill quickly looked around for danger, pushed the plank all the way out and pulled himself up. He gave his hand to Glenna, helped her out and then took her to the horses waiting for them nearby.

He helped her mount, swung up on the horse he would now call his, and led the MacGreagor mistress away. In less than an hour, he would pick up Ralin, wish his brother well, and keep going. The life of his mistress was now in his hands and he intended to make sure nothing happened to her, or his precious wife.

*

Unlike other clans, the MacGreagors did not build fires inside the wall at night. Wild animals could not get in, everyone trusted everyone else and there was no need. So when the first families were ready to go, they slipped through the back door of the Keep unnoticed by anyone who might be watching them from the hillsides. They carried with them a few pots, a few keepsakes and all their extra clothing.

Ten at a time, the people met in the great hall, hugged Neil, went down into the tunnel and then up the other side to start their new lives. It went much faster than he expected. Guards posted in the towers came occasionally to report, but so far they had not seen any MacDonalds. Neil guessed they were hidden out of sight waiting for the blue-black of dawn.

At last, only Neil's guard of ten men remained inside the wall.

They were ready, all they needed was the first sign of the attack. While he waited, he walked once more through the place he called home. In Leesil's room, he noticed the hand mirror that once belonged to his grandmother. He would have been unhappy when he realized he left that behind. The handle was made of finely carved wood and when he tucked it inside his shirt, he made sure the glass faced away from him.

The idea of losing his home was not as devastating as it might have been. The land his ancestor fought for had been difficult to hang on to for generations. The MacGreagors had a good life there, he would miss visiting the graves of his parents, but once he saw the vast lands of the north, this home did not seem so very wonderful. It was certainly not worth dying for.

He walked through the room that once belonged to his parents, saw nothing he wanted and went to look out the window. The first rays of dawn were beginning to illuminate the meadow where his mother and her horse once did tricks. He did not remember it, but his father's description would be a good memory to hold in his mind.

Then he smiled at the thought of leaving Laird MacDonald to deal with the King of England. How many good kings could the English produce before a bad one tried to conquer all their land?

No, he was not all that sad to be leaving.

Even so, he did not intend to give up the MacGreagor hold without some sort of retribution. He went back down the stairs and touched the shoulder of each of the ten men. "'Tis time." He went to the table, picked up a candle and then walked to the back door.

Neil held the door open and as each man passed, he lit the man's torch with his candle.

As quickly as they could, they lit the timbers leaning against the hidden doors and then the ones at the base of the guard towers. Beginning in the back, the men set the roofs of cottage after cottage on fire and worked their way down the paths.

Inside the Keep, Neil spread MacGreagor plaids soaked in animal fat up the stairs, over the table and along the walls. Then he used two to make a straight line down the middle of the room.

His sweetest revenge was not yet and he wanted to see it for himself, so he went out on the landing. The cottages in the back were in full blaze and the men scurried up the steps to stand beside him. Some of the iron chain links had been removed and when he gave his nod, the last two men released the ropes and the aging bridge began to fall.

It shattered into a million pieces.

The last two guards ran to the stables, opened the doors and let the horses out so they could escape over the broken bridge as best they could. Then the men ran to the Keep. If the MacDonalds were about to attack, the noise of the fire blocked any sounds that would notify them. Now their race was against the smoke and the fire.

Neil followed the last man in, waited for each to disappear down the ladder and then lit his own torch. He got as far down the ladder as he could, tossed the torch onto the plaids, made sure they lit and quickly pulled the trap door closed.

CHAPTER XIII

Walrick stood in the open window of his cottage and stared at the full moon. Something was keeping him awake. The animals did not appear to be upset, no storm was approaching and all his adopted children went to bed happy and well. Yet as soon as he closed his eyes, he opened them again. Something was stirring his heart and for the life of him, he could not figure out what it was. So he stared at the moon until the sun began to rise and still he could not sleep.

*

Steppen was on the move again in the early morning light and might not have gone back, but she heard a loud crash and knew it had to be the bridge. She knew Neil and the men planned to take links out of the chain so it would fall when the MacDonalds tried to lower it. If it fell, it meant the MacDonalds were inside and MacGreagors were dying.

She hesitated for just a moment before she decided she would see this sight for herself. Someone had to witness it and tell Justin when he was old enough. By the time she eased out from behind a tree on the top of the hill, the entire hold was on fire.

MacDonalds were sitting on their horses outside the moat. Inside the wall, she could not see a MacDonald or a MacGreagor. The fire was too smoky and intense to see anything…but she knew without seeing, that the MacGreagors were dead. Instead of fighting, the cowardly MacDonalds were burning them to death.

Orange and yellow flames consumed the roof and licked their fury out the second floor windows of the Keep. The thick smoke billowed straight up and she pushed away any thought of what was happening inside. Instead, she began to look up the road for Neil and Glenna.

Neil promised he would meet her in England, but where was he? She looked in every direction, but there were no MacGreagors riding anywhere. They were all trapped inside the wall. Neil and Glenna were both dead…they had to be.

She could look no more and turned away.

Steppen was numb. Her home was gone, her laird was gone, and her mistress was gone. All that remained was Neil MacGreagor's son, and a heavy sword with a gold blade that meant nothing, now that everyone who knew the legend was dead. Her eyes began to fog over with tears.

Just then, she remembered the people outside the wall, turned back and quickly wiped her tears away. She could only see a few from the hilltop, but their cottages were not burning nor could she see smoke rising farther away.

She remembered Neil's words exactly. She was to save the sword and give it to his son when he was old enough. The thought that she would never hear Neil's words again made her started to cry. Neil cannot be dead -- he just cannot be. She allowed herself another few seconds of sadness before she got mad.

How dare the MacDonalds burn her beloved laird and

mistress! Someday she would shove the gold sword down the throat of the MacDonald laird herself.

Below, the MacDonald warriors were beginning to move and she realized she was too close. Quickly, she stepped back into the forest and headed away. She didn't notice the weight of the burdens on her shoulders or the child in her arms. She was so distraught and enraged, she did not notice anything.

Where could she go? Where could she hide? One thing was certain, if Neil and Glenna were dead, there was no point in going to Jessup. Steppen loved her sister-in-law, Jessup, but she was English and raising Justin with the English was unimaginable. No, she must raise Justin with the clans in the Highlands. She would go north, take a good husband, raise Neil's son and come back one day to avenge the MacGreagors.

*

Steppen walked through the trees for what seemed like hours, stopped and finally fell to her knees. "My burdens are too heavy." She hung her head and tried to catch her breath. "I cannot do this."

Something in what she said or did made Justin laugh, and she abruptly realized the precious life in her arms, was now hers to love and cherish. She kissed his soft cheek and steadied her resolve. She was Steppen MacGreagor and she would find a way to save them or die trying.

The little boy laughed again and when he reached out his hand, she caught her breath. Someone was behind her. Slowly, Steppen turned her head. Just two feet away stood the beautiful black stallion. She released her held breath, set Justin down and got up.

Could this be the same horse she saw Neil with in the meadow? He was huge. Never in her life had she seen such a big horse. Carefully, she reached out and touched its head just to make sure it was real. The horse did not move, so she patted his nose and smiled. "Might you give us a ride?"

When the horse nodded, it frightened her. She grabbed Justin and backed away. Horses do not speak Gaelic, that much she was sure of. She stared into the horse's eye for a long moment before she realized she was seeing her own reflection.

Horses sometimes nod for no reason at all, she thought. It was just a coincidence he nodded after she spoke. She looked around for a log to stand on and when she found one, she climbed up. Yet she was still too far away to mount. She glanced at the horse, then at the ground and back at the horse.

She stepped down and rolled the log closer. Then she got back up, patted the side of the horse's neck and set Justin on its bare back. "I beg of you horse, do not move." She adjusted the heavy sack so it was down the middle of her back, shoved the sword out of the way, grabbed a hand full of mane and swung up.

The horse waited for her to seat Justin in her lap, and then began to carry them down the Cameron side of the hill – to their new life.

-end-

STEPPEN

CHAPTER I

The fires in the MacGreagor village were burning hot when the last MacGreagor pulled himself out of the tunnel. He put the plank back in the ground and covered it with leaves. Then Neil led his men to the place in the forest where their horses were hidden. The successful escape of his wife, his son and most of the MacGreagors rested on getting the MacDonald warriors to chase him. Most MacDonalds had no idea what he looked like, but surrounding himself with ten men would get their attention.

The warriors he chose to stay with him were carefully hand-picked; they had to be unmarried so their minds were not on the safety of a wife and children. After that, he considered their skill as horsemen, fighters, hunters, and the builders they would need to be to settle a new land.

The eleven MacGreagors mounted their horses and walked them in plain sight up the road toward the burning village. However, the MacDonald warriors were so mesmerized by the fire, they sat unmoving on their horses outside the moat, watching generations of MacGreagor history go up in smoke. Some had their swords drawn, but found no one to fight and forgot they were holding them.

Horses without riders escaped through the hole where the raised bridge had blocked intruder entry for years. Some horses went into the water on top of the shattered bridge and came up the other side unharmed. Others were not so lucky, and still other horses managed to stay on the narrow passageway between the wall and the moat until they could find a less dangerous place to cross the water.

Neil waited and marveled at the MacDonald commander's total lack of understanding. Did he really think the MacGreagor laird would burn his own people alive? On the other hand, the longer it took the man to sort out his options, the more time the MacGreagors had to escape.

Neil estimated there were a hundred warriors within sight and another four to five hundred he could not see surrounding the moat. It was less than half the number of available MacDonald warriors and the rest, he guessed, were waiting at the Ferguson hold, where they expected the MacGreagors to show up.

He sent Steppen and Glenna south and the plan was to draw the MacDonalds away by going east. However, just letting them give chase was not good enough. For months, Lucas MacGreagor planned exactly where they would ride and which paths they would take. If all went well, the MacGreagors would have the last laugh.

The minute the MacDonald warriors spotted them, Lucas led the MacGreagors at a dead run back down the road, and then east toward Ferguson land. He looked back often, as did the others, to make sure they were still being followed. At first, the MacDonald commander and a considerable number of warriors gave chase, but little by little some fell away and the MacGreagors knew exactly why. There were much shorter routes to the Ferguson hold. The MacDonalds hoped to get there first and cut the MacGreagors off. Lucas turned the MacGreagors south instead of north.

They rode through a wide meadow, then up a hill and down again until they reentered the forest. Then Lucas held up his hand to slow them. He carefully led the men single file off the path, through a narrow passageway between two trees and sped off again.

The last MacGreagor stopped, pulled the long handle of an ax out of his belt, got ready and waited. At the first sign of the speeding MacDonalds, he threw the ax. The blade hit its mark perfectly and sliced the rope that kept the two sawed off trees from falling. Both trees crashed to the ground at the same time causing the leading MacDonald horses to rear up and almost dump their riders. The MacDonalds cursed and watched the MacGreagor ride out of sight.

Afraid of a second trap, the enemy cautiously made their way around the fallen trees, but now they were minutes behind instead of seconds...or so they thought.

In the distance they heard laughter.

For another hour the chase continued with the MacGreagors leading them south and then east again. Neil and his men stayed just out of reach, exhibiting their superior skill as horsemen. Occasionally, a MacDonald tried to hit one with an arrow, but shooting a moving target while riding on a moving horse was not something they were skilled at.

Once more, Lucas slowed, carefully led the men off the path and then back on again at the edge of a clearing. He pulled his horse to a halt, let the others pass and then whispered to Neil. "You will want to see this." Lucas took the MacGreagors to the other side of the clearing where they hid in the trees to watch.

The trap was set and the MacDonald commander and his warriors rode right into it. Before they knew what was happening, the floor of the forest gave way and men and horses alike fell into the giant hole.

The MacGreagors rode on and just as they hoped, the surviving MacDonalds collected their dead, gave up the chase and went back the way they came.

*

As tired as they were with no sleep the night before, Neil was comforted by the knowledge that the MacDonalds had not slept either. So when he decided to find a place to hide and spend the night, he did not fear closing his eyes.

He prayed for the souls that were lost, the safety of his family and the families of all the MacGreagors. He prayed for a new land where they could live in peace, closed his eyes and went to sleep. There would be time enough for worry in the days to come.

*

Perhaps knowing William Ferguson for only one day before they married meant their love was not as deep as Taral would have liked, but their physical attraction more than made up for it, and for the first few days of their marriage they were happy. Taral, who hated all the talk of war, wanted to feel safe and knew her husband would take her to live with the Fergusons. Therefore, she would not be trapped inside the wall when the attack came. To her, the union with William made sense.

What did not make sense was what happened the day the MacDonalds finally attacked the MacGreagors. Even at that distance, some heard the faint crash when the bridge fell and not long after, the smell of smoke filled the air. It might be a forest fire, some speculated, but by midmorning what happened was abundantly clear. A MacGreagor man brought ten people inside the Ferguson's tall wooden wall seeking safety.

The three small families were in the courtyard telling Taral and William how they escaped through the tunnel, just as all the other MacGreagors did. Taral noticed Laird Ferguson standing on the top step of his keep listening. It was not until he nodded that the horror began. His men, Ferguson men, cut down the MacGreagor men from behind.

Taral gasped and turned to hide her eyes against her husband's chest. The women screamed and tried to shield their children, but both the women and children were quickly dragged away. At the edge of the courtyard, several MacDonald warriors stood ready to receive the captives and carry them off. Each had a sickening display of satisfaction in his expression. The look on the face of the Ferguson laird, who once called himself Neil's friend, was stone cold and Taral felt sick.

Taral tried to protest, but William pulled her back, held her close and kept whispering in her ear, "We cannot help them. We must leave here and save ourselves." He had to say it four times before Taral let herself hear it. At last, she nodded and let him take her away.

He opened the door to his cottage, followed her in, closed the door and pulled her back into his arms. "I am ashamed to be a Ferguson this day. We will both become MacGreagors. Do you know how to find them?"

She pulled back and looked into his eyes. She knew exactly how to find Neil, but there was something in William's voice...something insincere. She needed a moment to think. What did she really know about William? If he was unhappy with the Fergusons, why not become a Kerr or a Forbes? Why try to find a clan that had no home -- unless there was another, more sinister reason? Taral lied. "Nay, I do not know where they went."

"They cannot be far, perhaps we can find them. Gather your things, we will leave tonight."

Taral watched him walk out of the cottage, did as she was told and then sat on the bed clutching the cloth sack with all her belongs inside. She heard other screams, closed her eyes, covered her ears and tried to block out the noise.

Her husband did not come back until very late, but he did take her safely away. Like thieves in the night, they slipped outside the wooden gate, mounted their horses and rode away. Yet Taral was not a stupid woman and the lack of guards questioning their actions was far too obvious.

*

That very day, a MacDonald rumor began of a great battle that killed everyone inside the MacGreagor wall. A second Ferguson rumor reported all were saved, going out instead through a tunnel. The other clans were not quite certain what to make of the two opposing rumors.

The war ended before it even began and the victory, no matter how hard the MacDonalds tried to portray it as such, was no victory at all. The much lusted after MacGreagor keep, village and drawbridge were all in ruins. For a time, MacDonald warriors hunted for hiding places, found a few MacGreagors and killed when they could. Yet a one-on-one fight with a man trying to protect his family gave none of them bragging rights, no matter how much they exaggerated the story.

By the next day, Laird MacDonald was satisfied just to have the land, the loch and the extra women. Therefore, he was not inclined to continue the war and called his warriors home.

CHAPTER II

Steppen was numb. Justin was being such a good little boy, but if they did not stop soon, she was going to fall asleep sitting up. The lack of sleep during the night before was nothing, compared to the emotional exhaustion of losing everything and everyone she loved. She was still too stunned to cry.

When Justin got hungry, she discovered someone packed bread in the cloth sack, and for that she was very glad. She also found a short dagger and a leg strap, which she quickly tied on under her skirt.

Not long after the sun reached the height of day, the horse found water and stopped. She discovered a flask in the sack and filled it, but when she realized she would have to tie it around her waist, along with everything else she was carrying, she dumped half the water out. The horse, she knew, would find water again when it got thirsty.

She walked a ways with Justin in hand and the horse followed. For a moment, she entertained the idea of hiding the sword somewhere on Cameron land, just to relieve herself of the weight. That moment passed quickly. Somewhat refreshed after a time, she found a high rock and got them back on the horse. The horse, she realized, was being as good as Justin, so she remembered to lovingly pat its neck.

Not once in her life had she ever been off MacGreagor land and Steppen had no idea where the horse was taking her. They passed through meadows, patches of forest, small clearings and went up and down hillsides. The sun stayed behind her back in the afternoon so she assumed she was crossing Cameron land. Where Cameron land ended, she did not know. At least, she was wearing a Cameron plaid and would probably not be bothered or suspected of anything.

She wondered how long it would take before all the Camerons knew what happened. Probably not long. That kind of gossip would cause warriors to go out of their way to spread the word. MacGreagors intermarried with Cameron's too, and there would be many a broken heart when they heard. Many would vow vengeance but that vow would be forgotten with time. Most vows were.

Her own heart was broken, but she dared not think about that now. When night finally came, she missed her warm bed and only had enough strength left to make sure they were well hidden in the forest. She spread the plaid, pulled Justin into her arms, covered them both, and instantly fell asleep.

*

Whatever bothered Walrick the night before was gone finally. He did not understand it and because such rumblings in his heart had never happened before, he knew not what to make of it. So he pushed it from his mind and when night came, he too quickly fell asleep.

*

Except for the placement of the sun in the sky, it was difficult for Neil and his men to know where they were. For all they knew they were in England, and the last thing they wanted was to start a war there. For half a day, they saw no other living soul and decided to start back.

The thing that bothered Neil most was the lack of information, so he split the men into teams, sent them to learn what they could, and instructed them to meet up with him near Jessup's home. He kept only two guards with him and all the men protested, but he insisted. They all needed to know what was happening and he personally needed to know if Glenna and Steppen survived.

*

For years Jessup's family called it the throne room, because her crazed brother fancied he would be King of England one day. God help England if that ever happened. Jessup MacGreagor had auburn hair, warm brown eyes and lived in an English manor, surrounded by English cottages, at the end of an English style road. The other end of the road became a path that led straight into Cameron land in the Highlands. Her English life was completely different from the one she shared with the Highlanders.

When Patrick MacGreagor came into her life, she had a daft brother, an aging mother and an invalid uncle to care for. All that changed once she married him and went to live with the MacGreagors. With Patrick's family, she was free and she loved being free, but after Patrick and her mother died of the plague, she went back to her English home.

Jessup kept the throne room just as it was. It had golden

figurines, jewel laden goblets on various tables and her brother's red cloak was still draped across the back of the throne. Indeed, everything looked just as it did the day she brought Patrick there, except now her MacGreagor plaid was lovingly folded on a table.

It was to the throne room Jessup went when she wanted to remember Patrick, and it was to this room Neil came a few months ago. He showed two of his men how to enter the tunnel, told Jessup what he suspected and then asked her to notify the king. As it turned out, the king was there that very day.

He did not promise, but Jessup hoped Neil would bring Glenna and Steppen to her for sanctuary. To enable them to find her manor easier, she cut off strips of a MacGreagor plaid, wrapped them around trees where the English road became a path, and hoped MacGreagors would spot them. After that, she checked daily to make sure the cloth had not been removed.

Each night she came to light candles and leave apples, cheese and bread on a table in the throne room, just in case. Therefore, when she opened the door at dusk and saw a MacGreagor kilt on a man with his sword drawn, she shrieked her delight. "Finally! Where are Neil and Glenna?"

Timidly, Glenna peeked out from behind Gill. "You are speaking Gaelic?"

Jessup put the platter down on the table and then put her hands on her hips. "Do you have any idea how happy I am to see you?" She grabbed Glenna's hand, pulled her forward and wrapped her arms around her. "I have been on my knees praying for days, Glenna MacGreagor. I would never have…"

"Is Steppen here?"

Jessup looked concerned. "You are the first."

"Neil sent her to you. She has Justin with her."

"Justin?"

"Aye, we have a son. He is but two." Glenna nodded to Gill who put his sword away and drew Ralin out from behind him. "This is Gill and his wife Ralin. We are starving."

"Of course you are. Come, I will feed you." She opened the door wide thinking they would follow, but when they did not, Jessup went back. "You need not be frightened. The plague was no kinder to England than to Scotland and I am alone here. I have three servants, who come in the day, but they are loyal and they will not betray you. One taught me how to speak your language and is looking forward to meeting you." She put an arm around Glenna and ushered her through the door. "I have no reason to stay here, you know. I have missed my MacGreagors something awful, and intended to go back to you soon. So I thought I best learn the language."

"Instead, we come to you." Glenna smiled. She had forgotten how much Jessup liked to talk and it was so good to be able to understand what she was talking about. She was relieved to know it was not all nonsense like she suspected.

"And you are more than welcome," Jessup continued. "I have many empty rooms and can hide most if need be. Will they come here, do you think?"

"I do not know."

"I see." She sat Glenna down at the table in her kitchen and motioned for Gill and Ralin to sit, while she began to fill bowls with food she was keeping warm near the stone hearth. "Steppen was to come to me before now?"

"Not before now possibly. We could not give her a horse without drawing attention to her."

"Then she is on foot."

"Aye."

Jessup put the first bowl down in front of Glenna and then handed her a spoon. Glenna moved the bowl over in front of Ralin who promptly gave it back. "You are with child, eat."

"With child? How wonderful," said Jessup. "I assure you there is plenty. Do eat, then I will let you bathe and sleep as long as you like…although the place gets a little noisy in the mornings. We have considerable land and many to work it." She set another bowl down for Ralin and then one for Gill.

Jessup took a seat and was quiet so they could eat in peace. She tried not to think about how long it had been since they ate, and how hungry her sister-in-law, Steppen, might be. She assumed Glenna would bring Steppen with her and was not that concerned before. Now she was frantic.

Steppen was only fourteen when Jessup left and could not be more than seventeen or eighteen now. She was a woman, but no amount of growing up prepared a girl like Steppen for the outside world, where men were a bigger danger than wild animals. Not only that, Steppen had Neil's child and would be willing to die protecting him. Jessup could not stand the thought of her being out there alone. "Tomorrow, I will find Steppen myself."

Glenna took hold of Jessup's hand. "You cannot, the MacDonalds will kill you. Besides, Steppen knows how to hide very well and you would never find her. We must wait for Neil, he will know what to do."

Jessup decided they could bathe in the morning and when they finished eating, she took Gill and Ralin up the stairs to one bedchamber and Glenna to another.

"Tell me what happened." She sat on the bed and listened to Glenna tell about the horror of knowing war was coming, about all of Neil's hopes, the fire she could see as they rode away, and the fear of being chased. Jessup could not imagine it.

She hugged Glenna, tucked her into the soft English bed she knew Glenna would not stay in long, and went back to the throne room to say her prayers and wait for Steppen.

CHAPTER III

The next morning, Jessup found herself asleep in a chair in the throne room. Steppen had not come. She roused herself, stretched away her sore muscles and went to check on her guests. She found Gill and Ralin in the foyer staring at a gold figurine.

She smiled, went to stand next to them, picked up the piece and handed it to Ralin. "You may touch them. They are outrageous gifts and if the world knew, I would be constantly besieged by thieves. Some came from the King and others were purchased by my wealthy uncle or brother. They are very valuable, or so they say."

"I have never seen gold like this before," said Gill.

Ralin giggled, "I have never seen a cottage like this before either. Do all the English live like this?"

"Nay, only the ones who know the King. Some live in cottages like the clans and some live in places a lot worse." Jessup put a finger to her mouth thoughtfully. "Glenna tells me Neil will take you to search for new land. I hope to go with you and I was just wondering if some of these things might make our way a little easier? Perhaps we might trade for new land."

"Perhaps," said Gill.

"Then while we wait for Neil, we will gather it and decide what to take."

Gill smiled. "And bury the rest?"

Jessup returned his smile. "That is not a bad idea."

*

Taral MacGreagor Ferguson killed a man.

William, her husband of only a few days before the attack, brought with them a full flask of wine when they escaped from the Ferguson hold. Frustrated that his search for the MacGreagors had been fruitless, on the third night when they rested, he eagerly began to drink. The more he drank, the more he was willing to reveal his true motive for wanting to find the MacGreagors.

The reward for killing Neil was the promise of becoming the MacDonald's second in command. It was a much coveted position and he wanted that kind of high esteem badly enough to marry her and betray her clan.

Taral was sick at heart and meant to leave him that night after he passed out. But he began to insult everything about her and in a fit of anger, she confessed she lied and knew exactly how to find Neil. William reached out to strike her and it was the last thing he ever did. She avoided his strike and shoved her dagger into the upper part of his stomach instead. It pierced his heart and when he fell away dead, she was not sorry.

She quickly gathered her things, mounted her horse, took his horse away with her and found a new place to bed down. The next morning, she came upon the most welcome sight in the world. She saw two people and a little girl walking a path, and thought she recognized them. Taral let out two short MacGreagor whistles and slid down off her horse. With quiet cries of joy, she ran into the arms of Dugan, Mayze and their little girl, Kenna.

Taral was home. They were four people and two horses with no land, but they were MacGreagors and anywhere with other MacGreagors was home. Once all four were mounted, she turned them toward Jessup's and prayed they were not too late to find Neil.

*

The wait for Neil only took three more days after Glenna made it to Jessup's. He left his guards outside and when he opened the hidden door in the wall and stepped into the throne room, Gill, Ralin and Glenna were asleep on the floor. A lone candle still burned on a corner table and he took a minute to stare at his beautiful wife before he put it out, sat down, stretched out beside her and took her in his arms.

"You are safe," she whispered.

"Aye." He kissed her lips and then settled her on his shoulder. Soon, they were both asleep. Just inches away, Gill and Ralin cuddled and went back to sleep.

In the morning, Neil was up before the others. He quietly searched the entire house and when he knew Steppen and the boy were not there, he sat down at the table in the kitchen and put his head in his hands. Something had gone wrong. It was the morning of the sixth day and maybe it was too soon to panic, but it was six days after all, and they could be anywhere by now. They could be captured, killed or just lost. How long did he dare wait for Steppen? His men were outside, the clan was counting on him to find new land and...how long could he wait? And if he did not wait long, would Glenna ever forgive him?

*

It was not in her nature to steal, but from her hiding place Steppen could see the men on the paths no longer wore Cameron plaids. She remembered hearing the Camerons and their neighbors were not always friendly, and therefore wearing Cameron colors might not be a good thing. Stealing seemed like a necessity.

The first time, she watched a woman walk to a river, waited for her to undress and go into the water. Then she raced over, grabbed the woman's plaid off a rock, left the MacGreagor plaid and hurried away. She successfully escaped, but she was sure her pounding heart was going to kill her.

She quickly mounted, rode off, and stopped a safe distance away. Then she cut off enough material to cover Justin's small kilt and hastily pleated the rest around herself. It was a full hour after she remounted and let the horse take them away, before her nerves calmed.

In their travels, she did not encourage the horse to go this way or that. However on some days they went west and on other days more toward the north. The horse did not follow the beaten paths, therefore she saw few men and managed to avoid the ones she saw.

Of all the problems the world had to offer, unfamiliar men worried her the most. She was well armed and all MacGreagor women were trained to fight, but men had the superior strength. She could handle one or two at a time perhaps, but not more than that. Twice she was spotted by men on the paths and got away before they could get to her. On every occasion, she shook with fright for what seemed like hours.

Each morning she expected the horse to be gone. Each morning he was still there and Steppen hugged his neck to show her appreciation.

Then on the sixth day, she spotted an elder woman sitting in front of a cottage she might otherwise have mistaken for abandoned. The roof looked as though it might cave in at any moment and a strong wind would surely blow the walls down. However, the old woman did not seem concerned, and after watching her for a time from her hiding place in the forest, Steppen decided to approach. She hoped the woman might know where to find the giant.

She slid down off the horse, dropped her heavy sack on the ground and took Justin's hand. The two quietly walked to the edge of the woods and once Steppen decided there was no danger, they walked out. The cottage door was open, but no fire was lit, making it too dark to see if anyone was inside. Therefore, she decided she would keep the doorway in sight just in case.

The woman was even older than Steppen guessed and although she and Justin stood right in front of her, it took the elder an extra-long time to notice them. Then she seemed to wake with a start, "Mercy on me, who are you?"

"We mean you no harm. What clan is this?"

"Are you lost, lass?"

"Nay, just passing through. May I know what clan you are?"

The man inside the rundown cottage was dirty and wore a long beard, uncombed hair and a nasty grin. He peeked around the corner of the opened door and listened intently to the chatter between the young woman and his mother. He would like a pretty wife like that one. Yes indeed, she was a pretty woman.

Asked Steppen, "Have you heard where the giant lives?"

"He lives in the north. Do you seek him?"

"Only if we happen to run across him in our travels. My husband is hunting for our evening meal in the forest and then we will move on." The woman did not offer food and Steppen did not stay. She thought she saw movement inside the cottage and it alarmed her.

The mention of a husband made the man reconsider his intentions. He still wanted her, but not enough to fight a husband. He stayed hidden inside and reluctantly watched the pretty woman and the boy walk back into the woods.

CHAPTER IV

All seven of his children were lined up like stair steps in front of Walrick. They stood outside in the courtyard where a goat was tied to a tree, and four other children waited to play, once the punishments were doled out.

Walrick looked his middle daughter square in the eye and frowned. "You must not hit your brother."

Katie put her hands on her hips, stomped her foot and narrowed her eyes. "You will not punish me."

"Where did you get that foolish notion?"

"You said if we did something out of love, we would not be punished."

Walrick closed his eyes and rubbed his forehead. "So you are telling me you hit your brother out of love?"

"I love him enough to hit him, you see. He was about to pull Catherin's hair, and for that he would have been punished, am I right?"

There were days when being a parent was not at all how he wanted to spend his time. The line between right and wrong was very, very thin and Katie took everything he said literally. He took a deep breath and slowly let it out. "For one, we do not hit except in war. For two, if you love your brother you will allow him to reap his own punishment. A man must be responsible for his own actions and his sister must leave him to it. Do you understand?"

"Not at all."

"I thought not." He began to pace in front of the children and rub his neck. "Katie, you will not hit anyone ever again. That is a command." He stopped directly in front of her, waited for her to finish rolling her eyes and then reluctantly nod. Then he went back to pacing. "As for you, Clifton MacClurg, you know the rules. Men are never to hurt a lass and that includes pulling hair. We protect our lasses, not hurt them."

One year younger than Katie, Clifton did not look at all frightened. "I am your son, do not forget. Are you going to kill me?"

"Kill you? Nay, but I will have you stand beside me all this day, and tell everyone your crime." It had exactly the effect Walrick hoped and the little boy gasped. If he only suspected it before, the MacClurg laird was certain now -- the children needed a mother and Walrick needed a wife to handle the constant squabbling of seven children.

*

England was such a foreign place for Neil to be, and staying inside an English manor was stifling. He walked the rooms repeatedly and looked out every window. When he wasn't doing that, he walked the tunnel and opened the outside door, just in case Steppen was having trouble getting in. She was not.

He and Gill went into the woods, took food to the men waiting there and checked on the horses. The horses had already been checked on regularly, but it was something to do. When that did not satisfy Neil, they mounted and rode to the place where Jessup tied plaids around the trees.

Then on the third day of his confinement, two more guards stepped out of the trees to greet their laird. He smiled, slapped one on the back and grabbed the arm of the other. "What news of the clan?"

"The news is good for most," Geddes answered. "The MacDonalds stopped searching for us five days ago and people are coming out of their hiding places. Some died, but we do not know who or how many."

"I did not expect Laird MacDonald to give up so easily."

"Everyone is surprised, but who can explain why Laird MacDonald does anything? The man is witless and best of all, he is not our problem any longer."

Neil grinned. "Indeed not. Come, I will feed you and then you can tell me everything." Neil took them to a place where they could hide their horses, led them through the tunnel and then enjoyed their expressions when they entered the English manor. He waited until the Glenna and Ralin greeted them, took them to the kitchen and let Jessup feed his men.

With everyone gathered around, he listened to his warrior's accounts and then took Glenna's hand. "If they are no longer searching for us, 'tis time to leave."

Glenna knew this was coming and bowed her head. They had waited eight days and if Steppen could, she would have come by now. "Perhaps we will find them on the way."

"I pray you are right. If not, I will settle us on new land and come back." Neil watched her bravely nod and then looked at Jessup. "How many horses may we have?"

"Six. One for me to ride and five to pack."

"Good. The lads will help you pack the horses, but if they say something must stay, you will not argue. Agreed?"

Jessup puckered her lips. "Does that mean I cannot take my bathing basin? I did not quite get the hang of swimming in a loch when I lived with you, and I have grown quite fond of my basin."

Neil smiled. "We will teach you to swim."

"I knew you would say that. Oh well, best we get started." She took Ralin's hand and led her out of the room. She was determined to take the basin, even if she had to wear it on her head. "Gather every comb and brush you can find. I do not..."

Neil watched the hungry men devour stew and another half loaf of bread, and then turned to Glenna again. "Jessup tied a cloth around a tree to show us the way here."

"I saw that when we came."

"Suppose we do the same? We could tie strips of plaid to show Steppen which way we have gone." He watched his wife's eyes light up. He smiled when she quickly stood and rushed out of the room, and then he looked at his men. "When a lass is upset, give her something to do. My father taught me that and it was very good advice."

Geddes looked concerned. "Your wife does not look well."

"She is with child. We will cross Cameron land quickly, but then we will move slowly and stop often for her sake. I do not intend to lose two sons. Besides, we will need to hunt along the way."

"And tie strips of plaid," said Geddes.

"Aye, Glenna will keep us busy doing that."

*

"Why are you surprised my husband will let you go with us?" asked Glenna. She finished cutting up one MacGreagor plaid, set the last strip in her pile on Jessup's bed and picked up another plaid.

"I am a lass and a burden."

"My dear, you misunderstand. Without lasses, the clan disappears and rebuilding a strong clan is on the minds of our men right now. They will gladly take you with us and treat you like a queen." She paused and thought for a moment. "You do plan to remarry?"

Jessup sighed. "I have yet to see an Englishman who tempts me, but if a MacGreagor…"

"My husband chose ten unmarried lads to protect him and I saw the way those two in the kitchen watched your every move. You will not be unmarried long."

Jessup smiled, "I will be trading gold and jewels for a husband, but let's not tell them, shall we?"

Glenna smiled. She was quiet for a moment, but then her smile faded. "Neil is tired, he misses our son, although he will not let me see, and the journey will not be easy."

Jessup set the box of tightly packed sewing supplies down and looked out the window. "He has aged."

"Aye, he walked the floor at night for months trying to decide what to do. Now he fears he made all the wrong decisions and the people are lost to him."

"Especially Steppen and Justin."

"Aye, but I am convinced I would feel it if Justin were not still alive. No one loves him more than Steppen and she is taking very good care of my baby. I am sure of it."

"I agree."

"What will happen to your land?" Glenna asked.

"It belongs to the King and he will pass it on to the next Baron, and the one after that, and the one after that, until the end of the world. By then, I will not care."

CHAPTER V

The second time Steppen stole a plaid, she took it off a rope stretched between two trees outside a newer cottage. The sun was bright, she could see inside the open door and when she was certain no one was home, she went in, took a loaf of bread and a chunk of cheese off the table too. She dashed in and out so fast she forgot to leave a plaid behind as payment and had to go back.

She was so terrified and breathing so hard, she nearly missed the rock she needed to stand on to get back on the horse. The life of a blackguard would be the death of her, she thought -- even if she didn't get caught, and getting caught was out of the question. She shared the badly needed food with Justin and hoped they were not eating someone else's only food. Too late to worry about that now.

By the time the men finished loading the packhorses, the sun was nearly up. They helped Glenna, Ralin and Jessup up and then mounted their horses. When they left Jessup's small English courtyard and started up the road, they numbered three women, six men and one child on the way.

When they came to the place where the English road became a Scottish path, eight more men stepped out from behind the trees. Thrilled to see them all safe, Neil slid down to greet them, and when Lucas nodded toward the trees, Taral came out followed by Dugan, Mayze and little Kenna.

Neil took Mayze in his arms and hugged her tight. "I cannot tell you how happy this makes me." He kept his arm around her, touched little Kenna on the head, and then grasped arms with Dugan. He let go of Mayze and wrapped his arms around Taral.

"I killed William," Taral said.

Neil drew back and looked into Taral's eyes. "Did he deserve to die?"

"Aye and I would do it again."

He nodded. "Tonight when we stop you will sit by me and tell me what happened." He looked at Mayze and then back to Taral. "I say we find a new home." He waited for each to nod, hugged them both again and then picked up the child. He handed little Kenna to his smiling wife, waited for everyone to mount their horses and then motioned them on.

Thus, the MacGreagors increased their numbers by nine men, one child and two women -- one of them beautiful and newly unmarried. If nothing else, Neil was going to enjoy watching to see which MacGreagor men would win Jessup and Taral's heart.

*

Walrick had to admit she was a pretty woman and looked to be about his same age. She was attentive and patient with the children, even his, whom he thought were getting more and more out of hand every day. Women, he decided, were born with more patience than men.

Janell did not often look at him, however, and therefore it was hard to tell if she was interested. Then again, he was not altogether sure he was interested. He could not decide if she was around him more often, or if she always had been, and he was noticing her more often. She set his noon meal on the table, poured him a goblet of water, smiled and then left.

It was when his children acted up that he thought about taking a wife, but the thought passed as soon as the children mellowed out. He kept his heart sealed up so tight, he hadn't really noticed any of the other women either. Yet this woman somehow had his attention.

Carrying buckets of bath water up and down two flights of stairs each day was not easy, but Walrick liked giving that chore to the men who needed to build their muscles most. He did not sleep in the Keep, but he maintained the third floor as his private dwelling, where he could be alone, bathe, and look out the windows in all directions. The large bathing basin was the one possession he kept after he threw Knox off the land, and he was glad he did.

It was after his bath, after he put on clean clothing and looked out the window, that he saw Janell walking one of the paths in the glen. She was indeed a pretty woman even from a distance.

*

For days, Gelson noticed his laird noticing Janell and he was disturbed. She was not a bad person particularly, but she was not above lying to get what she wanted, and what she appeared to want now was to trick a man into marriage, just as she tricked his brother. Now she was a widow and Gelson feared she was about to sink her claws into his unsuspecting laird. This, he intended to prevent.

If Laird Walrick MacClurg had a weak spot, it was that he trusted women too well, and would not see Janell coming. The thing to do, he decided was to alert everyone else and elicit their help. So when Janell looked as though she were about to fall, on purpose, right in front of Walrick, Finley caught her just in time.

Walrick saw the whole thing and was impressed with Finley's quick reaction. His teachings about protecting women seemed to be catching on. Yet the look on her face surprised him -- she looked annoyed. "Are you hurt?"

Her expression quickly softened. "Nay." Janell brushed past both Walrick and Finley, walked on down the path and went into her cottage.

She did not thank Finley for saving her and Walrick found it puzzling, but dismissed it as just her being embarrassed. Finley, on the other hand, realized Gelson was right; Walrick needed protection. The women in the MacClurg clan did not like Janell at all, and having her for their mistress would cause problems for everyone. Still, how do you keep a man from falling in love? There was a way, Finley thought, and hurried away to consult with Gelson.

*

She was just standing there with her berry basket in hand, staring into the forest, when Walrick noticed her for a third time that same day. He dismissed the young warriors he was training and walked to her. "What is it?" Janell was not startled by his sudden appearance and she turned around to face him.

"I confess I am frightened."

"Of what?"

"Someone said there was a wild boar in the woods yesterday. Do you suppose 'tis gone by now?"

"I heard no such rumor."

"No? I am surprised." She smiled then and lowered her eyes. "Perhaps I dreamed it."

When she raised her eyes again, he noticed they were a pleasant green that went well with the touch of red in her brown hair. Her smile was friendly and there was something seductive about her. "Perhaps."

She started to walk up the path and was pleased when he walked with her. "I am a widow. My husband was killed in a hunting accident, and he left me with no children. I do so love children, but it was not to be."

He kept his hands clasped behind his back. It had to be years since he walked with a woman and he liked it. "I am sorry to hear that."

"They say your wife died as well. Tell me about her."

Janell's question did not please him. He was not ready to talk about Kindel even after all this time, and especially not with someone he did not know. "Were you born here?"

"Aye. I was…"

Gelson was several yards away when he spotted them. He had to do something quick, or Janell would draw Walrick into the forest, and who knew what might happen then. "Janell," he shouted and began to quickly walk that way. He smiled and kept right on smiling until he reached them.

She was smiling too. "Gelson is my brother-in-law."

"I did not know that," said Walrick.

Gelson nodded. "Aye and I have been neglecting her. I should be guarding her when she goes to pick berries. Do forgive me, sister." He got exactly the kind of reaction he expected. Her mouth held her smile but her eyes were glaring. He ignored "Sister, are you aware that Finley is...well, he finds you pleasing."

She was truly shocked. "What?"

Gelson put his arm around her shoulder and began to guide her into the forest. "Surely you are not surprised. You are a young lass with no husband, and you should at least give the lad a thought. Finley is a good lad, you must admit."

Walrick walked away. If one of his men preferred her, then she was off limits.

*

Steppen finally found paradise. She was tired of riding a horse, getting up, getting down, finding water, not finding water, going for two or three days without a bath, and eating what little she could find or steal. At last, the horse took them to a stream and when she got down and dropped her heavy cloth sack on the ground, she took Justin's hand and walked into the forest to look for food.

That's when she found them -- bush after bush loaded with ripe raspberries. She shrieked her excitement, pulled some off, gave them to Justin and began to fill her empty stomach. The horse, she noticed, was grazing on the grass in the small clearing, so when they were finally full, she spread her plaid and put herself and Justin down for a long, much needed nap.

She woke up to discover another surprise under a tree not far away -- mushrooms.

It was a good place with ample water and food, so they rested there for two whole days. She shot a game bird the first day and a rabbit the second, she washed their clothing, hung them over tree branches to dry and watched the color return to Justin's cheeks as he played. The horse stayed and she was still amazed.

Before she left the next day, she had mushrooms and berries crammed into every possible place, even in her flask.

CHAPTER VI

For the most part, the MacGreagors remained quiet the whole time they crossed Cameron land. Some of the guards wore Cameron kilts to make it appear the MacGreagors were being escorted, or perhaps were captives. It was a good plan. Neil kept them two days south of the Cameron village, just in case Laird Cameron had made an alliance with Laird MacDonald. After the plague, very little was heard from the Camerons and Neil had never met their new laird. He did hear, however, that Laird Cameron was terrified of Laird Campbell.

*

On the morning of the fourth day, he breathed a sigh of relief and instructed the guards to put on their MacGreagor kilts. He also awoke to find they were joined by six more MacGreagors, two men, two women and two children. He was thrilled, heartily welcomed them and led the clan north.

When they stopped for the night, they all gathered around, to hear the story of how the newest members escaped and all the latest gossip. It was the gossip they were interested in most. To no one's surprise, the MacDonalds were claiming a great victory. The bridge was un-repairable and the MacDonalds had no idea how to build a new one. Everything inside was a total loss and the MacDonald laird was furious when he heard about the fire. He planned to live there himself.

Neil smugly smiled. He was also pleased there were no rumors of Laird MacDonald getting his hands on Neil's son. It wasn't much, but there was some comfort in that. The war was behind them by ten days and the farther they traveled, the more they began to feel the excitement of good things to come.

*

Knox MacClurg was a vile man who enjoyed the suffering of others. Deposed as laird of the MacClurg Clan by Walrick, he was equally as incensed as he was vile. Three years earlier he was set loose a good five days south of the place he called home, with no horse and no food. For the same three years he nursed his anger and swore his revenge.

He became a decent hunter, a good thief and a vagabond, while slowly making his way back north. He did not take up with any other clan; after all, a laird does not change clans. A laird is either a laird or he is dead -- and Knox was neither. The real reason he'd been run off, he convinced himself, was because the giant was bedding his wife.

Knox did not particularly care for the wife he'd been tricked into marrying, but she was his property and no other man could have her, unless her husband set her aside or was dead. Knox had accomplished neither of those things either, and the thought of her in the giant's bed galled him. His conjured up mental images consumed him so completely, in three years he wasted not one moment thinking about his twin son or daughter.

The woman sitting with the little boy, on a log near the small fire, was a beauty to be sure. Her face was square, her long hair was a golden blonde and her dark eyes captured his attention immediately. Yet it was not because of her beauty Knox sought to do her harm -- it was the magnificent black stallion he wanted, and he was willing to kill her to get it. He certainly could use a horse and one like that could be bartered for a lesser horse, a few more weapons and badly needed supplies.

The one thing he found unfathomable, however, was the horse's lack of a bridle. Knox did not have a bridle and capturing a creature like that required at least a rope of some sort. Hidden behind a bush, he nodded to no one but himself. He could steal the bridle he saw hanging on the outside of the farmer's rabbit hutch, and come back. The woman and the horse might not be there when he got back, but it was a chance he would have to take. Satisfied with his decision, he slipped quietly away.

*

Knox MacClurg was not the only one who knew Steppen was there. From the top of the hill, Gelson spotted her as soon as she entered the long glen. He watched her for quite some time, decided she was indeed alone with a child, and suspected it was yet another woman trying to find the giant. He too was drawn to the magnificent black horse. It looked a great deal like the one Walrick had when Gelson and his men first found the giant.

If it was the same horse, he wondered how she managed to capture and control it. None of the MacClurgs were able to, and they kept trying until Walrick told them to let the horse be. Of course, that enabled the horse to just wander away, and Gelson was sorry to see it go. A few colts from that stallion would have improved their herd immensely.

He decided the horse was something Walrick would want to see, and it was a good excuse to get him away from the temptation of Janell, so he went home to get him.

*

Steppen was tired of being on a horse, the berries and mushrooms were gone, Justin needed to run and play, and the poor horse had to be worn out. She had not seen a village or any travelers in two days, they were in a peaceful glen with ample water, and she doubted they were in any danger.

She slowly looked around. If the horse finally decided to leave, they could manage. The creek didn't look like it would dry up any time soon, the trees were big enough to give them shelter from the rain, and she suspected the hunting was good. Maybe they could find more berries.

She watched Justin try to catch a butterfly, and then noticed an eagle glide from one end of the glen to the other. It was a magnificent bird and she watched to see if it would come back. Yet the warmth of the sun made her sleepy, Justin was tired and nothing sounded better than a short nap before they headed off again.

*

When she woke up, Steppen felt the danger. She sat up and stretched, as anyone would just waking up, but she did not look around. Instead, she allowed her good instincts to let her know where the intruder was, and then nonchalantly got up. First, she tied the sword back on, and then adjusted her dagger strings so she could pull it quickly.

Her movements woke Justin, so she helped him stand up and then whispered in his ear, "Be very quiet." When the little boy nodded, she took him into the trees. She went just far enough away to hide the boy behind a tree and still see what was happening in the clearing.

*

With the woman gone, Knox stepped boldly out from behind a bush, held his bridle up and began to walk toward the horse. So intent was he on having the horse, he did not hear the men approaching behind him.

Gelson and Walrick arrived and dismounted, just in time to watch Knox's first attempt at capturing the stallion. The horse managed to back up just in time. Still unaware he was being watched, Knox tried again. Again, the horse backed up.

Gelson could not help himself and began to laugh. Knox spun around and found himself once more, face to face with the giant. His color began to drain, but he was not sorry it had come to this. He aimed to face the giant again someday, and this day was as good as any. His was a loathsome life, he was tired of it and death would be welcome. Slowly, he tossed the bridle away and drew his sword.

The intention was not lost on Walrick who also drew his sword.

Gelson put his hand on Walrick's arm. "Did I ever tell you what this lad did to my mother?" Gelson turned his glare on Knox and slowly drew his own sword. "I have waited years for this."

Walrick stood aside and put away his sword. The battle was short and soon the coward lay dead in a heap on the grass. Gelson cleaned his sword, put it back in its sheath and went to stand beside Walrick. The worry over Knox was finally behind them.

Nevertheless, the war between Steppen and Walrick had just begun.

*

From her hiding place behind the trees, she recognized him. He was Walrick MacGreagor -- in the flesh, looking just as healthy as a man could, and that made her furious. For months, she missed him, wondered where he was, and feared he was dead. He was not dead, not dead at all, and she would never forgive him for not coming home.

"You may come out now, 'tis safe," said Walrick.

Safe for her maybe, but not for him. She was mad enough to pull her dagger and run Walrick through. For a moment, she considered not going out. Perhaps in a while he would go away. On the other hand, he was Walrick and never had she known him to just go away. Steppen took a deep breath and let it out. She reached for Justin's hand, walked out of the woods and kept going until she was face to face with Walrick.

"We will not harm you. What is your name?"

She let go of the boy, folded her arms and stared at Walrick. Was he serious? Didn't he recognize her?

Perplexed, he wrinkled his brow and looked at Gelson. "Perhaps she cannot speak."

"I can speak very well when I have something to say," she said.

"I see. I am Walrick and this is Gelson. May we know your name?"

Steppen needed to think for a moment. What game was he playing? She was the little girl who followed him everywhere; asking all sorts of questions. Was it possible he did not remember her, was he lying, or had she changed that much in three years? "I do not care to say my name."

"Why not?"

"I do not like you."

Walrick's eyebrows shot up. "You have decided that already? How have we upset you? Have we just killed your husband?"

"I have never seen that lad before in my life. He only meant to steal my horse."

At almost the same moment, all three of them looked, but the black stallion was nowhere in sight. Steppen sighed and closed her eyes. "Now see what you have done."

"I have done nothing to frighten your horse away."

Gelson liked this woman. She was pleasing, determined and brave enough to stand up to the giant. Most women swooned or became speechless. This one, Gelson decided, would provide stiff competition for Janell, and that pleased him very much. He looked at the little boy and then knelt down. "What is your name?" The little boy didn't answer so he asked the next logical question. "How old are you?"

"His name is Justin and he is two," Steppen answered.

It was Walrick's turn to fold his arms. "You have no horse, no food and a laddie to care for. You will come home with us."

Steppen stood her ground. "*You* will not tell me what to do. I have taken care of the laddie for…God knows how many days, and I can do it for as long as need be. You may leave us now." As soon as she said it, she regretted her words. More than anything in the world, she wanted to go home with Walrick. Anywhere with him would be home and she was so tired of being alone. Steppen walked back to the log, sat down and began to add more twigs to the fire.

CHAPTER VII

"Then I will stay here with you. I am Walrick MacClurg and we do not leave helpless lasses alone to fend for themselves."

She was instantly livid. She could not decide which made her the maddest -- that he thought she was helpless or that he'd taken another name. She tightened her fists and gritted her teeth. Before she knew it, he was standing right in front of her.

"Are you unwell?"

"Will you please stop asking so many questions?"

Walrick exchanged a confused look with Gelson and then glanced around. "We will gather your things and take you home." This time it did not appear she was going to argue, so he picked up a wooden bowl, an empty flask and put them in the sack. Next, he began to fold the plaid she laid out for their nap, and watched Gelson put the fire out. He wondered if he dare speak to the woman, but decided to take a chance. The most she could do was bite his head off again. "You have few belongings."

"We left in a hurry."

"For what reason did you leave in a hurry?"

She put her hands on top of her uncombed hair and tried to think how much she should say. It was, after all, his home and his people too and the news would come as a big shock. "There was a war."

"I see."

She wanted to scream -- No, you do not see! You were not there and you should have been! Upset with herself for thinking she should protect him from the shock, she stood up and began to pace away her fury. "Everyone burned." She stopped to see his reaction, but there was no flicker of recognition in his eyes.

Walrick had no idea what to say to comfort her. He did not recognize the colors she wore, nor had they heard news of a war. At length, he turned away, finished packing her things, drew the strings and put the strap over his shoulder. "Did your husband die?"

She gritted her teeth. "Must you keep asking questions?"

He shrugged, waited until Gelson mounted his horse and then handed the boy up. "The lad is too thin. He needs food and a warm bed." He swung up on his horse, leaned down, put his arm around her waist and pulled her up. He sat her in front of him, and then waited while she put a leg over and got settled before he nudged his horse forward. He was surprised when she put her hand on his arm in a familiar manner. Most women tightly crossed their arms when a stranger held them on a horse. Shyness was definitely not one of this woman's short comings.

"How far is it to your home?"

"Not far. We will be there before dark."

Had she been in the arms of a stranger, she might have felt uncomfortable, but he was Walrick, and she had been in his arms on a horse since she was ten. She thought of the sword, quickly felt her side to make sure she still had it, and let out a sigh of relief.

"'Tis a lad's sword," said Walrick.

"It belonged to the lad's father. I am to give it to Justin when he is grown. Do you mind if we do not talk? I am very tired."

"You may lean against me, if you like."

How very generous of him, she thought. Steppen would rather wring his neck, but she was exhausted and leaning against a man she had known all her life was very tempting. Instead, she took hold of his arm and leaned around to look back at Justin.

Gelson smiled. "He is nearly asleep. I have a two-year-old. I will take good care of him."

"Thank you." It was a relief to have the boy in someone else's care for a change. She loved Justin dearly, but he was getting heavier every day. It was not until she turned back around that she realized she was already leaning against Walrick.

"Are you cold?"

"Nay and stop asking questions."

He rolled his eyes, "Do forgive me."

"You need not be so mocking."

"I am mocking? You have hardly said a civil word." The woman in his arms did not argue. Instead, she got quiet. Perhaps she would sleep now and he would be glad if she did. Her words were angry, but the way her body was slumped against him let him know her true exhaustion. He had a thousand questions. What was her name, where did she come from and why did she feel so familiar in his arms?

"He frightened me very much."

Walrick could barely hear her whisper and leaned a little

closer. "The lad who tried to take your horse?"

"Aye, I almost did not notice him watching me."

He tightened his arm around her waist in response. "I will not let anyone hurt you."

She nodded, lifted her hand and wiped the tear off her cheek. Then she wrapped both her arms around his upper arm and put her head against his shoulder. It was hitting her finally, how alone and how terrified she had been, not just today but every day of their journey. She was safe in Walrick's arms and what she really wanted to do was turn, confess who she was, let him hold her and welcome her home. Still, she waited all that time for him to love her. How could he not come home?

Walrick smiled. Steppen used to hug his arm that way when she was little. Suddenly he realized it was not all the beautiful MacGreagor women he missed, it was Steppen. He missed her smile, her boldness and her endless questions. He especially missed the look in her eye when she was about to ask a question she knew no one could answer. He almost laughed remembering his favorite question. At twelve, Steppen wanted to know who lit the sun every morning before it came up. They both pondered the question for quite a while before she decided it was the archangel Michael.

Now a woman was hugging his arm the way Steppen did and he missed her even more. He was tempted to draw the woman closer. Instead, he said. "Go to sleep, I will not let you fall."

"Thank you." How wonderful that sounded. She could finally sleep on a horse without fear of falling off or accidentally letting go of Justin. She sighed…finally, but she could not sleep. She told Neil she 'sometimes' watched for Walrick to walk back over the bridge, but it was a lie. She watched for him every day for three long years. She worried about him, fretted over him and loved him. Walrick had no one left and neither did she. Her brother Patrick would have wanted the two of them to be together, but Walrick would not come back and it hurt her every day for three very, very long years.

The woman in his arms seemed to have kept herself clean, but her hair had not seen a comb for a long time. He thought about her seeing the people burn and running with the boy from a war. No woman should have to endure either of those things and he wanted very much to make everything right for her again. He wanted to wrap his other arm around her too, but he didn't give in to the urge.

Steppen was cold but too stubborn to admit it. "Do you have children?"

"Aye, seven."

She sat up so fast; she almost hit his chin with her head. He had seven children in three years? His poor wife. On second thought, how does a woman have seven children in three years? Even three sets of twins could produce only six. Maybe this clan believed in more than one wife. That had to be it, Walrick was a bigamist.

"What has upset you?"

"I do not wish to discuss it."

He rolled his eyes. For a moment he thought they were about to have a conversation, but she seemed to get annoyed over everything he said. "Where were you going when we found you?"

She settled back against him, but everything was different. A few minutes ago she had dreams of becoming his second wife, now she feared becoming his third or fourth wife. "I have heard there is a giant in the north who is a fair lad. He does not make lasses marry against their will. I hope to take a husband someday, but I do not wish to be forced."

Walrick tried not to smile, "You have heard of the giant?"

"Aye, do you know where he is?"

"I do. If you like, I will take you to him. However, I fear you will be disappointed. The rumors about him are not all true."

She turned around to see his face. "How so?"

"Well, he is no bigger than I am."

She looked disappointed. "I see." She glanced at the top of his head. "I suppose to some you are big enough to be a giant."

"I suppose. You do not seem surprised by my size."

"I have seen bigger. Are there many unmarried lads in your clan?"

Her question annoyed him and he was not sure why. "Gelson, how many unmarried lads do we have?"

Justin was sound asleep on Gelson shoulder and he took a moment to consider his answer. "Thirty five if you do not count Finley." He reminded Walrick of Janell on purpose, so his laird would compare her to the woman in his arms.

"Finley will make a good husband for Janell," said Walrick.

Gelson grinned. "Aye."

CHAPTER VIII

Walrick's attention quickly returned to his unexplained attraction to this woman. "What sort of husband do you hope to find?"

Steppen was with the man she wanted to marry -- once she forgave him for not coming back. Since she always imagined herself married to him, she had not thought of what sort of man she wanted. "You will ask me no more questions."

"Good, go to sleep."

She decided not to argue and relaxed against him again. "Will we be welcome in your clan?"

"Aye."

"Most lads have to ask their laird before they invite someone to live among them."

"I am the MacClurg laird."

"You are what?" She was seething again. So that is why he did not come home, he wanted to be a stupid laird more. It was a good thing he was already married. If she married him, she would be a stupid mistress, trapped in her stupid home half the time, just like Glenna. Oh no, that was not going to happen to Steppen. "Stop the horse, I need privacy."

As soon as he halted, she swung her leg over and slid down. In a huff, she stomped off into the forest.

Walrick waited until Gelson pulled his horse up next to him. "What do I keep doing to upset her?"

"I have no idea, but you fancy her, am I wrong?"

"You are not wrong."

"She will make you daft before you win her."

"Aye, but what can I do? I already prefer her." Walrick smiled at the little boy. With seven already, what difference would one more make? Eight children. At least now, he would have help -- that is if he could get this woman to talk to him. "You are a good laddie." He smiled a second time when the boy nodded and then went back to sleep.

*

Steppen did not need privacy nearly as much as she needed to cool off. The Walrick she knew would not have multiple wives and would have come home if he could. Maybe this was not the same man. Maybe he just looked like Walrick...was as handsome as Walrick and had the same name. After all, Walrick was a common name. Maybe she should get to know him better before she judged him so harshly.

If it was the same Walrick, she was going to be very disappointed. It did not bother her when he married Kindel. Everyone loved Kindel and they were a perfect match. Yet she would be a good wife for him too...unless he already had a wife, or two, or three. The only way to find out was to ask him. She took a deep breath, straightened the latest plaid she stole and walked back out.

When she came back, Walrick was gone and it alarmed her.

The dapple-gray horse was still there so she relaxed. She decided he wanted some privacy too, so she went to talk to Gelson. "Is the giant married?"

Gelson liked her very much. She was very direct, did not let Walrick get away with a thing and she would make a good mistress for their clan. His laird needed a woman like this one. "Nay."

"But you are."

"Aye, my wife is Jonrose."

"And you have a son. Is it your only child?"

He offered her a drink of wine from his flask. "We have another on the way."

She was happy for the wine, it would help her sleep...if they ever got to the MacClurg home and she could finally lie down. "That is good news. Thank you for the wine."

As soon as Walrick came back, he mounted his horse and lifted her back up. He hoped she would leave her legs draped over one of his so he could see her face occasionally, but she settled herself back the way she was, with her back to him. He pointed, "Do you see that smoke in the distance?"

"Aye."

"That is home." He almost regretted taking her there. This was the woman he waited for and he didn't even know he was waiting. When he got her home he would have to share her with the clan. Walrick wanted her in his arms for as long as possible. He let the horse move at a leisurely pace and smiled when she went back to hugging his arm. "What do I say that annoys you?"

She hated how good it felt to be near him and feared she might not ever feel it again. She closed her eyes to memorize the moment. "I am not annoyed."

"You are not annoyed?"

"Well perhaps I was, but I am not now."

"I see, then we can talk?"

"We can talk. I have many questions."

"Will I be allowed to ask questions?"

She ignored him. "How many wives have you had?"

"Wives?"

"Aye, if you have seven children, you must…"

"I have had one wife, who passed. Do you have a husband?"

"We are not talking about me."

Walrick rolled his eyes yet again. "Why are we not talking about you?"

"Because I have never married. There, are you satisfied?"

He was surprised. The woman had a son, has never married and the possibilities of how that happened were endless. He wondered, but was afraid to ask, if she had been forced. She would tell him when she was ready, he decided.

Steppen was trying to figure out how he could have fathered seven children in three years with only one wife who passed. The wife was Kindel, naturally, but if he fathered…uh oh. "So you and your wife had seven children before she passed. You do not look that old."

"I am twenty four and my wife gave me no children before she passed."

"I see, you have seven children and no wife. You have seven

or perhaps eight concubines then."

"What?" he asked.

"The priest said a concubine is a lass you bed, but do not marry. You have children with your concubines."

"The children were orphaned by the plague. They call me father and I claim them as mine."

Steppen let her head fall forward and was grateful he could not see her face. She was completely ashamed of herself. Of course, it was exactly the sort of thing the Walrick she knew and loved would do.

They were both quiet. She tried to find a way to apologize for jumping to the wrong conclusion, while he tried to understand why having seven children made her so mad. At the same time, both noticed Justin was awake and having a wonderful time talking to Gelson.

The boy was talking more than he had in days and Steppen wondered just how much he understood of what happened. He didn't seem upset when they watched the village burn, and didn't fuss much on the way. She hung on to Walrick's arm and looked back.

It was getting harder and harder not to hug her when she did that. For all her anger, she was the most exciting lass he had been around in a very long time. "Do you want him with us?"

"Nay, he is happy there. I have never heard him talk so much. It will be good when we can rest and he can run and play. We have traveled for many days."

"I hope you will stay with us. I live in a three story keep, but I do not sleep there. The children live on the second floor and so do the lasses who tend them. You will stay on the top floor if you wish."

"Thank you."

"I will order a bath and some clean clothing, but I fear you will need to wear MacClurg colors."

Steppen could hardly object to that. She had no idea whose colors she had on now, and anything clean and not stolen would be a pleasure. "I appreciate your kindness very much."

"However, I cannot say who you are unless you tell me your name."

A name? Now what was she going to do? Steppen was not a common name and she still didn't know why he didn't come back. "Do you own all this land?"

"The MacClurgs claim all they can hold. I have been with them for less than three years."

Something suddenly occurred to her. "Are these people at war?"

"They tell me there is so much land the people here do not fight over it. I tend to believe 'tis true."

Steppen was greatly relieved. "Where did you live before you came here?"

"I am not sure. I am lost."

Steppen caught her breath. Lost? She could not help herself, she looped her arms around his upper arm again and hugged him. Tears began to rim her eyes. She never thought about him being lost. "You do not know where you are?"

"Nay. I remember my people, but…'tis a long story."

"Tell me?"

He didn't want to talk about it with Janell, but telling this woman seemed so natural. She was hugging his arm again and this time he could not resist. He tightened his hold and drew her to him. When she did not resist, he kept her there. "I hardly understand it enough to tell you. When Gelson found me, six months had passed since I left my home. I have no memory of that time or how I got here."

"And you do not know how to get home?"

"I asked, but the people here have never heard of my clan or the clans who live around mine. I meant to go look for them, but then I found the children and they needed me."

CHAPTER IX

Just then, Gelson let out a soft whistle signaling riders approaching. All of them sat up straighter. Gelson quieted the chattering Justin, pulled his horse to a stop next to Walrick's and put his hand on his sword.

As the men approached, Walrick leaned close to her ear. "I know these lads. Do not be frightened, they will not hurt you." Walrick's greeting to the strangers was warm. "What news of the south and the east."

The oldest one smiled, "You are fortunate today. We bring fascinating news from the south, though the rumors be confusing. There has been a great war between two of the clans."

Walrick felt the woman in his arms stiffen and knew this was probably the same war. He almost didn't ask, but there was only one way to know if it was the same war. "Are all dead?"

"Therein lies the mystery. One rumor says yea, but the other says all inside the wall survived. The people escaped through a secret tunnel and the invaders were tricked."

"A wall?" gasped Walrick.

Steppen could hardly breathe. "A tunnel? They lived?"

"Or died, depending on which rumor you believe," the stranger said.

"Was there a fire?" she asked.

"Aye, all the cottages inside the wall burned. Do you know this rumor?"

"I was there." The jaws of the strangers dropped, but she didn't seem to notice. Instead, she spoke her thoughts out loud. "Of course there was a tunnel. He often talked about the one he saw in England." Steppen's eyes began to light up and a plan was forming in her mind. She quickly glanced around -- this land was perfect and she had the perfect way to bring the MacGreagors to it.

She turned to look at Walrick. "Have you ever seen the golden sword?" She moved his hand away and quickly untied the strings to her sword.

Walrick was still thinking about the wall. Was it the MacGreagor wall? Did they finally go to war with the MacDonalds? Was it his village that burned? If so, who was this woman and why was she close enough to see the fire? "What?" he finally muttered.

Steppen put the sword handle near his hand. "Draw my sword, Walrick."

His mind was racing and he did not trust himself to draw it without cutting her. Still, he did as she said, took hold of the handle and slowly began to pull it out of the sheath. Inch by inch, the golden blade caught the light. The men stared and Steppen's smile grew wider as it came all the way out and he held it up. She had not taken it out even once to look at it, and in the full sunlight it glistened bright enough to almost blind them.

She put her hand on Walrick's arm and pushed until he was holding it high above their heads. Then she turned to the strangers.

"This is the MacGreagor sword. You are very privileged to see this sword. Few ever have. When you speak of it, say 'tis kept safe by a woman and a laddie. But you must also say the one who touches the sword and is not a MacGreagor will surely die."

Just as carefully, she helped a speechless Walrick guide the sword back into the sheath. Then she watched the strangers bow at the waist as though she were a queen and quickly ride away. Steppen smiled. "The MacGreagors will come to us once they hear."

"Who are you?"

"Still you do not know who I am? How could you not know me?" With the sword and sheath still in her hand, she swung her leg over, slid off the horse and began to yell at him. "I waited every day for you to come back. I love you and you do not even remember me." Consumed by her hurt and her anger, she walked away determined not to cry and not to ever let him touch her again.

He quickly dismounted and followed her. "Steppen?"

She was so furious, she didn't even hear him. "Do not misunderstand, I loved Kindel too, but she died and it was not my fault." Steppen stopped and turned to face him. "I never wished her to die, but she did and when she was gone, I wanted you to come back to me. I wanted you to love me the way you loved her, not the way you loved Patrick's little sister or that lassie you used to take riding. I wanted you to love me…the grown up lass, but you did not come back!"

"I did not know."

For a very long moment, she stared into his eyes. He was

right. How could he know a little girl loved him so completely or that she grew up still loving him? Finally, she closed her eyes and lowered her head. "It was not your fault. I see that now."

"Steppen." He thought his heart would burst when he took her in his arms. She was his Steppen, his only link to the MacGreagors he loved so much, and the woman he knew he wanted to spend the rest of his life with. She was all that and more. Steppen was his reason for being. At first, he held her like she was still that little girl, but soon, he was stroking her hair and kissing her head. "I have missed you so."

All her life she wanted him to hold her like that and when he finally kissed her, she was afraid she would melt into him. Without even realizing it, she dropped the sword. "I do not want to be the wife of a laird. I do not want to live inside a wall and never be allowed out like Glenna."

He repeatedly kissed her face and when she wrapped her arms around his neck, he lifted her up. "The MacClurgs have no wall."

"No wall?"

"Nay and I will give up being a laird if you hate it that much. But I will not give up the children."

She smiled. "No, you must not give up the children."

Walrick kissed her again, lowered her back down to the ground and then closed his eyes when she put her head against his chest. "You feel so good in my arms."

"Do I? I grew up."

He raised an eyebrow. "That you did." He stepped back and held her at arms length. "Tell me about your son."

"My son? Oh, of course you do not know. Justin is not mine, he is Neil's son."

Walrick looked back at the sleepy little boy in Gelson's arms. "I should have seen the resemblance, he looks just like Neil."

"Will you wear the sword for me? 'Tis too heavy."

"Aye." he picked it up, began to tie the strings around his waist and wondered if she realized she was stroking his arm. He might go mad if she kept that up. "I love you."

"You used to love me."

"Nay, I love you now."

"How can you? You do not even know who I am now."

He stepped back and finished tying the sword around his waist. The new strings Neil made for it were just long enough. "How long must I know who you are now, before I am allowed to love you?"

"At least longer than a few hours. I have changed a great deal."

"Have you stopped asking questions?"

"Well no, I suppose not."

"You have not stopped hugging my arm when I take you riding."

She giggled. "You remembered that?"

"I loved it when you did that and I love it still. Only then, you were too young...to love the way a lad loves a lass. Patrick would have had my head if he knew."

"Knew what?"

"That I sometimes wished you were older." He grinned, kissed her once again and then lifted her into his arms. "I am taking you home."

"Good." When he got her back to his horse, he set her down, mounted and then leaned down to draw her to him. This time she put her arms around his neck, closed her eyes and did not let go after he lifted her. She heaved a sigh of relief and then remembered they were not alone. She opened her eyes and winked at Gelson. "We are old friends."

He returned her smile. "I gathered that. Welcome home."

"Thank you. You have no idea how happy I am to be here." She motioned for him to pull his horse up beside Walrick's and then sat sideways in Walrick's lap with her legs over one of his so she could talk to Gelson. "Justin is the only son of Laird Neil MacGreagor. I was to take him to England, but I thought all were dead and I let the horse bring us here instead."

Gelson looked perplexed. "'Tis not your horse?"

"Nay. After the fire, the horse came to us in the forest and it has stayed with us until now."

Walrick hugged her again. "Tell me what happened."

"We knew they would attack, it was only a matter of time. The Fergusons and the Camerons refused to help. Neil sent me away with the boy first, and we tried to sleep in the forest, but I could not. It was a full moon, and…"

"This last full moon? I could not sleep that night either. Go on."

"I heard the bridge fall just before sunrise and went back. By then the place was on fire. I thought they were dead. Do you think they are still waiting for me at Jessup's? Should we go back and find them?"

He quickly kissed her lips. "You need to rest. Besides, they will come when they hear about the sword. The legend demands they recover it. You did a very good thing."

"If...they hear about the sword."

"They will hear. No rumor will spread over Scotland faster than one about a golden sword."

Alan MacGreagor and his wife heard the rumor about the sword first. Survivors of the war, they began to move steadily north on the first day. They reasoned Neil would come that way and perhaps they would find each other again. In only five days, they met up with another MacGreagor family who wanted to see the giant. Why not? They had no other place to go. The mere mention of a golden sword made them smile. They doubted there was such a sword, but it might be Neil's way of gathering them, so they continued north to find the sword, the woman and the boy. If they happened to see the giant on the way, so much the better.

CHAPTER X

Alan and his wife were not the only ones who guessed Neil would go north instead of east or west. In a short two weeks, Brendan MacGreagor collected seven families. Among them were two hunters, three farmers, and a builder complete with tools, six women, eight children and a small flock of sheep. Once they were well away from Cameron land, they put their MacGreagor colors back on and wore them with pride and honor.

Rumors began to spread among the other clans about groups of people calling themselves MacGreagors who were on the move, but had no particular place to go. More rumors reported firsthand accounts of the war and how stupid they made the MacDonalds look. The MacDonalds, it was said, actually thought a whole clan committed mass suicide. Stupid MacDonalds! Still, those rumors were about the MacGreagors who fled into Cameron land to the east.

Once the people passed Ferguson land and traveled west, they were welcomed into other clans such as the Kerr and the Forbes. The plague had diminished the numbers of those clans also, and well trained MacGreagor warriors were a welcome sight. Yet fitting into a world, not at all like their own, was hard. The women, whom some thought of as beautiful, were not easily accepted and the men, who did not care for the way women were treated, were unimpressed.

Therefore, when the rumors reached them, they were more than happy to have a direction in which to go finally. How to get beyond MacDonald land was not an easy question to answer. No one was quite sure how big MacDonald land was, and especially how far north it stretched. The reasonable thing to do was to go south and hold their breaths until they crossed Ferguson land, their old land now held by the MacDonalds and the Cameron land.

The extent of possible danger and hard travel made some question just how badly they wanted to be MacGreagors again. Others believed a chance to live in peace, in their old familiar ways, was worth the risk. By virtue of their numbers and their love for each other, some one hundred and fifty of the remaining MacGreagors were on the move -- taking with them the rules for love and survival that had served them all very well for generations.

As the number of people moving north began to grow, so did the rumors and the gossip.

"...three lads, who were not MacGreagors, died trying to steal the MacGreagor sword."

"...nay, it was not the giant who had the sword, but the King of Scotland. Who would dare try to steal the sword from the King of Scotland?"

"...the lass was actually an old lass and the laddie, a nephew of the King of England."

"...the lass is so bonnie, none can look upon her face save the MacGreagor who comes to claim her sword."

*

It was not that the rumors were so outrageous; it was the fact that they reached Neil and Glenna at all. They had grown to nearly a hundred and they were carrying what Jessup claimed was half the wealth of England. No one believed that was true.

The men kept the women and children inside their circle as they moved and protected them from attack. Yet they were becoming so large in numbers, strangers no longer approached them daily. Naturally, the size of the men was also a deterrent and few wanted to fight them.

Glenna's color improved daily, and she kept busy finding places to tie strips of blue MacGreagor cloth around the trees for Steppen to follow. She could not have guessed how many MacGreagors were following the strips of blue and were grateful for her efforts.

A stranger, wearing a kilt of an unknown clan, was not deterred and could not believe this group of travelers had not heard the latest gossip. First, he told of the great war where everyone died, and then he told of a golden sword and a woman, who killed the seven men who tried to take it away from her. There was a boy, but the stranger could not say how he was involved. He did say that the King of Scotland was heard to say...

"But where did the lass go?" asked a confused Neil.

The stranger rolled his eyes. "To live with the giant, where else? Who could tame a dangerous lass like that one, but a giant?"

It was only then the man noticed how big Neil was. Even sitting on a horse, Neil was considerably taller than the stranger.

Suddenly unsure he could get away fast enough; the stranger made his excuses and rode off. All of Scotland was being overrun with giants!

Neil motioned for his clan to keep going, but his smile grew with every step the horse took. At length, he looked at his beaming wife. "Steppen is alive."

"And so is our son."

"Aye, now all we have to do is find the giant."

"How big do you think the north is?" Glenna asked.

"I do not know, but we will find them. I will not rest until we have found them."

*

Steppen and Walrick stood by the river and watched the rushing water. He wrapped his arms around her from behind and kissed the side of her head. "Is a week of knowing the lass you are now, long enough to love you?"

"Well, let me see. I slept for the first two days and refused to get out of the bath for another day after that. So you have really only known me for four days."

"I nearly went daft waiting for you to finish your bath."

She turned in his arms and hugged him. "I always dreamed of getting married in the MacGreagor colors, but my plaid is...who knows where it is. How long do you think it will take them to get here?"

"We do not even know how long it took you to get here."

"Aye, but we know the war was on the full moon. Can we not tell by that?"

"You are as wise as you are bonnie. Would you be willing to look at the moon with me later?"

She lifted her lips to his. "I would like that very much."

"And then, will I be allowed to say I love you?"

"You are a very persistent lad."

"I am a lad who is truly in love and I want you to marry me now, this day. But we could wait for a few more days…or weeks if you insist. Just do not ever leave me."

CHAPTER XI

MacClurgs chopping wood in the forest were the first to see them. The men stopped to watch as the dot that began small in the distance, steadily grew. Before long, it was clear a large number of people were moving up the glen toward their village. The eldest let out the whistle to let others know of the arrivals, and the whistle was then passed from man to man, until the people inside the MacClurg keep stopped to listen.

Walrick raced up the three flights of stairs, pushed the coverings aside and looked out the window facing south. "Steppen!"

Steppen was already out the main door and running down the path. Walrick laughed and flew back down the stairs. He hurried out the door, grabbed his horse's reins off a tree branch and mounted. He nodded for his men to join him and watched Gelson pick up Justin.

Steppen was running and the people were still a long way off, so he rode to her and slowed. "Would you care for a ride?"

She was laughing and crying all at the same time and when he pulled her up, she wrapped her arms around his neck and hugged him tight. Then she turned, sat in front of him and when Gelson pulled his horse alongside of Walrick's, she reached over and took Justin. She settled the boy in her lap and then wiped the tears off her cheeks.

The rest of the MacClurg warriors moved in close to protect their laird and for a moment, Steppen feared the MacGreagors might think it was a trap or the start of a war. Suddenly she thought of something.

Walrick thought of it too and halted. "Lean forward, love." When she did, he drew the MacGreagor sword and then held it high above his head, turning it ever so slightly back and forth so the bright sun was sure to make it glisten.

As soon as the MacGreagors saw the sword, they began to race forward, and when they were close enough, Neil raised his hand and they came to a complete stop. He could not believe his eyes and at the sight of his son and Steppen, he had to swallow hard to hold his emotions in check.

Slowly Neil walked his horse forward. The man with Steppen did the same and it was only then that Neil realized the man was Walrick. He pulled his horse to a halt, got down and walked to his son. He grabbed hold of both the boy and Steppen, pulled them to him and turned to his family.

Instantly, the MacGreagor's cheered, dismounted and rushed forward. As soon as Glenna got there, Neil handed Justin to her and then swung Steppen around. "You did it! You saved him!" He set her down and then slapped a waiting Walrick on the back. "Where the hell have you been?"

"Here, waiting for you. Welcome home."

"Here?"

"Aye. 'Tis good land and we live in peace."

Steppen hugged Glenna and walked back to Walrick. Then something made her glance up. "Look!" She pointed at the top of the hill.

The stallion's shiny black coat sparkled in the sunlight as he stood looking down at the MacGreagor family in their new home. Then he turned, started down the other side of the hill and disappeared.

~ End~

EDANA

CHAPTER I

Slade was an extraordinarily handsome man even by MacGreagor standards, although he did not seem to know it. With women, he was friendly, helpful and courteous, but never more so with one than the others. His curly, deep brown hair and dark brown eyes made more than one young woman daydream about him, but he was not yet ready to take a wife and father children.

He very much wanted to be a cabinetmaker. The MacGreagors had many fine furniture builders, so when Neil needed warriors more, Slade did not object. Most people were pleased with the simple designs of the chairs, tables and beds the other carpenters made, but he was not. What he loved was building very strong furniture, carving wooden decorations and affixing the delicate slabs to his fine furniture with small wooden pegs.

Slade MacGreagor hoped, now that the war was behind them, the clan would need fewer warriors and more carpenters -- if he could find the clan.

A good warrior, he was one of the twenty men Neil chose to take people outside the wall the night the MacDonalds attacked. The destiny of his group was in his hands, and once they got through the tunnel and up on top of the ground, he decided to take them to his aunt in the land of the Camerons.

It was a risky move since the new Cameron laird was not a friend of the MacGreagors, was afraid of the MacDonalds, and was not inclined to hide or protect any fugitives. However, Slade's aunt and her husband were farmers and lived a considerable distance north of the main Cameron village. Laird Cameron paid little attention to his northern clansmen and the MacDonalds did not much care what they did either. It was the perfect place.

It took three terrifying days of walking, hiding, staying off the beaten paths and foraging for food, before the three MacGreagor men, two women and five children, under the age of eight, finally made it to his aunt's cottage. By then they were exhausted.

A month later, it was obvious they could not intrude on the kindness of Slade's family forever, and hiding an extra eleven people became more difficult each day. At the same time, they were not willing to jeopardize the lives of the children by taking them on a long and treacherous journey -- to a place they might not find. So after careful consideration, they decided Slade would find Neil and come back for them.

He set out with a borrowed horse, two cloth sacks filled with provisions and a keen sense of direction, which he hoped would serve him well. He wore a green Cameron kilt over his white shirt with his MacGreagor kilt underneath.

Slade went west until he was certain he was out of Cameron land and then turned north. It was the way he suspected Neil would go.

His days were long and his nights were lonely. He hid often from men on the paths and sometimes wondered if there was any use trying. Who knew how big Scotland was or if he would ever find Neil?

On the eighth day, the fog was heavy, he could not be absolutely certain which way was north and the horse needed rest. So he did a little hunting, checked his provisions, bathed in a creek and fell asleep dreaming of a cabinet he intended to build one day.

On the morning of the ninth day, he opened his eyes, looked up and discovered a stripe of MacGreagor plaid tied around a tree. Without taking his eyes off the cloth, he slowly sat up, got to his feet and touched the cloth with the tips of his fingers. It was not a dream and he was elated.

Half a day later he found another one, reached up and touched it as well. Then he realized each had been tied at the edge of a meadow -- find the next meadow -- find the next strip.

Finally, having some sense of where he was going and what to look for, gave him more freedom to watch for game, and he was rewarded. He halted his horse, slowly reached over his shoulder, withdrew an arrow and loaded his bow. With expert marksmanship, he released the string and brought down a game bird. Pleased with himself, he got off his horse, ran to his kill, made sure it was dead and tied twine around its neck. Next, he tied the twine to his belt and resumed his journey.

*

Laird Walrick MacClurg and Laird Neil MacGreagor had a lot to talk about. A few hours earlier, the MacGreagors entered the land of the MacClurgs and found Walrick, Steppen and Justin waiting for them. After all the greetings and hugging, the two men finally slipped off together to climb the hill and look down on the glen.

Neil was exhausted and after riding a horse for days, it felt good to walk. Once he got half way to the top, he stopped in a clearing and turned to look back. The landscape below took his breath away. "'Tis grand." He slowly turned to see the lush green glen, the intermittent forests, the meadows and the mountains beyond. "I have dreamed of a place like this."

"From the top 'tis even more glorious and it goes on forever. The clans do not fight over land, but you best not try to take their lasses."

Neil laughed. "There is always a shortage of lasses."

"I am pleased you have agreed to stay."

"We are tired, this land is more than I could have hoped for and we will stay if your clan allows it."

"I am convinced they will."

In the glen below, Neil and Walrick could see the MacGreagors sitting on their plaids on the glen floor. Not all wore the MacGreagor colors and instead of a sea of blue, they were a patchwork of greens, yellows, reds and blues. The MacClurg women offered them hot food while the MacClurg men gathered near the Keep to talk about combining the two clans.

Walrick put a hand on Neil's shoulder. "I have been telling the MacClurgs about you since Steppen found us. They are a small clan and need more of everything, especially warriors to protect them."

"How did you manage to have food ready for us?"

Walrick found a log and sat down. "We dug three pits several days ago, filled them with beef and deer, built fires on top and let them slowly cook."

"You were certain we would come?"

"Steppen was. It was her idea to show the sword to strangers hoping you would hear the gossip. Neil, she went back when the bridge fell, saw the fire and thought you were dead."

Neil sat down on the log next to Walrick and closed his eyes. "So that is why she did not go to Jessup's."

"Aye."

"We heard the lass with the golden sword went to live with the giant."

Walrick rolled his eyes. "Allow me to introduce myself."

"Do you mean you are the giant?"

"I am not even as big as you are. Now I suppose they will call this the land of the giants." Walrick enjoyed the sound of his old friend's laughter, and then went back to watching the MacGreagors in the glen. "The people are tired. Steppen slept for two days after she got here."

"Aside from believing we were dead, was it very awful for her?"

"She cried once she felt safe enough, but from being afraid, not because of something that happened to them. She was very brave and...she is very pleasing when she is asleep."

"You have fallen in love with Steppen?"

"I have. I have always loved her, only now she is grown up."

"Patrick would be pleased."

"I hope so. I would not want him haunting me."

Neil grinned. "Why have you not married her yet?"

"At first, she wanted to wait until she could get married in a MacGreagor plaid. Her plaid is somewhere this side of the land of the Camerons, and she has no idea whose colors she was wearing when she got here. Then about a week ago, our priest died."

Neil suddenly caught his breath. "The priest! I knew I was forgetting something."

Walrick was appalled. "You did not bring the priest? But we cannot marry without one and ours will not be replaced for weeks…maybe months."

"I do not often know where our priest is. He does not fall under my command, you know. The people call him when he is needed and he comes and goes as he pleases. Usually when I need him, I have a devil of a time finding him." Neil began to rub the back of his neck. "He was not inside the wall, that much I do know and I doubt he stayed on MacGreagor land once the attack began. He is no fonder of the MacDonalds than we are."

"Did very many of our people stay?"

"I do not know. We heard some of the lads were killed, but we do not know who. Their wives and children were carried away, and I hope to go back and rescue them."

"But they did not kill the priest?"

"Even Laird MacDonald is not stupid enough to kill a priest. Perhaps the priest will come when he hears about the sword."

"I hope so, I am not a patient lad."

Neil smiled. "I remember."

"You did not bring as many as I expected. Tell me what happened."

Neil explained the escape, his fear that the MacDonalds would give chase if he brought all eight hundred at the same time, and how they started from Jessup's with only a small band that grew along the way. Now they had just under a hundred men, women and children. "...we are hoping the others will follow. I fret about them constantly. They must feel I have deserted them, and I find it far harder to live with that, than I imagined it would be."

"Will you go back yourself to find them?"

"I want to very much, but Glenna is with child and I cannot leave her. I will send some of the lads back after they are rested."

"Perhaps they will find the priest. I have seven children who need a mother."

From the hillside, Neil watched Glenna take their son in her arms again and kiss him repeatedly. Then he realized what Walrick said. "Seven children? I cannot wait to hear this."

It was Walrick's turn to explain all that had happened, including the discovery of the children in the forest. Then he explained about Knox, about the old ways of the MacClurgs and about Gelson. "He is a good lad and the MacClurgs honor him."

"Will I be forced to fight you to become laird of both clans?"

Walrick rolled his eyes. "I will surrender and save us both the trouble."

"Then if the MacClurgs agree, I will make you my second and

Gelson my third."

"And you will find a priest."

Neil smiled and slapped him on the back. "Aye."

CHAPTER II

It was not polite to interrupt their mistress, so Taral held back and waited for Steppen and Glenna to stop talking before she cleared her throat. As soon as Steppen threw her arms around her, Taral burst into tears. "I did not believe I would ever see you again."

Steppen held her tight for several long moments. "What happened? The last I saw of you, William was taking you to live with the Fergusons."

Glenna wore MacGreagor blue, Taral had on the yellow of the Fergusons and Steppen wore MacClurg green, but none of them cared. Glenna took Taral's hand and encouraged her to sit down on the plaid she had spread on the ground. "Steppen, 'tis not a good story. Perhaps it can wait for later."

Taral could not contain herself. "William is dead."

Steppen slowly sat down and as soon as Taral joined her, she put her arm around her friend's shoulders. "Did he die in the war?"

"Nay, I killed him."

Steppen glanced at the pained look on Glenna's face, lowered her eyes and bit her lip. "Perhaps we *should* discuss this later."

"Oh Steppen, you must help me. I am twice widowed, no other lad will want me and now I am..."

"What?"

"I believe I carry William's child."

Glenna wrinkled her brow. "Are you certain? It has hardly been a month."

"Well no, but I am past my time and if I am with child, who will want me?"

Steppen smiled and tried to calm Taral. "My dearest friend, we are surrounded by lads who do not have wives. Finding a husband will not be a problem -- choosing which one will be."

"Aye, but I already told everyone I killed him. Now my third husband will fear me?"

"I hope so," said Glenna. "All lads fear their wives will oft them in the night, as well they should. A wise lad does not let his wife go to bed enraged."

Steppen frowned, "They cannot fear us if they cannot marry us, and right now, that is impossible."

Glenna swished away a dragonfly, kissed Justin's cheek for the hundredth time and then let him curl up in her lap. "What do you mean?"

"Our priest died. I asked Walrick to wait until you got here and now I am sorry I did." When Glenna's mouth dropped, Steppen grinned. "Why are you so surprised? I have loved him all my life. It just took this long to make him notice me. The golden sword helped. Wait until you hear how he found me...or rather how I found him. I was..."

The eldest of the MacClurg clan was a man named Cobb. After the MacClurgs discussed things among themselves, it was

Cobb who sent a message up the hill saying the MacClurgs wanted to have a word with Neil. Now, Cobb was the one standing in front of the small gathering determined not to let the young MacGreagor laird get the best of him. "If we say nay, where will you go?"

Neil was a full head taller than most of them and needed no podium from which to speak. Yet he made his voice loud enough for all to hear. "I do not know."

They were gathered in front of the large three-story stone keep Walrick sometimes lived in, and as they talked, the MacGreagors began to gather behind the MacClurgs just to listen. It was their future they were discussing and they all wanted to hear it firsthand.

Walrick walked forward until he was standing at Neil's right hand and folded his arms. "Where he goes, I go also."

Several of the MacClurgs gasped. "But you are our laird," argued Cobb.

"I used to be your laird. Knox is dead, I have taught you all you need to know, and I do not wish the burden. Find a new laird."

A man in the back shouted, "Gelson will lead us." Several others grumbled their agreement, but not very enthusiastically.

"Is that your answer then?" asked Neil.

Gelson shook his head, went to stand on the other side of Neil and faced his clan. "Nay, 'tis not. I go where Walrick goes and if he follows Neil MacGreagor, so do I."

Cobb turned to glare at Gelson. "You would leave us with nothing?"

"'Tis *you* who would leave us with nothing. We need the MacGreagors and you know it. We need them to teach us, to protect our women and children, and God help us if these giants ever decided to dislike us. Only a stupid lad would decide against joining our two clans together."

Cobb wrinkled his brow, put his hands behind his back and glared. "Are you calling me stupid?"

Said Gelson, "I am."

Cobb was not about to back down. "The lad just lost a war, I remind you."

Neil raised an eyebrow and looked at Walrick, "He has a point."

"I do?" asked Cobb.

"Aye you do. A better lad might have stayed and fought to the death. Of course, they had three warriors to every one of ours and most of us would have died. They wanted our widows, you understand, and I thought to cheat them out of the pleasure."

Cobb considered that for a moment and then lowered his gaze. "You willingly gave up the land?"

"'Tis not as beautiful as this and the south of Scotland is far more crowded."

Walrick nudged Neil. "Tell him the worst of it."

Neil looked confused. "The worst?"

"I will tell them…the MacGreagor land is far too close to England." Walrick nodded and then enjoyed the gasps of the MacClurgs.

"No wonder you were willing to leave." Cobb thoughtfully put a finger to his chin, "Did I hear that you set the place on fire yourselves?"

"We did. However, we were not able to bring much with us. If you are willing, we need the use of your tools and your advice for building new homes. Most of ours were already there when we were born and we are not skilled. We especially need the help of the MacClurg elders to advise us, as we lost most of our elders in the plague."

"I see." Again, the elder Cobb took his time considering the possibilities. "Will we be MacGreagors or MacClurgs?"

It was Walrick who answered, "A clan always claims the name of the laird and Neil is a MacGreagor. But all lads should keep their Christian names. I say we leave it up to each lad to choose for his own family?"

"And the colors?" Cobb asked.

On this question, no one seemed to have a ready answer. Then the weaver, Effie, spoke up. "We shall each wear our own colors for a marriage and a burial, but the weavers can combine all the colors and make new plaids."

Neil smiled. He was going to like this woman and decided to ask her opinion often in the future. "'Tis a fine idea. Perhaps you could make samples and let the people choose their favorite design."

Pleased that he so easily accepted her advice, Effie grinned. She was going to like this laird. "I will be honored."

Elder Cobb cleared his throat. "How many MacGreagors should we plan for?"

"We were seven hundred and eighty-nine before the war, but some died and some have stayed behind. Others may not be able to find us and for those, I will send lads back."

"And find a priest," Walrick put in.

Again, Cobb was thoughtful. "We could stretch a MacGreagor plaid between two trees on the top of the hill. That might help."

Neil's smile began to widen. "Then you have decided?"

Cobb turned to face the crowd. "I will hear your 'nays' now." He waited an appropriate time and when he heard no replies, he gave his nod. "We are yours. Welcome home."

The exhausted MacGreagors cheered, and began to greet their new clansmen with slaps for the men and hugs for the women. Abruptly, Walrick held up his hand to quiet them. "Before I give over my clan, I have one more command. I have known this lad all my life and he looks ten years older than the three years since I last saw him. For the next two days, I will be laird while he does nothing but rest. Agreed?"

Again, the crowd cheered.

It was done then. Neil walked through the crowd and looked into the eyes of each MacClurg so they would feel they could trust him. Then he went to join his wife and son.

The MacGreagors were home at last.

CHAPTER III

Walrick sent men to Laird Graham to explain what was happening, and to secure wheat for bread, straw for the builders, tools they could barter or borrow, wool for the spinners, dye for the wool and an invitation for him to visit at his earliest convenience. He also sent messages to their other neighbors, hoping that by doing so, they would not see the gathering of such numbers as a threat.

He sent the hunters out, gave up his third floor to the MacGreagor women for their rest, and ordered men to carry up a constant supply of water for baths. He showed the men where to bathe in a loch nestled between two hills, sent guards up on top of the tallest hill to watch for intruders, as well as more MacGreagor families, and kissed Steppen every time their paths crossed.

*

Old habits were hard to break, and even though there could not possibly be any danger in a valley where they could see forever, two guards followed Neil and Glenna as they took a rare walk together. Neil put Justin down, drew his wife into his arms, kissed her lovingly and then pulled back to examine her face. "You look tired, love."

"No more so than you. Walrick is right, this war has aged you."

He made sure Justin was not too far away and then held her close again. "I am fine, or at least I will be when the others have found us. For now, all the MacGreagor lasses who are with child are to rest."

"There are three of us, you know."

"I did not know. Who?"

Glenna giggled, looped her arm through his and urged him to resume their walk. "One is your fault and the second is Mayze."

"Mayze, how wonderful. She and Dugan should have at least a hundred children. Who might the third be?"

"The third is our most troublesome and I fret about her. 'Tis Taral, she is upset because 'tis William's child and I have no words to comfort her. She also fears the lads will shun her because she killed her husband."

"She is not thinking clearly. On our journey, I happened to notice Geddes was never far from her. He waits because she is so newly widowed, but he has that look when he sees her."

"Tell him not to wait. If she is with child, the notice of a lad might be a comfort."

"Glenna you surprise me. I would expect you to be more cautious. We do not want her to marry just for the sake of being married. That is what she did when she married William."

"You are right. We must wait until she finds someone to truly love."

"And I am just selfish enough to want her to marry a MacGreagor this time. Taral has seen enough of unhappiness in her short life. Keep an eye on her and let me know what she needs.

I will not see her suffer another day."

Glenna took a deep breath and slowly let it out. "I am happy to see we are matchmakers still. I cannot wait to learn all about the MacClurg lasses."

"Aye, but first you will rest, Glenna MacGreagor."

"As you wish. There is one more thing."

"What?"

"Jessup wants to know where to hide the gold and silver she brought from England. And, you must hide the golden sword, now that it is not just a legend."

"I wonder how many generations will have to pass before it is a legend again."

*

By nightfall, all were fed and drifting off to sleep, when Walrick took Steppen's hand and led her to their favorite tree. He leaned his back against the tree trunk and then pulled her into his arms. "Happy, love?"

"I am so happy I am afraid to breathe. I did not truly think they would find us and I have been pinching myself all day. Walrick, they did not bring the priest?"

He puffed his cheeks. "So I heard. Do you know where he was that night?"

"I think he was with Victoria who was going into labor. What a night to be born and the poor lass was in labor."

"Why did she need a priest for that?"

"She always thinks she is going to die and she insists on last rites every time."

"So the priest was outside the wall and might have survived. Perhaps he will find us."

"'Tis all my fault, I should have let you marry me when I first arrived, I..." Suddenly, his lips were on hers, her guilt quickly dissipated and she could think of nothing but the passion in his kiss.

*

Morning came far too soon for some and not soon enough for others. Both Neil and Walrick were up early, mounted on their horses and once again at the top of the hill. Two of the trees were just close enough together and high enough to be seen over the tops of the other trees. So when Neil unfolded the plaid he had draped over his arm, and held the top corner against the tree, Walrick used a mallet to pound a wooden peg through the material into the tree. They attached the cloth in three more places, moved to the other tree and put four pegs through the cloth into that one. The plaid was now a banner and both moved back to survey their work.

"That should do it," said Walrick as they mounted their horses. They turned and for a long time, they sat silently looking at the beauty of the land in the sunrise.

*

Although it was supposed to be another day of rest, MacGreagor men offered to help keep the fires lit, move the horses to better pasture and chop wood. The MacClurgs seemed impressed, but in the days to come Neil and Walrick spent most of their time trying to keep a delicate balance between the feelings of the old clan and the new -- did the MacGreagors want to help or take over?

Because he saved Glenna's life and because Neil wanted to give positions of importance to an equal number of MacClurgs and MacGreagors, he appointed Gill his commander of the guards. Ralin was very pleased, although it meant she would see less of him. Their marriage was still very new and constant travel afforded them very little time alone. Yet things were bound to settle into a more common routine, where husbands and wives could enjoy each other more often. At least that is what Ralin hoped.

Dugan was and always would be the head of his hunters. Mayze, whom Neil treasured almost as much as he did Glenna, was also pleased to find her husband still among Neil's advisers. When he had them alone, Neil asked the couple to do one more favor - gather dead rose centers and keep them on hand in case they ever needed to make more itching powder. Both happily agreed.

The position of head of the carpenters went to a well-respected MacClurg, and the elder Cobb was asked for his opinion often. Walrick offered the names of two more MacClurgs who were assigned to keep track of the livestock and to make sure the farmers had all they needed.

*

On the top floor of the Keep, Glenna's eyes were open and when she rose up on one elbow, she smiled at the sea of women sleeping on the floor not far from her. She thought about how much there was to do, and said a quick prayer that her husband would know how to get them all organized again this day. So far, he was doing a very good job, but it was hard work with long hours and many decisions.

She missed being alone with him. The journey offered little privacy for the other married couples and none at all for them. Now they even slept on different floors. She considered dragging him into the forest where she could have him all to herself, but realized he probably would not go without his guard. Glenna sighed. All she could do was wait for more cottages to be built.

Neil's third in command was the one responsible for the clan's mistress and children, but there had been little time for Gelson and Glenna to get acquainted. If Gelson liked her, his duties would be far easier and it would be better still if his wife liked her. Maybe, Glenna thought, getting to know Gelson's wife was more important than getting to know Gelson.

Once she was dressed, her hair brushed and her morning meal finished, she asked Gelson to take her to meet his wife. He was pleased and as they walked up the path, they chatted about their small sons becoming best of friends. Abruptly, a man burst out of his cottage and nearly ran into Glenna. Embarrassed, the man quickly made his apologies, went around her, and headed on down the path.

A woman stood in the doorway with her hands on her hips and yelled, "You are witless, husband." Then she closed the door.

Glenna let a few moments pass and then knocked on the door.

"Mistress MacGreagor, I was not expecting you. Do come in."

Glenna smiled, walked in, nodded for Gelson to wait outside

and closed the door. "What is your name?"

"I am Blanka, Mistress."

"Blanka, you have shamed your husband in front of me."

The young woman looked stricken. "I did not know you were out there."

"Why not?"

"What?"

"Why were you not aware of who might hear you insult your husband? Do you think so little of him that you do not care who hears you?"

"Nay, Mistress, I love my husband."

"Do you? What precisely do you love about him?"

She stammered, trying to find the right words. "Well...he is a good lad. He is tender, caring and..."

"Have you told him this?"

She shifted her eyes, "I..."

Glenna intentionally softened her voice and gently took hold of the wife's shoulders. "Blanka, unless you are certain your husband will not be killed, you must never send him away with the kind of hurt I saw in his eyes just now. A lad with that on his mind is distracted and does not keep himself well guarded. Go after him. Tell him you are sorry and it will never happen again. Then be sure he knows you love him."

She was afraid she held the girl's shoulders too tightly and worried that the shocked look on her face might never go away, but then her words seemed to sink in and Blanka caught her breath. Like a bolt of lightning, she was out the door and on her way down the path.

CHAPTER IV

Glenna softly closed the cottage door and rejoined Gelson on the path. "Did you happen to hear all that?"

"Nay, what did you tell her?"

"I will let her say if she wants others to know. However, if the lads in this clan are to honor the lasses, the lasses must also honor their lads, by not yelling insults at them where others can hear."

Gelson was more than pleased. "I will pass the word." He took her elbow and guided her down an adjoining path. "My wife is named, Jonrose, and my son is Lorne." He opened the door to his cottage, peeked in to make sure his wife was dressed and then invited his mistress in.

It was an ordinary one-room cottage, clean and decorated as best a woman could with what little she had. Still, Jonrose managed a bowl of freshly cut flowers that made the room smell sweet and delicate.

Jonrose had a wonderful smile and bright eyes that she often turned to her husband. It was obvious she loved Gelson very much and Glenna was happy to see it. She sat down in the chair he offered her and smiled, "Jonrose. I need your help."

Gelson's wife was pleased. "Help with what?"

"We are too many lads and too few lasses. I want you to come to the Keep this afternoon and meet my friend, Jessup. The three of us must find a way to tempt more lasses to our clan. Will you help us?"

"Of course."

She stayed only a few minutes more and when Gelson walked Glenna back down the path, he too had a smile on his face. "You have just made a friend for life. She is very happy to be included in your..."

"Intrigue?"

He chuckled, "Intrigue."

"I did not ask out of kindness, I truly need her. She will know more about the neighboring clans than either of us, or at least know where to find out."

"Then I am even more pleased to be at your service."

The plan Glenna set out to accomplish that morning worked and she was happy. Perhaps there would not be as much strife between women as seemed to be developing among the men. Then again, how long can two sets of very different women get along without going to war?

*

It had become the custom of all the men to gather in the courtyard first thing in the morning, to hear what Neil wanted them to take care of that day. Neil tried to remember the names of the MacClurg men as he greeted them one by one, but he missed twice. He was just beginning to give his instructions when a woman ran to him. "What is it?"

"I wish to tell my husband I am sorry, and that I love him very much."

Neil smiled. "Perhaps you would also like to show him?"

She nodded, ran to her husband, threw her arms around his neck and kissed him passionately. When Blanka came back, she winked at Neil and whispered. "Do not keep him all night."

"I promise." He watched her leave and couldn't help but notice the grin on the husband's face.

There never seemed to be enough builders, enough tools, or enough hours in the day. The women thought looms should take priority so Taral and Ralin could help make the new cloth. When Neil refused, they complained for a time and then compromised by working on the existing looms in shifts.

Other women thought wooden bowls should be made first, and were even more important since everyone had to eat. That problem they also solved by eating in stages. Men kept the meat cooking in the pits while the women baked bread from morning until night. At least everyone had enough to eat, and after a war and days of traveling with little food, the MacGreagors were happy to have it.

With almost one hundred and fifty men to help, the building began in earnest the morning of the third day. The first completed cottage, all the unmarried men agreed, would house the unmarried women.

First, the men cleared the land and piled the logs near the village. Even with the ones Jessup brought from England and Laird Graham sent, only a few axes were available for splitting the logs into beams, to form the cottage frames and planking. Wooden pegs were shaped and then driven into the shafts of wood, to hold the frames together. Other men took turns using wooden shovels to mix mud with clay, heather and straw or hay for mortar, while others gathered rocks to use for hearths and to reinforce the cottage walls.

Later, a second wall lined the inside of the first one to add warmth and extra protection. In one particular cottage, the second wall was set far enough from the first to allow the hiding of certain English and MacGreagor valuables.

Instead of drapes to cover the open-air windows, the MacClurgs showed the MacGreagors how to make shutters. After that, thatched roofs were made using thick layers of heather and straw, arranged in such a way as to let the rain run off, and prevent it from seeping into the cottage.

In less than two weeks, ten new cottages were nearly finished and another fifteen were well on their way. After that, there were beds, tables, chairs, looms, carts, stables, corrals and all sorts of necessities to make, but all in all the people worked together well, -- or so Neil thought.

Eventually however, the MacClurgs could be found building one group of cottages and the MacGreagors another.

The children helped by finding rocks, the women helped mix mortar and when a new colt was born, they all stopped to admire it. On Sundays they rested, for if they didn't, the new priest might find out -- if they ever got a new priest.

Only twice did they have to stop for rain and when they did, Ralin and Taral talked four of the men into using the time to build two new looms. When the sun came back out, the drying of the walls began again. Yet it was Scotland and no one complained about the rain. When it didn't rain for a few days the people worried, but it always began again and life went back to normal.

At night when everyone was exhausted, Charlie played his flute, Earc played his fiddle and everyone's spirits were lifted. Therefore, the village surrounding the three-story stone and mortar keep, began to steadily grow with new paths, new places for children to play and extended guard posts.

Occasionally there was a sunrise filled with glorious color for Taral to enjoy and continue her conversation with God. She always remembered Dan in her prayers, but had not yet talked to him about the tiny life growing in her womb. She was not certain what to say.

Walrick had a wonderful idea. If they built a house of worship and started a rumor, maybe a priest would find them. It was worth a try and every one of the unmarried men were willing to help, although none were certain what a house of worship should look like exactly. They decided one room with a cross on the wall would do and then the priest could tell them what else was needed -- if they ever got a priest.

They could send word of their need of a priest to the King of Scotland, but Neil decided against that idea. He was tired of kings and would rather none of them knew where the MacGreagors were. Besides, the other nearby clans were without a priest too and he doubted there was little the King of Scotland did not already know.

*

Jonrose, Glenna and Jessup were like conspirators sitting around a small table on the third floor of the Keep. The mountain of folded bedding was piled in a corner and the women, who used that room as their temporary shelter, were outside taking walks, helping other women cook or tend the children. That left the three of them in rare privacy.

"I am amazed more lasses do not come to see the giant," said Glenna. "We heard such wondrous rumors of him in the south."

Jonrose stood up and walked to a window. It was her first occasion to be this high up and at first, she feared falling out. Timidly, she eased forward. "They did at first, but the other Lairds watch their lasses more carefully now." She inched just a little closer and looked down. Instantly, she drew back and had to steady her nerves before she could speak again. "Some lasses escape and come to us, but not many. My, but looking down makes me lightheaded."

Jessup nodded. "It makes me lightheaded too. Glenna, you must ask Neil to have straps attached to the walls for us to hang on to."

"My dear friend, I cannot ask anything that trivial of him until all the families are settled. But I will keep it in mind. Until then, what can we do to find more lasses?"

"A festival?" suggested Jessup. "Or maybe a contest such as who makes the best honey bread?"

Glenna smiled. "I like that idea, but wouldn't their men come with them?"

Jonrose puffed her cheeks. "The lads would laugh at us."

"She is right. We must think of something else," said Jessup.

Jonrose came away from the window and sat back down at the table. "Mistress, the MacGreagor lads are very handsome. Perhaps you might send them to the other clans with messages, or to search for something. Once the lasses get a look at how handsome they are…"

"Again, she is right," said Jessup.

"But what could they be looking for?" Glenna asked.

Jonrose grinned. "Wives. Have the lads tell who they are, where they live and that they are in want of wives. If even one lass hears it, she will tell the others."

"It might truly work."

Jessup giggled, "They might attract unsightly wives too."

"For a lonely lad there is no such thing as an unsightly lass. Besides, some of our lads are not all that handsome."

Jessup spoke before she thought. "But do not send Lucas."

Glenna stared at her friend. "Jessup, you have chosen?"

"If you tell Neil or Gelson, I will deny it. Your husbands will try to interfere and there are some things a lass would rather do herself." Jessup glared at both women and then smiled. "Would you believe he has not yet noticed me? I have been thinking about hitting him over the head."

*

Laird Ronan Graham and his guards cautiously showed themselves, and listened as the whistling down the valley began the notification of their arrival. Since that first meeting when he presented Walrick with a horse, the two men had enjoyed each other's company several times. Yet this was different. Even after being told the circumstances that brought the MacGreagors to this land, he needed to see for himself what was happening.

He slowly led his men forward, taking time to notice all the cleared land, the new buildings and the men wearing different colors. He hoped Walrick and Neil MacGreagor would ride out to meet him and he was not disappointed. When they approached without a guard and halted their horses, Graham nodded. "Your neighbors want to start a war."

"They fear us?" asked Neil.

"They fear you want their lasses and so do I."

Neil patted the neck of his nervous stallion to calm him down. "Of a truth, my wife is plotting to do just that. She feels all lads must have a wife and 'tis her aim to see our lads are not without."

Laird Graham almost smiled. "Has she thought of a way to do it?"

"Not that I am aware of. Would the clans be more at ease if I promise to alert them when she does?"

This time Graham allowed himself to smile. "I was afraid I might like you. 'Tis difficult to go to war with a likeable lad."

"Indeed it is. Perhaps you would like to meet my wife."

"That I would." When Neil turned his horse, Ronan Graham moved up to ride beside him. "Tell me, did you happen to bring any unmarried lasses with you? I am in need of a wife myself."

CHAPTER V

Slade was still seeking, and finding the blue MacGreagor cloth tied around the trunks of trees, when he heard a man and a woman arguing. How could they be so reckless? It was never safe to let people know your location in the woods. On the other hand, this was probably their land and they felt safe on it. The woman's voice was getting louder but the man's was not, so Slade quietly slipped down off his horse and crept closer.

He hid behind a tree, cautiously peeked around it and discovered three unhappy men facing an upset woman in a small clearing. The men were clean and well dressed, while the woman had smudges on her faces and wore tattered clothing. Her hair was uncombed, her hands and arms were filthy and her shoes were caked with mud.

"Edana, you are nineteen. Soon you will be so old no lad will have you. Be a good lass for once and do as you are told. I have already accepted payment and you must marry him, or they will have my head."

She put her hands on her hips, leaned forward and glared at him. "Father, you bartered us for seven sheep and three cows. I cannot decide if I hate you for selling us or for selling us for such a low price!"

Slade wrinkled his brow...us? Quietly, he went from tree to

tree until he spotted the others. Eight women, two each on four horses, were watching the argument in silence. Each was as dirty as the first and they looked like sisters with very dark hair and oval faces. Just as quietly, Slade went back to his first position.

Edana's father glared right back. "I barter you for the sake of your brothers. You would not like them to go hungry, now would you?"

"You did it out of greed and if they go hungry, 'tis because you do not teach them to milk a cow, grow a crop or hunt."

"You are well aware lads do not work. 'Tis against the laws of the clan. Besides…" He hesitated to think of just the right way to say it.

"Besides what?" she asked.

"You would not understand."

"What would I not understand? You can tell me; after all we will never see each other again."

Her father shrugged. "I need a wife."

"You are trading the nine of us for seven sheep, three cows and a wife?"

"With you gone, I need someone to tend us."

She stared at him in disbelief. "Indeed you do and may she be an unsightly wife who makes you miserable!"

"Now Edana, you would not truly wish that on me. You know I love you."

She still had her hands on her hips, but she was leaning still closer to him. "I know you are a simple minded old goat who uses the laws of the clan as an excuse for everything. I doubt we even belong to a clan, leastwise I have never seen a laird or any other followers. I will not marry and that is an end to it!"

His eyes grew wide. "But Edana, I have already accepted payment."

"Then give it back."

"I cannot. I have bartered the sheep for more land."

"More land?" She was incredulous. "Who barters for land when there is plenty to be had for nothing? Did the Kennedy brothers talk you into that? "Tis not their land, you are aware."

"They do not own the land?"

Edana closed her eyes and shook her head. "Father, you are hopeless."

He ignored the words that might have insulted any other man. "Nevertheless, I need a wife and all of my daughters need husbands."

"We do not need *Kennedy* husbands."

"How do you know, you have never seen a Kennedy save the brothers."

"I know they would rather buy a wife than try to win her, I know they are not above selling that which they do not own, and I know if they are willing to take up with the likes of you, they are not worth my notice!"

"The Kennedys are wealthy lads. They own very large flocks and considerable land."

"Then you marry them if you are so smitten. We will find our own husbands." She turned and started to walk into the forest. It was a planned effort to lure her father and her brothers away from her sisters. If the plan worked, her sister, Slava, would be able to hide the sisters in the forest before they were missed. When her father and brothers realized and began to search, she would escape and join them.

It was not a well thought out plan, but it was the only one they had, considering the news of their impending marriages only reached them minutes before they were taken away. On one of their previous rest stops, the women took the opportunity to rub dirt all over themselves, muss their hair and tear their clothing, hoping to be rejected by their future husbands. Still, escaping was a much better idea.

Edana's father rushed into the woods after her. "If I must, I will bind you, daughter."

Edana kept right on walking, and no one was more surprised than she, when Slade MacGreagor stepped out from behind a tree to stand between Edana and her father. He took up a steadfast position with his feet apart, his arms crossed and a rigid look on his face.

"Who are you?" asked her father.

"You will not bind this lass."

"She is my daughter and I will do as I please. Move out of the way."

"Do not make me draw my sword," said Slade.

Edana's father paused to look at the angry expression in the stranger's eyes. He was a great deal larger than most men and possibly larger than his two sons put together. He turned to look at his sons, only to find them cowering behind him. Their fear made him apprehensive too, but he tried to gather his courage. "Do you mean to kidnap my daughter?"

"She is welcome to go with me if she pleases, but she will not be forced."

Edana walked half way around the stranger so she could see his face. "May my sisters go with us?"

"If they wish."

She was not sure if she should trust him or not. "Will one of us have to marry you?"

"I do not want a wife." Slade answered. "When you are safely away, you may go wherever you like. We do not force lasses to do anything."

Her father spit on the ground, "Not force a lass? Whoever heard of such a thing?"

Edana turned her satisfied grin on her father. "We will go with him."

"What are you saying? If you go with him, the Kennedys will kill us."

"That will be your doing, not mine." Edana walked past her father and brothers, went to her horse, mounted and then nodded to her sisters. Without hesitation, the women followed her into the forest.

Slade didn't change his stance or take his eyes off her father. He marveled that he did not even have to draw his sword to frighten these cowards. These were the kind of men who would cut a man's throat while he slept rather than fight -- if they were brave enough to do even that. He waited a few minutes longer to give the women sufficient time and then, as if to make his point more clear, he narrowed his eyes. "If you follow, be prepared to fight."

"I will say you snatched them," her father swore.

"As you wish." Slade backed off until he was far enough away, and then raced to his horse, swung up and quickly followed the women. As soon as he reached them, he took the lead and hurried the women on. He glanced back often, made sure the women were keeping up and assured himself they were not being followed. He raced them across a wide meadow and up the side of a hill. Once they were near the top, he signaled for them to stop so he could watch and listen. He saw and heard nothing except his horse breathing, birds chirping and the leaves in the trees rustling in the breeze.

At length, Edana pulled her horse up beside his. "My brothers are not good trackers and my father is lazy. They will not likely try to follow us." At his nod, she led her sisters down the other side of the hill until she came to a small creek. Then she turned her horse into the water and began to follow it.

A full hour later, Edana halted the procession and looked back. The stranger was not following them. "We will rest here." She was not sure if she was glad he was no longer with them, or upset he was gone. As the eldest, she was often charged with protecting her siblings, but just now she had no weapons. Edana helped her sisters down, let them drink from the stream and let them wash their faces.

Repeatedly she looked for the stranger, but he was gone and she was terrified.

CHAPTER VI

"I hate being dirty," said Sheena.

Slava, the second to the oldest, wet a cloth and began to wash the smudges off her sister's face. "You would have loved it, if it kept a lad from wanting to marry you. Lads are little more than swine who think lasses are for the taking and not for the asking. They are…"

Sheen's eyes widened, "Slava."

"What?"

"That lad is right behind you."

She bit her lip and slowly turned. He was still on his horse and he was much larger than she first thought. Slava expected him to be furious and she supposed he had a right to be -- she had, after all, just called him swine. Yet his dark eyes held a glint of delight instead of anger. "Do forgive me, I spoke out of turn."

"I am Slade MacGreagor."

Edana was relieved and as soon as she spotted the large dog curled up in Slade's lap, she grinned and went to him. "A deerhound, how wonderful."

Slade quickly held his hand out to stop her. "His back paw is hurt. I do not think 'tis broken, but he will snap if you touch it."

"I see." She let the dog smell her hand, began to rub behind its ears and then looked up. Edana and her sisters had not been around that many unrelated men, except for the rare festivals they were allowed to attend, but she had seen enough to know this one was handsome. She tore her eyes away, gently lifted the dog and carried it to a place near the water, where two of her sisters sat watching. She knelt down, lowered the dog to the ground and as softly as she could, ran her finger down its leg, and then its paw. She did not feel a lump. "'Tis not broken."

To Slade's amazement, the dog let her examine his paw without so much as a flinch. The woman had the gift of gentleness and he liked that about her very much. She had the same dark hair as her sisters, but there was something about her eyes when she looked up at him. He quickly reminded himself he was not in the market for a wife. He had no clan, no home and nothing to offer a wife even if he wanted one…which he did not.

He got down off his horse, untied a rabbit he shot earlier and handed it to one of the sisters. "'Tis not enough to feed us all. I will hunt for more." He smiled when she half curtsied. "The MacGreagors do not bow or curtsey, except to our laird when there are guests. You need not do that for my sake."

The woman let out a held breath. "Oh good, I do not do it very well. My name is Nessa." She followed his gaze and began to introduce the others. That is Slava, she is second eldest. Charlotte is third, Alison fourth, Sheena is younger than I, and then there is Colina, Laura and Aleen."

Slade noticed Aleen was pouting and went to her. "What is it?"

"I am only eleven and I do not want a husband."

"Nor should you have one, you are too young," he said.

Her pout quickly turned to a smile. "That is what I think."

Slade patted her head and then went back to Edana. "Are you certain your father will not find us here?"

Edana puffed her cheeks. "He needs directions to find his own backside and so do my brothers. They are off hiding somewhere, you can count on that. Father promised to deliver nine brides to Laird Kennedy and now he cannot. The Kennedys will be furious and they will come looking for us. 'Tis from them we must hide."

"I see. How far away are the Kennedys?"

"From here? Half a day west."

"Do you know where we are?"

Edana stared at the sincerity in his eyes. "Are you lost?"

"In a way. I am trying to find my clan and I have never been this far north before."

"You mean you cannot recall where your clan lives?"

"Nay, my clan moved."

Edana frowned. "Moved? A clan does not move."

"This one did. I will explain it later. My clan has left markers on trees to show the way, but we have traveled east and not north. I must go back, find the markers and then go north again to find them."

Charlotte's eyes widened, "But west will take us back to the Kennedys."

"Then we must be very quiet and very careful -- that is, if you are willing to go with me."

Eight anxious sets of sisterly eyes watched Edana and waited for an answer. "Well, we cannot go back to our home, that is for certain. And having one lad to protect us is better than none, I suppose." She paused to think for a moment. "Will your clan welcome us?"

"Of that I am certain," Slade answered.

At fourteen, Sheena's blue eyes were still a little too big for her young face. "Will we be forced to marry the lads in your clan?"

"Nay, we do not force lasses."

Nessa nudged her sister, "Sheena, he said that already."

"I know, but I wanted to see if his answer would be different, now that we are away from our father and brothers."

Slade nodded to Sheena and then turned to Edana again. "The Kennedys will not know you are missing until nightfall. If we keep going, we should be well north by the time they start to search." He pulled the bottom of his green Cameron kilt up just enough to expose the blue one underneath. My clan has tied strips of this cloth around trees. Watch for them, they are up high." He let his kilt fall back down and then looked to each of them for their nod.

"The dog can ride with me," Edana said as they got back on their horses. The stranger put the dog in her lap. This time he took the lead and she watched their backs.

*

They did not find another cloth tied to a tree, but when Slade felt they had traveled west the same length of time they traveled east, he turned them north. As the evening hours approached and he knew the women had to be worn out, he let his horse lead them to a stream and then halted.

The clearing was small, they would lose the good daylight soon, and once it was dark, he knew no one would be able to see their smoke. "I will build a fire." He slid down, walked to Edana's horse and lifted the dog down, then he held out his arms to her, but she hesitated. "I will not harm you."

"I have no weapon to defend us from you."

"Aye, but there are nine of you and I am not good at keeping my eyes open day and night." She did not appear to find that answer satisfactory, so he began to untie the dagger and sheath from around his waist. Once it was free, he handed it to her. "Try not to hurt me unless I deserve it."

She still would not accept his help, so he walked away, helped the others dismount and then began to search for dry fire wood. When he came back, two of the women were preparing the rabbit and the others had their plaids spread on the ground. A small fire was already started with a pile of wood beside it.

When he looked surprised, Edana flashed a small piece of mirror his way. She waited for him to set his wood down and kneel beside her before she showed him how to reflect the light. "'Tis only successful when the sun is shining and the leaves must be very dry, but it saves time when it does work."

"I can see that. Thank you for showing me." Of course, he carried the usual flint and steel, but he did not mention it.

She watched him gather the wood back up and set it down closer to the fire. "In our clan, the lasses gather the wood."

Her words disturbed him. "Is that what your father taught you?"

She stood up and carefully tucked the piece of broken mirror under her belt. "Aye."

He added a little more wood to the fire and then started back toward his horse. "I will hunt for more food."

"But lasses do the hunting, 'tis our…"

"A MacGreagor would never let a lass hunt for him. You have been taught wrong." He took hold of his reins and began to mount his mare.

Edana hurried after him. "Wait. We have bread, my sisters and I can gather berries and it will be enough for tonight."

He studied the expression on her face. "You are frightened?"

Edana lowered her gaze. "We need you to protect us far more than we need to eat."

Slade was torn between feeding them and guarding them. "Perhaps you are right. You will feel safer when we are farther away from the Kennedys, and then I will do the hunting. Agreed?"

"I am a very good hunter."

He pulled his sacks down and let his horse wander off to graze. "I did not mean you were unable, but 'tis an honor for a lad to hunt for a lass."

Edana was completely confused, so much so, she couldn't think of anything else to say. Worry lines were deep in her forehead. At her instruction, four sisters went in search of berries while the others fetched the bread, finished preparing the rabbit and making beds around the camp fire. Edana tended the fire and tried to understand what the stranger was talking about. She always felt the men in her family did not work because they were lazy, but for a man to say it was an honor, was a completely new concept.

Slade spread a Cameron plaid on the ground not too far from the women, dumped the water out of his flask and refilled it with fresh from the stream. When he sat down, he noticed the youngest sister watching him. "Will your horses come when you call them?"

"Aye," answered Aleen. "We have raised them from birth and they obey us, but not our brothers. We taught them reverse, you see."

"Nay, I do not see."

Aleen was delighted to know something the strange man did not know. "If you tell them to go they will come, but if you tell them to come they will go...do you see?"

"That I do see."

"Our stupid brothers never did figure it out," Aleen continued.

"Then your father will not be upset that you took his horses?"

"Nay, they are our horses. He gave them to us and since he thinks they cannot be managed, he will not be sorry they are gone. He is a stupid, stupid lad."

Slade smiled. These women were not only beautiful, they were clever. He could not wait to get them home to a clan that would cherish them. Women being sold into marriage was an insult to all MacGreagors.

CHAPTER VII

The ten of them ate rabbit, bread and berries, and then gave the bones to a dog that was happy to have them. Finally, they bedded down...all except Edana, who was still not certain it was safe to close her eyes with a strange man in their midst. The dog curled up on her plaid while she stirred the embers of the fire with a stick.

Slade knew she feared him and hoped talking would ease her fear. "Why is he called a deerhound?"

Edana thought it was a stupid question, but answered it anyway. "Deerhounds are trained to hunt and kill deer. Many of the lairds have them; it makes the hunt far easier for the hunter."

"Then most of the lairds in this land are lazy?"

Edana started to grin, "I have often wondered that." She repeatedly ran her hand down the dog's velvety, reddish-brown coat. "They are very graceful dogs."

"He is too thin, are they not fed well?"

"They are naturally thin." She could feel Slade watching her, but she dared not look at him any more often than was usual for a normal conversation. She was not still afraid of him exactly, but he made her feel self-conscious -- something no other man had made her feel; the few she had encountered anyway. There had been two suitors in the past who asked for her hand, but neither of them gave her heart the least flutter. If this man did not stop watching her soon, she thought she might pass out. "You promised to tell us about your clan."

"That I did. We lived under the threat of war for years. Another clan wanted our land and they greatly outnumbered us, so when they attacked we escaped through a tunnel and now we must find a new home."

Slava quickly sat up, "I have heard of this war. Did your village burn?"

"Aye, we burned it ourselves."

Slava was enthralled, "We have heard all sorts of rumors. Did a lass really draw a golden sword out of the fire?"

Confused, Slade wrinkled his brow. "A golden sword? There is a legend, but…"

Edana tossed her stick away, folded her legs under her and pulled her extra plaid tighter around her shoulders. "I heard the lass went to find the giant."

"I do not believe in giants," said Aleen. Just the same, she got up, dragged her plaid closer to Slade and then curled up next to him.

"Neither do I." Laura, the second from the youngest agreed, moving her plaid closer to Aleen, and therefore closer to Slade as well. "Even if we are going north where the giant lives, I will not be afraid as long as you are with us. I like you, Slade MacGreagor."

He smiled and gently touched the top of Laura's head. "I like you as well."

Edana finally stretched out and covered herself. "Sleep sisters." She was still a little concerned, but she was too tired to stay awake worrying about what he might do. The others seemed to trust this man, and so far, he had not done or said anything to make them feel threatened. Perhaps they would be safe with him, and like he pointed out, they were nine against one. She wondered if they would have to kill him. She wondered that just before she fell asleep.

Slade waited until she closed her eyes before he lay down and tried to sleep. As tired as he was, it was not easy. That many women out in the open had more than one clan to worry about, and he wondered just how he could protect them. The answer, he decided, was to keep them in the trees. To his surprise, the dog got up, limped to him and then curled up beside him. He stroked the dog's head for a time, realized the dog would alert him to any danger and went to sleep.

*

The morning meal for nine women, one man and one dog consisted of more berries. Two of the sisters began to squabble over the way their things were packed, but when Slade held up his hand, they quieted. He was happy to see it and felt he would have a good measure of control over them as they traveled. He kicked dirt on the cold embers from the night before, and then helped Edana lift the younger ones into the laps of the mounted older women.

Yet when he went to help Edana, she refused his help. "I can manage." She watched him shrug, wait for her to mount and hand her the injured dog. "We are not accustomed to having lads help us."

He nodded as though he understood. "When you live with the MacGreagors, you will become accustomed to it. We enjoy helping our lasses very much and 'tis an insult when they do not let us."

An insult? Edana watched him mount his horse, held back until the others passed so she could protect them from the back, and thought about what he said. She certainly had not meant to insult him, but his touch made her feel...she could not quite describe how it made her feel. When he accidentally brushed his hand against the back of hers the night before, she felt awkward, shy and weak. That was it, weak. Edana had never felt weak a whole day in her life, and she did not like it one bit.

As well, there was that other feeling that made her long to be with him. She had never felt like that before either. She decided she would let him help her in the future, just so she could get used to it. Then she began to wonder about all those other MacGreagor men who needed wives. Were they as handsome as Slade? Would they make her feel weak when they helped her? Did the MacGreagors really let women choose their own husbands, or was this man just a very accomplished liar leading them straight into a trap?

*

By noon, fog began to obscure the sunlight and they were all showing signs of exhaustion. Slade was about to stop them, when the dog growled. He halted his horse and looked back at Edana. She was calm, but was also scanning the forest for any sign of danger. When no danger was easily spotted, she quietly lifted the dog out of her lap and then lowered him to the ground.

Limping less than before, the dog started off and Slade followed. In just a few feet, he saw what the danger was, slid down off his horse and hid behind a bush. In the misty meadow, several men wearing red kilts were off their horses looking for tracks. He could not hear what they were saying, but it was clear they were after someone and he hoped it wasn't them.

Suddenly, he felt movement beside him. He reached for his dagger and spun around, only to find he no longer had his dagger. Then he realized the person beside him was Edana. He was not pleased and gave her an angry look, but there wasn't time for that now. He quickly turned his attention back to the men in the meadow.

The dog was still softly growling and he prayed they wouldn't hear it, or that the dog would not go charging out, so he rubbed its ears to calm the dog down. Finally, the men began to mount and ride south. As soon as they were gone, Edana went back to her horse and the dog followed. Slade stayed a few minutes longer to make sure the men did not come back, and then he grabbed his reins, went back into the fog and found all nine women dismounted and walking the stiffness out.

He was furious with Edana, but tried not to frighten any of the sisters, especially the little ones. He left his horse to graze, knelt down and talked to the dog. "You are better this morning. Perhaps the lasses will give you a name sometime today." Then he stood up and glared at Edana. "You must never sneak up on a lad. Do you not know better? I might have hurt you."

Edana's own anger flared. How dare he chastise her in front of her sisters? "I needed to see what was happening."

"In the future, you will wait until I tell you 'tis safe before you come to see what is happening."

She narrowed her eyes and clenched her fists. "I thought MacGreagor lads honored lasses."

"A MacGreagor lass would never do anything that stupid. They trust us to know what is best."

"I am not a MacGreagor lass."

"You will be." He realized his temper was getting the best of him, looked away and began to rub the back of his neck. "I will be pleased if you do not do that again...ever."

Edana's temper was out of control too, she realized, and at length she gave her nod. "They are Kennedys."

Slade nodded. "I see. They went south so perhaps we have seen the last of them."

"We must be closer than I thought to their village. We should go east again," said Edana.

"Nay, we must find the MacGreagor cloths or we will be lost forever."

"I say we go east," Edana insisted.

Slade would have none of that foolishness. "I go north. Where you go is up to you."

CHAPTER VIII

Edana thought being the oldest was the devil's cruelest joke. She was used to making all the decisions, even for her brothers and her stupid father. She could handle who slept where and who had to do which chore, but those were not life and death decisions. She truly believed going east would insure their safety, but being without Slade frightened her too. For a second time she gave in to his ultimatum. "We will go with you."

He was relieved. It was unthinkable to leave nine defenseless women in the wilderness alone, and he would have gone with them if she refused. Fortunately she did not know that. "The fog will help hide us."

She untied the strings to his dagger and gave it back. "You may need this."

"Thank you." He guessed that meant she would not sneak up on him again, now that he could cut her. He guessed wrong.

As soon as all the women were mounted, he got on his horse and started off. This time, he did not offer to help Edana get on her horse. Touching her was a bit too much for him anyway. It made him think of holding her and kissing her, which he would not allow himself to do…if he could help it.

*

Laird Ronan Graham began to visit the MacGreagors on a

regular basis and Neil was not certain why, until Gelson asked to have a word with him outside in private.

As Neil's new third in command, and the man in charge of caring for his wife, Gelson would know if something was wrong with Glenna and Neil instantly became concerned. "Is my wife ill?"

Gelson wrinkled his brow. "Oh, nay your wife is fine." He saw the relief on Neil's face and smiled. "'Tis of another lass I wish to speak. I fear I have done her a grave injustice, or perhaps not. In any case, she is unmarried and not likely to find a husband in our two clans."

Neil leaned against the wall of the Keep and folded his arms. "You have confused me."

"The lass' name is Janell and she is my brother's widow. She took a liking to Walrick before Steppen arrived, and I feared she would trick him into marriage the way she tricked my brother. I could not let her become our mistress, so I asked others to help me prevent it. Now, even the MacGreagor unmarried lads know not to trust her, and she may never find a husband with us. However..." He paused to let Neil absorb all that he had said.

"Go on."

"I believe 'tis she Laird Graham looks for when he comes. He smiles when he sees her."

"So you are saying I should encourage a marriage?"

"Aye, before she thinks she needs to trick him. He was tricked once before, although not by the lass, by her brother. He would not take kindly to being tricked again."

"It would be a good match for both, then."

"Aye and a great relief to me," said Gelson.

"What do you suggest I do?"

"Perhaps you might introduce them the next time he comes. If you suggest they go for a ride or a walk, she will not feel the need to tempt him."

"Done then."

*

Everywhere Jessup went, it seemed Finley and Connell were there. She loved the attention, but she did not find herself attracted to either man, and occasionally she had to glare at them just to have a little privacy. Finley was a MacClurg and Connell was a MacGreagor. Both were pleasant to look at and both seemed nice enough, but she had her eye on a very handsome, very quiet and very MacGreagor man, whom she noticed before they left England. The problem was, he was one of Neil's protectors and he rarely seemed to look at her.

His name was Lucas and he created all the shrewd mishaps for the MacDonald warriors the day of the attack. Neil spoke of his cleverness often, when they stopped to eat and rest on their journey. Jessup suspected the praise of his talents sometimes embarrassed Lucas, but he did not say a word.

The very English Jessup, on the other hand, had no talents. All her life people waited on her, and she did not even have to dress herself. She knew how to read and write and how to make pictures using different color threads, but did not know the first thing about weaving, tending children or gathering herbs. When she was

Patrick's wife, she did little more than care for her elder mother and cook an occasional meal. Now, what small talents she had were of no value at all to her beloved MacGreagor Clan.

To make herself feel the least bit useful, she spent her days taking a flask of water from hard working man to hardworking man. It was a good way to get to know them better, but Lucas was never around and never needed her water. Little by little, it began to frustrate her until daily, hourly, and by the minute she came to know exactly where he was. In fact, she could swear when he saw her coming, he intentionally went the other way. She did not want to make her interest in him obvious, but she was not about to let him ignore her either.

Then one day she caught him watching her.

It was quite by accident, on a warm Sunday when nearly everyone was outside. She had just finished bathing, Glenna was brushing her long, beautiful hair and when she held up Neil's mother's hand mirror, Lucas was leaning against a tree behind her. He had his arms folded and, had that look in his eyes as he watched each time Glenna drew the brush the full length of Jessup's hair.

Jessup quickly lowered the mirror and smiled. So, Lucas MacGreagor noticed her after all. It was about time. Now all she had to do was get him to talk to her. Yet after all these weeks of silence, she wasn't sure how to do that.

*

Slade stopped and stared at the strip of blue plaid tied around a tree. Slowly, his lips curled into a smile and the relief he felt was overwhelming. At last, he found the right path and now they could rest for a second night, with him feeling much more peaceful. This time the dog captured a squirrel and had his dinner, while the humans hunted for berries. The number of bushes was fewer and held less fruit, but those, coupled with several mushrooms, staved off their hunger well enough. The women were tired and easily irritated over all sorts of little things. This night they were deciding who should ride with whom the next day and not agreeing at all.

Slade cautioned himself to stay out of it. He and the dog should just sit back, watch and let them settle things among themselves.

"You miss my meaning completely," Charlotte said.

"She does that intentionally," Slava put in and appreciated the nods of the other sisters.

Edana turned her angry eyes on her sister. "I do not."

Charlotte narrowed hers in return, "Aye you do. You are too overbearing."

Slade took issue with that and before he knew it, he had disregarded his own advice. "Does she keep you safe?"

Charlotte, who had hardly spoken a word since they were rescued from her father, turned to look at him. "Aye."

"Then she is not too overbearing. You need a leader or there will be chaos. Edana is your leader."

"Like a laird?" Nessa asked.

"Precisely like a laird."

"But what if she is wrong? She is sometimes wrong, you know," said Charlotte.

"All lairds are wrong sometimes, but what can the followers do? They must have someone in charge."

Nessa, Charlotte and the others paused to think that over. "Next time, I will be the laird," Charlotte said finally."

Edana smiled and quickly hugged her sister. "And what will you do when your followers do not obey?"

Charlotte giggled and started to spread the bedding. "I will oft them."

Everyone laughed and then began to settle down near the fire. Edana was surprised Slade took her side in the argument and it pleased her very much. She waited until he sat down and when she caught his eye, she nodded her appreciation. "I hate being the eldest."

"I can see why," he said.

Aleen pulled her cover up and snuggled closer to her sister, Laura. "I want to marry the King of Scots when I am big."

Slade covered himself, lay down and let the dog curl up next to him. "Why do you want to marry him?"

"So I can have all the riches in the world." She yawned, closed her eyes and fell asleep almost instantly.

Edana fixed her bed, sat down and when Slava began to laugh, she looked over. "What?"

"We have been gone two days," said Slava, "Do you think our brothers have learned how to milk the cow yet? If not, she is bawling something awful and making them daft."

"Too late," Charlotte said. "They are already daft."

Edana sighed and closed her eyes. "I doubt they went home.

They will probably hide until the Kennedys stop looking for them, and by then the cow's milk will be dried up."

"They do not know how to make the cheese anyway," said Alison. "Edana, why do you think Father chose to sell us just now? Why not last year or next year…why now?"

Edana turned on her side and tried to get comfortable. "I do not know. He must have done something wretched. Even if he had a wife, one lass could not do all that nine of us do every day. How did he expect to care for another seven sheep and three cows, without us to tend them?"

Charlotte rolled her eyes. "He lied again, there was no payment. He meant to give us away to save himself."

Edana touched her sister's arm and tried to comfort her. "At least we had a good mother who loved us, and now we are free of him. Rest sisters, tomorrow we will look to our future lives instead of our past."

CHAPTER IX

They were the first MacGreagors to find their clan by following the strips of plaid, and prayed they had finally come to the end of their journey, when they spotted an entire light blue plaid stretched between two trees at the top of a very high hill. They were a young couple and a baby, and their grins were wide as they rode their one horse up to the top and then down the other side. As soon as they were half way down, the man put two fingers to his mouth and whistled three times until every MacGreagor and half the MacClurgs were running to greet them.

The woman's sister-in-law snatched the child out of her arms, the brother lifted her, and even the husband got pulled off the horse and playfully roughed up. Then they were practically carried amid shouts of joy, until all three were finally close enough for Neil and Glenna to hug and welcome them home. As all the others had been, they were exhausted, so Neil kept them only long enough to hear how they found their way, and then sent them off to their well-deserved pampering and rest.

That afternoon, Neil gathered the people in the courtyard and mounted a nearby horse, so everyone could see and hear him. "'Tis time to send men back to find the others. Hector tells me they found us by following the cloth, but they lost the path often and more marks are needed. Unless you use them for warmth, bring your MacGreagor plaids to the Keep." Then he named the eight lads he wanted to go back.

Jessup held her breath and when Neil did not name Lucas, she was overjoyed. The women cut more MacGreagor plaids into strips, the men packed their supplies and eight accomplished warriors got ready to leave the next morning to search for lost MacGreagors.

*

It was another day of little to eat, exhausted women and a dog that was still slightly limping. It was also another day of keeping the women hidden in the dense forest, which meant slow going. In the morning, the dog rode with Edana but in the afternoon, Slade took him and for a second time, the deerhound suddenly came alert.

Slade immediately held up his hand to stop the small procession, listened and thought he heard voices. As quietly as he could, he put the dog down, dismounted and motioned for the women to stay put. Then he crouched down and slipped from tree to tree until he got close enough to see.

He first spotted two horses and a packhorse. Then he saw a man, wearing a MacGreagor kilt, lying on the ground with his hands and legs bound, and his mouth gagged. The man viciously struggled against his restraints, and his eyes were wild as he watched another man drag his wife out of sight. Slade recognized Arthur as the man tied up and that meant the woman about to be forced was Arthur's wife, Ulla.

Slade's mind quickly filled with rage.

He drew his dagger and moved quietly from hiding place to hiding place until he was close enough to act. The man had Ulla down on the ground, was on top of her and just as she was about to scream, Slade grabbed hold of the man's hair and yanked him off her. With fury in his eyes, he drew the blade of his dagger across the man's throat and ended his life. Then he shoved the man aside, quickly grabbed Ulla's arm, pulled her up and the two of them ran to her husband.

Together, they untied him and as soon as Arthur was mounted, Slade handed him the reins to the packhorse. Then he turned to Ulla, "Can you manage?" When she nodded, he quickly lifted her up on the remaining horse. It was then that he caught a glimpse of Edana's back and realized she had seen the whole thing.

Slade led Arthur and Ulla back to the others, saw that Edana was mounted, gave her the dog and turned to the sisters. "We must leave this place quickly. Be very quiet." He got on his horse and hurried them away.

As often as he could he glanced back, but not at the sisters...at Ulla. For a good hour or more, she held her head up high, but when he saw her lower her head, he stopped, got down and went back to her. He opened his arms and when she went into them, he pulled her down, held her, let her cry for as long as she wanted and kissed the side of her face. Then he lifted her into her husband's arms, accepted his grateful nod and walked back toward his horse.

Sheena could not contain her curiosity, "What happened?"

"Quiet," ordered Slava.

Slade gently took the younger woman's hand. "'Tis alright, we are safe now."

Sheena was not satisfied with his answer. "But I want to know what happened. Who are those people?"

"They are Arthur and his wife, Ulla. A lad tried to hurt Ulla, but she is fine now."

"Oh." Sheena was not certain if she should be happy or sad, so she just nodded. "I will be quiet now."

He was about to get back on his horse when he decided now was as good a time as any. He turned his glare on Edana. "I told you to stay back, you should not have followed me."

"You kissed another lad's wife."

"What?"

"Just now, you kissed another lad's wife. I saw you."

"Edana, we will talk about this later." He was still enraged and did not trust himself to keep his emotions under control, so he mounted and continued them north.

After a time, Slade began to worry about Edana. He was not fooled. He was certain she was not upset about him kissing Ulla; she had seen him kill a man and was having trouble accepting it. He did not blame her; it took days to get the mental images of the two MacDonald warriors he killed out of his mind. Now she had the same kind of horror to deal with and he did not know how to help her.

Edana was not thinking about the dead man. In her opinion, he deserved to die and she felt no regret. What disturbed her was Slade's actions. He held and kissed another man's wife and the husband did not object. Edana understood why the woman would need comfort, but why would Ulla want Slade to comfort her instead of her husband? It was a puzzle she could not put together.

Slade was more than a little concerned now. As soon as they stopped, all the sisters got down off their horses, and Arthur and his wife began to build a fire. Yet Edana had not dismounted and she didn't seem to notice when he took the dog out of her arms. "Edana." He held out his arms to her and if she let him, he would hold her. But she had not moved. "Edana let me help you down."

"You kissed another lad's wife."

"Ulla is a MacGreagor."

"Do you kiss all the MacGreagor wives?"

"Only the ones who want to be comforted. Put your hands on my shoulders." To his surprise, she obeyed and let him lift her down. When she did not let go, neither did he. She stared at his chest and he expected her to scream or cry or even hit him, but at length she calmly let go and moved away. Her words said she was upset about his kissing Ulla, but her actions were those of a woman in shock over seeing violence.

Slade would have followed Edana, but Arthur walked to him. He took hold of Arthur's forearm and smiled. "'Tis good to see you."

"I should not have let him get the upper hand."

Slade moved the two of them away from the women. "You have been a farmer for years, not a warrior. Have you found Neil?"

"Nay, but I have seen the cloth."

"We have as well. We will find them, I am certain of it."

Arthur nodded. "At least we gained a horse for Ulla and the packhorse carries salt."

"The pack horse is not yours?" Slade asked.

"Nay, the lad said he was on his way to deliver it to the Campbells, whoever they are. They might come looking for it when he does not arrive."

"Salt is more valuable than gold in the Highlands. Neil will be happy to see it, if we ever find him. Is Ulla hurt?"

"She says not."

Edana was suddenly standing right in front of him with her eyes narrowed and her arms tightly folded. Slade studied her determined expression for a moment and decided not to let her avoid the real problem. "You disobeyed me. A lass should never see what you saw this day. 'Tis unthinkable." He failed to notice the other sisters gathering around them.

"I have seen worse," said Edana.

At that, his eyes were on fire. "I do not care; you should not have seen this. In the future, if you do not obey me, I will take your sisters and leave you behind."

"You will not, they would never let you," Edana argued.

"I might," whispered Slava. She was standing next to Arthur and looked just as determined as her sister.

"What did she see?" asked Aleen.

Slade suddenly realized he had an audience. "'Tis nothing for you to fret about."

Ulla came over and put her arms around her husband. "A lad

tried to hurt me and Slade killed him."

Ulla said it so nonchalantly, Slade thought she was probably in shock too and changed the subject. "I wonder if there is any food on that packhorse." He watched all their eyes light up and then followed them. While he untied one bag, Ulla untied another and found it full of barley.

"Thank goodness," said Slava. "We will not starve after all."

Ulla was as excited as the others. "And we have salt to make it taste good, now all we need is water."

Slade had just started to look around when Slava grabbed his arm. "Listen."

"A waterfall?" Slade asked.

Charlotte excitedly clapped her hands and hurried off to unpack some clean clothing. "A bath! I hate being dirty."

CHAPTER X

Now, there were two men to protect the ten women. On the packhorse, they also found a dagger for Slava, and a bow and arrows for Edana. The evening meal was barley cakes and everyone ate their fill. Once all the bathing was accomplished, the sisters put on good clothing and then helped dry each other's hair.

Both Arthur and Slade sat on a MacGreagor plaid, petting the dog and admiring the individual attractiveness of each woman. "MacGreagor lads will be happy to see these beauties," Arthur whispered.

"Aye. Their father was about to sell them when I came along. The little one is only eleven, and I find it hard to believe a Highlander would wed one so young. Only four are truly old enough."

Ulla knelt down beside her husband and touched Slade's shoulder. "You should talk to Edana. 'Tis dangerous to let a lass go to bed that upset."

Slade smiled. "I am giving her time to think."

"She thinks she wants to strangle you."

He looked confused. "She must learn to obey me; there is no other way to keep her safe."

"That is not what upsets her."

"What then?"

Ulla studied the innocence in his expression. "You kissed another lass. Why do you think that upsets her?"

He considered it, closed his eyes and bowed his head. "I have given her no reason to think I prefer her."

"She does not need a reason. Edana feels responsible for eight other people, she is frightened and she is not thinking clearly. Once she feels safe, she may not even prefer you, but for now she believes you belong to her."

The idea that Edana might not prefer him once she felt safe bothered him, but he did not let on. He glanced her direction, noticed she was still brushing Colina's hair and decided he would wait and talk to her when she was finished.

Edana felt calm, a little irritated maybe, but calm enough. Having something to do helped and after brushing her sister's hair dry, she was beginning to realize how tired she was. She handed the brush to Colina and went to sit by the fire.

In a little while, Slade knelt down beside her. "You have been very brave."

"Would you really leave me behind?"

"Edana, I cannot keep you safe if you do not obey me. All kinds of things might have gone wrong today and I would never forgive myself if you got hurt. Promise you will not disobey me."

She ignored him. "Why did…"

"I will have your promise or I will answer no more questions."

She was too tired to stand up to him, and it appeared she would not get an answer to what bothered her most until she did. "I promise."

"Thank you. You want to know why I held and kissed Arthur's wife."

"Aye, she is a married lass and the church forbids such things. My mother taught us that."

"I have known Ulla all my life and she was frightened. I held her to comfort her, true, but she wanted to comfort me as well. I had just killed a lad for her sake and MacGreagors do not take such a thing lightly."

"And her husband did not mind?"

"Arthur would have been insulted if I had not held her."

Edana wrinkled her brow. "Insulted how?

"A person's touch is the most precious gift we can give to one another. Her touch is her way of thanking me, and she may thank me that way several more times, before she is over the upset of what happened. How could I not let her thank me? If I did not let her, her husband would see it as an insult. And one more thing, while I held her I told her she was safe over and over until she believed it. Do you understand?"

"Would you do that with all lasses?"

"I would. Of course, the lass must be willing. I might not kiss all women, but Ulla is like a sister to me, and I was not even aware I kissed her until you said it. All I thought about was what might have happened to her if I had not stopped him."

"The same as might have happened to us?"

Maybe she understood a lot more than he thought, and was not upset that he killed the man after all. The look in her eyes told him she was grateful, even if she was not yet willing to say it. "Aye, the same as might have happened to you."

She tilted her head to one side. "If her husband were to hold me, you would not object?"

"For that, I would have to call him out." He was as surprised by his answer as she was, and grinned hoping she would not notice his discomfort.

"You are daft."

"Have I neglected to mention that?" At last, he made her smile. "It has been a very long day. Sleep, the dog and I will keep you safe. Perhaps now that we have food, we will rest here tomorrow and let the horses graze." He waited for her nod and then went back to talk to Arthur.

*

It was another ordinary day for the MacGreagor clan. There was some excitement when Neil announced the newest cottage was ready for Taral and Jessup to move into. The families with small children were next in line, then the ones with older children. With any luck, the unmarried men could begin building homes for the wives they hoped to have someday. Little did they know their prospects were looking up.

Glenna plotted ways to attract more women and to get Neil alone, while Neil plotted ways to sleep with his wife more often. Jessup still couldn't figure out how to get Lucas to admit he wanted her. Taral did her weaving and waited to be sure she was with child. Walrick sent messengers to other clans in search of a priest, and once Laird Graham asked Janell to marry him, he also sent more messengers.

The MacClurgs and the MacGreagors were beginning to work together better and life was mellowing out. All that was bound to change.

*

It was their day of rest and when he walked to the edge of a meadow just for the exercise, Slade could hardly believe his eyes. A man wearing an unfamiliar green and blue kilt was standing on his horse at the edge of a meadow, tying a strip of MacGreagor plaid around a tree. Not far away, another seven men, dressed the same as the first, sat on their horses watching him. Who would do that but a MacGreagor? Yet whose colors were they wearing? It could be some sort of trap. A MacGreagor might have been forced to tell another clan about the marks and these men wanted to misdirect them.

If he decided it was a trap, Arthur and the women were just over the next ridge waiting and he could quietly leave…but what if they were MacGreagors and knew how to find Neil. Was the possible danger worth taking the chance?

The man finished tying the strip, sat down on his horse and looked as though he was about to leave. It was now or never. With a racing heart, Slade let out a short whistle, not too loud and not too soft, he hoped. Instantly, the men in the meadow turned to look his direction. Then the man who had just tied the plaid, returned with the same whistle. It was a MacGreagor!

Slade nearly tripped over the dog trying to get out of the forest and then started to run. The closer he got to the men, the more familiar they looked. Soon they were down off their horses waiting to welcome him with slaps on the back and arm holds.

"Am I ever glad to see you. I have ten lasses, the Kennedys are looking for them and I need help."

"Ten lasses? Are they unmarried?" asked one.

Slade grinned. "Arthur and Ulla are with me too. The other nine are sisters who were being sold into marriage by their father." He neglected to mention only four were old enough to marry, and he almost said to stay away from Edana, but he didn't. "How far are we from Neil?"

"You are almost there. Another two or three hours. We will help you guard them. Where are they?"

"On the other side of this hill." He waited for one of the other men to mount, took hold of his arm and swung up behind him.

*

At the sound of eight horses coming their way, the women were about to panic, but Arthur moved to stand in front of them, faced that direction and drew his sword. When Slade whistled, Arthur put his sword away and relaxed. "'Tis MacGreagors."

"Oh good," breathed Slava.

As the warriors broke through the trees, the four eldest sisters caught their breaths. Never had they seen such large and muscular men.

Slade quickly got down. "We are only a few hours from home and they will guard us on the way." The men spread out to watch in all directions, while the women gathered their things and got on their horses. Slade led the way out of the forest into the meadow, and soon the MacGreagor guards were flanking the women on both sides.

Aleen leaned around her sister until she caught the eye of one of the guards. Then she gave him her best frown. "I am only eleven and I do not want a husband."

He nodded. "Nor should you have one. You are not old enough."

"That is what I think, too." Normally by now, Edana would have scolded her for talking, but this time she didn't. This time they were riding out in the open and Aleen liked being guarded by men. It made her feel safe. She had a thousand questions she'd been storing up and with someone willing to answer, there was no stopping her. "I want to marry the king of Scots. He has vast riches, you know. I am hoping..." Not once did she notice the man glancing at, and sometimes smiling at her older sister.

CHAPTER XI

When the whistling in the woods began to signal a relatively large group of friendly visitors coming down the glen, everyone was anxious to see who was coming. Steppen grabbed Walrick's hand and he was quick to steal a kiss before they set out to join the gathering crowd. Hopefully, they were about to see the priest.

Neil lifted Justin up on his shoulders, put his arm around Glenna and waited in front of the Keep. They were all surprised when a man and woman broke out of the visiting entourage and began to gallop toward them, but then someone recognized Arthur and a shout went up. Still, the other newcomers held back and everyone was curious to know why.

Arthur finally got close enough to announce that Slade found nine beauties requesting sanctuary with the MacGreagors, which made Glenna grin from ear to ear. "Slade," she whispered under her breath, "now there is a lad who can attract more lasses."

It seemed like it was taking forever to get down the glen and Slade could not wait to see his clan and Neil. There was something extremely lonely about not having a clan or a laird.

To Edana, it looked like paradise, even with its half-finished cottages. All the people were smiling and just as Slade said, there were men everywhere, most of whom were handsome. At least she thought so. Suddenly, one of them had his hands on her waist, waiting for her to put hers on his shoulders, so he could help her down in the courtyard. It was a tradition she might like getting used to after all. The stranger's smile was infectious, and although she was trying not to get too excited in case the MacGreagor laird rejected their request for sanctuary, she returned his smile.

Slade was not pleased. The fact that he was so torn apart when she gave her smile to another man shocked him. He had to turn away to keep from seeing the way she looked into the man's eyes or stayed in his arms longer than he thought was necessary. Instead of watching any longer, he went to see Neil. On the way, he got several hugs from women happy to see him, and when he got into the great hall, he even got one from Glenna, which surprised him. He quickly looked to see if Neil was about to take his life, but his laird was smiling. Neil's smile widened when Slade told him about the salt.

*

Seated at the table inside the Keep, Neil agreed to let Slade go back to the land of the Camerons, to collect the ones he left behind, and insisted he take several fresh horses. The dog sat quietly by Slade's side and did not mind when Glenna reached out to pet him. The dog was not just a good watch dog; it would comfort the children, so Slade decided to take the dog with him.

Walrick sat at the table quietly listening to the account of what happened to Slade, and the people he took out through the tunnel. Then he could wait no more. "Did you happen to see which way the priest went?"

"You do not have him?" Slade asked.

Walrick closed his eyes and took a deep breath. "The lad has fallen off the face of the earth."

Neil laughed. "Love is a wondrous thing, unless there is no priest to perform the marriage ceremony."

"I will keep an eye out for him when I go back," Slade promised.

Walrick got up and slapped him on the back to welcome him, "You do that." Then he walked out of the room still a frustrated man.

When Slade finished talking to Neil and Glenna, and went back outside, Edana and her sisters had been whisked away to be fed, indulged and rested. For days, they were never long out of his sight and not knowing where they were just now bothered him. Finally, Taral noticed his distress, and whispered that all nine and Ulla were on the top floor of the Keep having warm baths. He smiled and thanked her.

*

The men Neil sent to search for the lost MacGreagors were not all that anxious to leave again, now that there were beautiful women to look at and get to know. Neil only granted them one more day before he expected them to go out again. He thought by then, Slade would be rested enough and could go with them instead of setting out alone.

That evening, Edana and her sisters asked Neil if they could show their appreciation for their sanctuary in a very special way. With the flutist to accompany them, the nine sisters stood in the courtyard, raised their voices in perfect harmony and sang an old ballad. It was the most beautiful thing the clan had ever heard, they were mesmerized and insisted the sisters sing more songs.

Glenna was especially pleased. Once word got out about this, the other clans would come to hear them. Perhaps they would bring their women, who would carry back word of all the handsome unmarried men. It was something to think about and hope for anyway.

Slade was just as taken aback as the rest of them and when Edana sang the moving words of the love song, she looked right at him. There was hope, he thought. Now he understood why the Kennedys wanted all nine sisters instead of just the ones old enough to marry. He quickly walked to Neil to warn him. Once the Kennedys heard where the singing sisters were, they might demand their return. It could mean war.

Neil considered it. He was about to send nine warriors away and he might need them here more. On the other hand, the sooner they gathered the rest of the MacGreagors, the sooner they would have many more warriors to defend the sisters. One thing was for certain, these nine sisters were worth defending.

*

After Edana finished singing, received the admiration of several eligible men, and strolled away from her sisters without accepting the offers of any of them, Slade went to her. "I need to tell you something, will you walk with me?" She nodded, he took her elbow, turned her away from the village and then let go. It was not yet dark, but it soon would be, so he was careful not to take her too far away. "I will be leaving in the morning."

That was not at all what she hoped to hear. "Why?"

"There are other MacGreagors waiting for me to bring them."

"How long will you be gone?"

"Not too long, I hope. I know the way now, but the children are young and we will not be able to travel for long hours."

"Then you will need this." She carefully pulled the piece of mirror out of her belt and put it in his hand.

"Thank you. I will be careful not to break it."

She watched him tuck it into his belt and then looked up at him. "Do you think we will ever learn your ways? 'Tis difficult for me to let lads do things I thought we were to do all these years. My sisters are having the same problem. I am quite certain we have offended at least ten or twelve lads already."

He smiled. "You will learn more quickly than you think. But if you are unsure, Ulla will help and it would be good for her to have new friends. Helping you will help her."

"To keep her mind off of being attacked?"

"Aye, her husband is feeling unworthy just now for allowing himself to be captured. He will need hard work to help him heal too. Ulla makes bowls out of wood, perhaps she will show you how."

"Is hard work the MacGreagor way of healing all hurts?"

"I had not thought of it like that, but I suppose it is."

"Even a broken heart?" she asked.

"Especially a broken heart."

"Then I will be working very hard."

He took her hand and made her turn to him. "Is your heart

broken?"

Suddenly shy, she refused to look at him. "It will be...while you are away."

He lifted her chin with his fingertips. "When a MacGreagor lass is hurting, 'tis a MacGreagor lad's hope she will let him hold her." He put his hand on the back of her head and gently pulled her to him. Then he closed his eyes and wrapped both arms around her. "Do you know what frightens me most?"

"What?"

"That you will find you love another while I am gone."

"I could never love another; I love you and you alone."

"I love you too. If we are betrothed, perhaps I will not fret so much. Will you wait for me and when I return, will you marry me?"

"I will." At last, she lifted her lips to his.

*

Each day after the men left, Neil waited for the Kennedys to show up, and each day when they didn't, he went to sleep grateful. The building and hunting continued, as did the weaving and the bowl making. Sometimes the sisters would begin to sing for no reason at all and encourage others to join in, but most just wanted to hear their wondrous voices and stopped working to listen. Neil didn't mind. How could he, he was one of their biggest admirers.

Glenna had a new project -- where to hide the sisters when the Kennedys showed up. She began to notice there were several more men than normal working on the new cottages, hoping the sisters would sing. They were MacDuffs and Grahams she would soon discover, and for just a brief moment, she missed that old stonewall and the drawbridge that could keep the sisters safe.

CHAPTER XII

Taral was upset. She finished her time on the loom, stormed out the door and quickly walked down the path. Without a thought as to where she was going, she crossed the open courtyard, passed the playing children, went beyond the last cottage and started down the floor of the valley.

She did not see Neil nod to Geddes or notice when the man began to follow her.

Once the clan chose a new pattern and color combination for their plaids, she tried hard to get it right, but it never quite suited her and daily her frustration grew. For years, she created the blue ones and it was difficult to remember to incorporate the green. Or maybe she just wasn't concentrating. She had no cottage of her own, which a woman twice widowed should have by now, no privacy, although Jessup was rarely there, no husband, and...no good reason not to let herself cry. So when she got a respectable distance away from the others, she let her tears flow.

Geddes stopped, clasped his hands behind his back and waited. He wanted to go to her, but the woman had enough trouble without feeling as though a man was interested in her too soon. There was, after all, a certain length of time set aside for mourning, and she was a widow of only a few weeks. Yet it was difficult to see her cry so hard and not reach out to her. Finally, he could stand it no more and cleared his throat.

She was surprised to find she was not alone and tried to quickly dry her tears. "How long have you been there?"

"Neil does not want the lasses who are with child to walk alone."

That made her tears flow anew and she began to sob. "You know about the baby? Does everyone know?"

His heart was breaking for her, but still he did not open his arms. "Would you like me to hold you?"

"Not just yet."

He understood and tried to comfort her with his soft words. "There are few secrets in a clan."

"I was not yet ready to talk about it, 'tis just too awful."

"You do not want this child?"

Taral dabbed at her tears with her cloth. "I do not want this child to be William's. I married the wrong lad and now my child will pay for it. I am so ashamed."

It was all he could do to keep from taking her in his arms. "No one else feels you should be ashamed."

"They do not?"

"Nay, they think you are very brave."

"I am hardly brave. I killed this child's father. What do I tell him when he is grown?"

"William was about to strike you."

"Aye, but..."

"A lad can easily kill a lass and William knew what he was doing. You will tell your child you killed his father to save his life."

Taral turned to see the look in his eyes. "I did not know about the baby then?"

"Nevertheless, 'tis what happened. William was a Ferguson warrior. I trained him myself and if his blow had not killed you, it could have left you addle brained or unable to move. The lad had great strength."

"You knew him?"

"I did."

"Did you know he was…?"

"I would have warned you before you married him if I suspected anything."

She nodded and then took a deep breath to clear away the last of her tears. "Will you walk with me?"

Geddes heart skipped a beat. It was more than he could hope for and even better than holding her just to give her comfort. It meant she valued his company and wanted to talk to him. It was a hopeful sign that someday…maybe. "I am honored."

She brushed the hair back off her face and began to walk. "I did not love him. With all the talk of war, I thought I would be safe if I were a Ferguson."

"We were all frightened."

"Even you?"

"Even me. A lad has all the same emotions as a lass, we are simply taught to react to them differently."

Taral stopped and turned to him. "Will another lad love William's son as his own?"

"I cannot speak for other lads, but a child is not at fault for anything a parent does."

She liked his answer very much. It was not as though she had not noticed Geddes during their long journey, or since they arrived. It was that she was such a jumble of emotions, considering the attention of a man was the last thing on her mind. Now she would like it if he held her. She would like that very much. "Does Neil truly believe all lasses who are with child need special protection, or does he think you and I will make a good match?"

Geddes smiled. "Either way, Neil is a very wise lad."

She returned his smile. "I am not yet inclined to fall in love or take another husband."

"I know, but you still need someone to care for you and keep all the other lads away until you are ready. I would like to be that someone."

"You are a very good lad. Tell me, if you had a son, what would you name him?"

When she resumed her walk, he was pleased with her. She was back to being that old familiar, good humored Taral that everyone loved so much. And this day she was walking with him. God willing, there would be a day when he would become more than just someone to watch over her. "I have not thought about that. My father's name was Neil."

She giggled. "Neil is a good name but one in this clan at a time is enough. My father's name was Gillies, but I am not all that fond of the name. Do you know your grandfather's name?"

*

The days were long and the nights were even longer for both Slade and Edana. Edana found she missed him so much, she hurt in her heart. It was true, hard work was the only thing that made the time go faster. She had a lot of talents, but discovered most of what she knew how to do was the duty of the MacGreagor men -- such as shoeing horses, herding sheep or milking cows. Learning how to make bowls out of wood seemed an appropriate endeavor, so while she learned she had Ulla also teach her sisters.

Of course, teaching nine women required they be outside where the men could see them, and maybe get them to sing. Some days the hopeful men drove Ulla daft.

Edana knew other men wanted her and it was impossible not to notice, but her heart belonged to Slade, and the ache in it would not be healed in the arms of someone else. So she continued to make bowl after bowl for as long as she could get enough wood chips.

*

Slade finally made it back to the MacGreagors waiting for him at his aunt's on Cameron land. He gave his aunt a bag of salt as payment for provisions and she was thrilled. He told her about the marks on the trees in case other MacGreagors passed that way, and then began to take his charges home. As he predicted, they had to shorten their travel time for the sake of the children. At least he had enough horses and he could take them straight north instead of having to go west first and then north. It saved a considerable amount of time.

He thought of nothing but Edana and sometimes had to

chastise himself for thinking about her, instead of being more aware of the dangers around them. He remembered every word she said and how she said it. He especially remembered her kiss and how she felt in his arms. He let both moments pass far too quickly and charged himself to hold her for a very long time when he next saw her. Then he had to chastise himself again for thinking about her too much. Each day seemed be a vicious cycle of thinking about her and chastising himself. Maybe he just didn't want to stop thinking about her.

Sometimes he worried about the other MacGreagor men and the temptations they provided, but he pushed those thoughts away quickly before he lost his mind.

Finally, it happened. He found a marker and remembered the meadow. No long after that, he found a whole group of MacGreagors, consisting of one man, twenty-six women and an equal number of children, who escaped from the clutches of the MacDonalds. With them, they brought packhorses loaded with tools, food and supplies.

It was late in the night when one of the women decided to tell Slade what happened. As he suspected, their husbands were murdered by the MacDonald warriors and the women and children were carried away. It made him furious.

"Laird MacDonald was so enraged when he learned MacGreagors burned their own village, he lined all the captured lasses up," she told him. "But he chose wrong. Bonnie was clearly daft even before the war and he dragged her away intending to force her. But she had a knife hidden under her skirt and cut him.

He killed her, true enough, but his injury did not heal. He got the fever and died.

After that, people started to believe they had seen daft Bonnie on the paths late at night. Then, they claimed seeing other MacGreagor dead, and the new MacDonald laird wanted no part of that. So we were let go and even given horses and food to take with us. He could not get us out of their village fast enough. Now, MacGreagor land sits empty with most afraid to step foot on it."

Slade smiled and could not help but ask, "Was it the MacGreagors who claimed to see daft Bonnie first?" When she nodded, he had to stifle his laughter so he would not wake the others.

CHAPTER XIII

Again, the whistles repeated up the MacGreagor glen announced new arrivals, and everyone stopped what they were doing to see who it was. To their amazement, most were women and children, but the only one Edana could see was Slade, and she started to run.

He had never seen such a beautiful sight as her running to greet him. Others were running toward them also, but he saw no one but her. Slade raced down the glen and barely got the stallion halted before he got down and let her run into his arms. He kissed her repeatedly and swung her around. Then he remembered what he promised himself -- he promised to hold her forever and never let her go, and he nearly didn't.

He wasn't the only man ecstatic that day. Slade not only brought women, who in time might choose new husbands, but in the midst of the women was…the MacGreagor priest.

-end-

SLAVA

CHAPTER I

She was a very private person and about this, Slava had not said a word to anyone, including her eight sisters. It happened one day when she was herding her father's sheep and she almost did not see him. He was just crossing their land on his way to somewhere else, or so she thought, and when he spotted her, Laird Kennedy and his twenty-man guard paused to stare. When he came closer and she found him to be a pleasing man with shoulder length blond hair. She meant to ask him why he wore her same colors, but when he spoke to her and she looked into his exciting eyes, she forgot.

He stayed and talked to her, helped her herd the sheep and laughed at stories she told about her sisters. His eyes were kind, his voice soft and when he touched her hand, she felt she would lose all control. Laird Kennedy even offered her a taste of his sweet wine and asked her to visit the Kennedy village soon. She hoped it meant he had chosen her -- for in her heart, she had chosen him.

Slava declined his offer to visit unless her sisters could come with her. At the time, she thought she was doing her sisters a favor -- they would be relieved of their tiresome labors, they would be together and each could eventually find a good husband.

However, her father could always be counted on to turn a good thing into a bad one. He heard Laird Kennedy's request and saw it as a way to turn a profit. As if that were not bad enough, when her father admitted he sold the sisters, Edana got upset, which upset the others. On their way to the Kennedys, Slade came along, rescued them from their father and took them to live with the MacGreagors.

The MacGreagor men were very nice and very handsome, but Slava could not quite get Laird Kennedy out of her mind. Edana was in love with Slade, and if the sisters were going to stay together, Slava would have to forget her heart's desire and marry a MacGreagor. Yet it was not that easy. Every time she saw a couple in love, it reminded her she was never going to see that kind of happiness, and it broke her heart.

*

The MacGreagors took every possible opportunity to celebrate. They delighted in the marriage of Walrick to Steppen, the completion of more cottages, the marriage of Laird Graham to Janell, and when more MacGreagors managed to find their way to the new land, they celebrated even more. The sisters sang for every occasion and finally got the painfully shy Mayze to add her glorious voice. Slade wanted to wait until he had a cottage to take Edana to before they married, and she reluctantly agreed. She would have lived under a tent made of deer hides just to be with him.

All in all, everyone seemed happy -- everyone except Slava.

She turned down every request to take a walk or to go for a ride, and even refused to let men help her with the work, unless it was something she found too heavy. The men glanced, watched and sometimes gawked at her, until she felt like she was constantly on display. She hated the feeling very much and soon began to take long walks alone to avoid the unpleasantness.

Still, people noticed. Neil and Glenna were both concerned and the sisters were aware, but no one could get her to say what was wrong. When they asked, Slava only smiled and reassured everyone she was fine.

The sisters noticed everything about everyone, and it was easy to see when one of their own was becoming unwell. It frightened them. Slava had long dark hair with blue eyes and it was no wonder the MacGreagor men admired her. She was truly a beauty and her sisters always thought her the most becoming of them all. She was also the most gentle and the most easily put upon by others. Still, none noticed anyone taking advantage of her, she ate well, did not appear to have any physical ailments and the sisters had but one choice -- make Slava tell -- by force if necessary.

The chore of finding out fell on Charlotte, with whom Slava was the closest. She looped her arm through Slava's and just walked with her beside the river for quite some time without saying a word. When it was obvious they were getting too far away and Slava did not seem to notice, Charlotte turned them around. She hoped her sister would want to talk about it, but it did not appear she was ever going to. They were nearly back where they started when Charlotte finally asked, "What is wrong, sister?"

"What makes you think something is wrong?"

"Well, let me see. It could be because you are second from the eldest, I am third and no one knows better than I when your smile is not true."

"I suppose that is so." Slava turned her troubled eyes away so her sister could not see.

The clear water reflected the colorful sky, a gentle breeze fluttered the leaves in the trees and the air smelled of freshly cut wood. Slava even spotted a Golden Eagle lazily gliding through the air. Everything was peaceful except her heart.

"Sister, what…"

"Are you happy here?" Slava asked.

Charlotte was taken aback by the question. "'Tis better than milking cows, shoeing horses and chasing sheep all day long."

"But if we become MacGreagors, how will we know we could not have been happier with some other clan?"

"I suppose we cannot know for sure. Still, there are several very handsome lads…"

"Aye, but we have seen so few other lads in our lives, how do we know there are not handsome lads in other clans?"

Charlotte was not at all sure where this conversation was going, and she was beginning to get even more concerned. "I suppose that is true too. Laird Graham is not unsightly, nor are the other lads he brought to stand up with him, when he married Janell."

"There, you see, we can have our choice of lads in any clan."

"Aye, but Edana will soon marry Slade and we cannot all be

together unless we stay here."

"But why must she be happy and the rest of us not?"

Charlotte stopped walking and turned to face her sister. "You might as well say it. You know I will not let you rest until you do. Who is this lad who tempts you away from the MacGreagors?"

Slava dropped her eyes and hung her head. "You will hate me when I tell you."

"How could I hate you for being in love? I dream of it daily myself. Just tell me, sister."

Slava took a very long, very deep breath and then quickly spit out the words, "'Tis Laird Kennedy."

Her mouth dropped, her eyes grew wide and her loud voice attracted the attention of sisters, Aleen and Colina. "Nay, it cannot be!"

Colina, third from the youngest, started to run and reached Charlotte first, but Aleen was not far behind. "What is it?"

"Slava is in love with Laird Kennedy."

The two younger sisters stood with their mouths open, which made Slava close her eyes and turned her back to them. Then Aleen began to run to fetch the other sisters. Before long, eight women, from the ages of eleven to nineteen, stood facing Slava -- some with their hands on their hips, some holding their heads in their hands and all with a look of horror on their faces.

"But we hate the Kennedys," Nessa breathed.

It was Edana who realized what the news truly meant, found a rock to sit on, and stared at the water in the river as it cascaded over large and small rocks. "We vowed to always stay together.

How did this happen?"

Slava had tears in her eyes when she sat down beside her eldest sister. "He came while I was tending the sheep. He talked to me for a long time and…"

"And you preferred him?"

"Aye." Slava studied the troubled expressions on all their faces. "Truly sisters, there is no need to fret. We will stay with the MacGreagors and we will be happy."

Edana put her arm around Slava's shoulders. "All save you. How can I be happy knowing you are not?"

Slava's tears began again. "I cannot be the cause of your misery either. What are we to do?"

Charlotte bit her lip. "Sisters, they are watching us and Slade is coming. They know something is wrong, what shall we tell them?"

CHAPTER II

Edana thought for a moment and when she looked, Neil had come to the river and looked as though he was about to head their way also. "Tell them 'tis a private matter and we wish to be left alone." She watched Charlotte go to Slade, wait for his nod and then come back. Then she watched Slade report to Neil. By then, all the sisters were sitting on rocks close to her.

"Thank you, Charlotte." Edana tried to comfort them with her smile. "Perhaps there is a way to settle this."

"How?" asked Aleen.

"We will all go to the Kennedys, see if we like it there better, and if Slava still loves him."

"Aye," said Alison, "and if she does not still prefer him, we can come back. I know the MacGreagors would let us."

Edana nodded. "I know they would too. 'Tis settled then?" She looked from face to face and then saw Alison's frown. "Alison?"

"What if she does still love Laird Kennedy? Will you stay with her even though you are betrothed?"

"I will. I am the eldest and 'tis my duty to make all of you happy if I can. I promised our mother."

Nessa was not convinced that was sound thinking. "But what if some want to stay and others do not? You cannot make us all happy, 'tis not possible."

Edana lovingly touched the end of Nessa's nose with her finger. "We have not had to decide anything as grave as this before. I suppose that is why God made nine of us. With eight, we might be four on each side, but with nine one will always break the tie."

"Then half of us could be happy and half of us not?" asked Nessa.

"This is all my fault." Slava wiped the tears off her cheeks. "Edana, you are the only mother the little ones remember and now I have ruined everything."

Edana shook her head. "'Tis your fault for not telling the rest of us, but not your fault for falling in love with a Kennedy. I am convinced we do not think clearly when we fall in love. Once we are with the Kennedys, perhaps I might find I do not love Slade as much as I thought."

Charlotte looked horrified, "Do you mean, when we fall in love, 'tis not forever?"

"I do not know, perhaps not." Edana admitted. "Walrick loved his wife very much before she died, and now he loves Steppen very much also. I guess we can love more than one lad, but how will we know unless we go to the Kennedys and find out?"

Slava did not believe a word of it. In all the days around the MacGreagor men, she had yet to find one that enticed her away from the feelings she had for Laird Kennedy. A woman might love two men, but not at the same time. Edana was just trying to make her feel better and she loved her sister for it.

"You are too late," said Edana.

"What?" Slava asked.

Edana kissed her sister's cheek. "You are thinking you should not have told us, and you are also thinking of refusing to go to the Kennedy Clan for my sake. But you are too late. I have made up my mind and if the others agree, we leave in the morning."

Whenever Charlotte wanted to cheer them up, she pointed to each and counted them. "One, two, three…" They were well aware none of them were missing, and her counting always made them laugh. It also got their attention.

Charlotte stopped counting. "I think a journey will be good for us. How often have we traveled? Not very often and never all of us together. I remember a time when we wanted to see the world."

Edana giggled, "It was you who wanted to see the world and you were only twelve."

"Well I still want to see the world. Like you said, we have known so few lads, how can we choose husbands unless we have seen other clans? I say we go to the Kennedys." She raised her hand and watched as one by one, the others also raised their hands. Even Slava raised her hand, although she was the last and it took several moments.

Edana took a relieved breath. "Good, we will have a word with Laird MacGreagor and then gather our things." She stood up, helped her sisters stand up, put her arm around Slava's waist and started to walk toward the Keep. "I do not see that anyone needs to know about Laird Kennedy. We will simply tell them we choose to leave."

*

He had only been back inside the great hall for a few minutes before the sisters came in and Neil was shocked by their announcement. "You do not like it here?"

As was their custom, Edana spoke for all nine sisters. "You have been very kind and we like it very much, but we wish to visit other clans."

In the company of women, he always stood and when Glenna put an arm around him, he was grateful for her support. He could not remember any woman asking to leave the MacGreagors and now nine of them wanted to go. He abruptly narrowed his eyes. "Has someone hurt one of you?"

Edana was genuinely surprised by his question. "Nay, none of us are hurt. We simply want to…we want to see other clans."

"You are aware 'tis dangerous for lasses to travel alone in the Highlands. At least let my guards see to your safety."

"I can protect us. I have done it for years, and we are not so easily captured as you think."

"What can we offer to get you to stay?" asked Glenna.

"Nothing, but we do hope you will let us come back once we have finished our visiting."

Neil tried to smile. "Of course you may come back, but I insist you let my lads guard you, 'tis not…"

Edana squared her shoulders, "Laird MacGreagor, you do not understand. We are nine sisters who have taken care of ourselves for most of twenty years. Slava fought and killed a wild boar. I have killed three lads and Charlotte has killed two. We are not so helpless as to need your protection. We shall leave in the morning alone."

In stunned silence, Neil watched all nine file out of the great hall. At length he tightened his arms around his wife, "I was not expecting that. How will we live without them?"

"They will be back. At least Edana will be back, she loves our Slade very much."

"I hope you are right. Slava was crying earlier, I am convinced something more is happening and I am determined to find out what. God help the man who has hurt one of them."

Telling Slade the bad news was going to be the hardest part and Edana waited until the last possible moment. Any other evening, she would have been with him, but he was honoring her earlier request to leave them be. Just before time to retire for the night, she found him leaning against a tree at the edge of the courtyard.

His eyes instantly lit up and he opened his arms. "I was hoping you would come."

"I prefer that you do not touch me."

"Not touch you? You are about to become my wife, why am I not allowed to touch you?"

"My sisters and I are leaving in the morning." Edana bowed her head to let her words sink in. It was all she could do to keep from crying, and it was important not to let him see how upset she really was.

"Have you stopped loving me?"

That was the question she feared most. She thought about it a lot before she went to find him. Which was kinder -- telling him she still loved him but may not come back, or setting him free? As hard as she tried, she could not make herself set him free. "I am unsure."

Slade took a deep breath. He knew something was wrong, but he didn't think it was this. "You are unsure."

"I need time away."

"You just had time away. I was gone nearly a month, was that not time enough?"

"Nay, it was not."

Slade put a hand on top of his head and tried to make his mind work, in spite of the hurt that was starting to consume him. "Is there another lad? Someone you neglected to tell me about from your past? Do you go to him to find out?"

"Nay, there is no other lad."

"Then what?"

"Please do not ask. We must go away and that is all." She did not hug him and she did not kiss him...she didn't even look him in the eye. Edana merely walked away.

CHAPTER III

Although her heart was breaking for her sister, Slava couldn't help but be excited about seeing Laird Kennedy again. Edana, on the other hand, was curled up in bed and doing her best not to burst into tears. In the courtyard, Slade paced and tried to understand what was happening, while inside the Keep, Neil and Walrick were making plans.

Neil sighed, "I had no idea the sisters were accustomed to killing, but after what Slade said about their father and brothers, it should not surprise me. Slava even fought a wild boar. How many lads have done that and survived?"

"None that I am aware of. Who will you send to follow them?"

"Our best is Geddes. If anyone can track the sisters without being spotted, 'tis Geddes."

*

Everyone gathered at the edge of the village to watch them leave and everyone was upset. The sisters were dressed in the clothing they arrived in, their hair hung loose around their shoulders and now that they were well rested, each was even more beautiful than when they first arrived. They tied their bundles on the backs of the elder ones and just as they had when Slade found them, they mounted two on each of four horses. Edana rode the fifth horse and kept her arms free in case she needed to protect them.

She still had the bow and arrows belonging to the man who attacked Arthur and Ulla, but Neil worried that it was not enough. He gave Edana a dagger, waited for her to tie the sheath around her waist and then lifted her onto her horse. She nodded her appreciation and without even looking at Slade, she turned and headed the five horses down the glen. None of the sisters looked back. They could not. Each had tears in their eyes and they did not want the MacGreagors to see.

The unmarried MacGreagor men were unhappy, the women would miss the singing, Glenna's matchmaking hopes were dashed and Ulla, who spent a great deal of time teaching them how to make wooden bowls, started to openly weep. She threw her arms around Slade to comfort him and he appreciated it, but he doubted he would ever find comfort again.

Jessup, on the other hand, got mad. This proved life was temporary and no one knew that better than she. Love could be lost in the brink of an eye and it wasn't going to happen to her a second time. She wanted happiness and she wanted it before the man she loved suddenly decided to leave or worse -- died. Determined, Jessup walked straight to Lucas, tightly folded her arms and brazenly looked into his eyes. "I am sorry to hear you are going blind."

"I am not going blind."

"Is that so? Then why is it you cannot see me?"

She started to turn away, but just in time, he reached out,

caught her around the waist and pulled her to him. "I was afraid you would deny me."

"I did not think you were afraid of anything."

"Only you." He lowered his lips to hers and took her breath away.

*

Geddes was Taral's protector, her friend and her confidant, especially when she wanted to talk to someone about the baby. She was definitely carrying the child of the man she killed and she was learning to accept it -- with Geddes help. So when he took her arm and urged her to walk away from the others, she willingly went with him.

"Neil wants me to follow the sisters to see where they go."

"Alone?"

He smiled. "Does that mean you fear for my safety?"

"Perhaps. You do know how to fight, do you not?"

"With lads, aye. Against a bonnie lass I am helpless."

She poked him in the arm, "Then you must avoid all bonnie lasses."

"Except the ones I am sent to follow?"

"I suppose you cannot help that." Taral wrinkled her brow and folded her arms. "Must you leave now?"

"Very soon. Will you be well until I come back? I will not be here to keep all the unmarried lads away."

She giggled, "I will ask Jessup to protect me."

He couldn't help but return her smile. "I should go now." He hesitated just long enough for her to stop him.

"Wait. I…"

"You what?"

"I…"

Geddes searched for the meaning in her eyes and then hoped he guessed right. "Would you like me to hold you?"

She quickly went into his arms. He held her close and made himself remember how delicate her feelings still were. He wanted to very much, but he did not dare kiss her. "I will only be gone a few days." He quickly pulled away while he still had control and hurried to his horse. He mounted, looked back and then smiled. He already had Taral's image seared into his mind, but this time she seemed to have some feeling in her eyes and the feeling was for him.

*

Slade was so distraught by the time Ulla walked away, he did not even notice Neil standing beside him. His eyes were glued to the sisters and he prayed Edana would turn and come back to him. She did not and too soon, the sisters were out of sight.

"You must not follow her." Neil waited, but the man did not seem to hear. "Slade, a lad in love does foolish things."

"I do not think I can endure this."

"You have no choice. We must honor their wishes or they will not come back."

At last, Slade had a glimmer of hope. "You mean there is a chance they will?"

"They even asked if they could. I believe there is something left undone and they go to settle it."

"Did they say that?"

"Not exactly. Try not to fret, Geddes will follow them and at least we will know where they are. If you are wise, you will have a home ready for Edana when she does come back."

Slade knew his laird was right. To keep from losing his mind, he needed to work and building a home for her, and the decorated furniture he'd dreamed of building for months, was the best work he could think of.

*

"Are you certain you can find the Kennedy Clan?" asked Sheena. Already she was tired of riding.

Instead of in the trees, Edana kept them in the open as they traveled. "I am certain. A few years ago father took me with him to barter wool with the MacClurgs and I remembered their glen. He did not take me to the Kennedy village, but he pointed the way and it should be easy enough to find."

"I remember that," said Slava. "Father said he would not go near the Kennedys, because they were dreadful people."

"True and getting around their land took an entire extra day."

Colina laughed, "If father did not prefer them, then we most likely will. What do you think they are really like?"

Edana was happy to answer, "According to the brothers, Laird Kennedy got his teeth knocked out in a fight and was very old, almost forty as I recall. He died a few years ago. I wonder why the new laird has not yet taken a wife."

Nessa rolled her eyes. "Perhaps he is simple like the brothers and just now thought of it." She glanced at Slava's frown. "Well, 'tis possible."

Colina caught her breath, "You do not suppose they are *all* like the Kennedy brothers, do you? They laugh at jokes that are not funny, run around in circles when we tell them they cannot do something, and gulp down their food as though they have not eaten for a week."

"I doubt they had anyone to care for them save us," Charlotte put in. She adjusted the heavy bundles again and tried to sit up straighter so her back would stop aching.

Aleen wrinkled her brow. "I wonder if they have died by now without us."

"Nay, they have found someone else to pester. That is the one thing they are good at." Charlotte chuckled, "Or…once father did not come back, they moved right in and are sleeping in our beds."

Nessa laughed too, "Aye and they have taught themselves how to cook, clean, milk the cow and make their own cheese. I hate making cheese. I hate it very much."

"So do I," Aleen said. Suddenly her eyes brightened. "Now that father is gone, we could go home, throw the Kennedy brothers out and live in all happiness by ourselves?"

"'Tis not a bad idea," said Alison. She urged her horse to go a little faster so she could keep up. "We could forget being in love and just dream about it instead. After all, we cannot be certain marriage will make any of us happy. Look what it did to mother."

"She is right." Nessa sighed. "Did you see how that one MacGreagor lass's husband was? He tried to tell her everything to do and say. I would not like a husband like that at all."

Edana shifted her position and looked back. She pretended her only concern was talking to her sisters, but it was clear she was watching something behind them. "That is why we must choose our husbands carefully. Mother said to spend time with them, find out what they think about, what they love and if they easily lie. If a man lies to anyone at all, he will not be a good husband." Edana finally stopped her horse, sighed and looked at Slava. "We might as well let him ride with us."

"We might as well." Slava turned her horse around until she faced the back of the procession. "Geddes, we know you are there."

Sheepishly, he moved his gelding out of the trees and walked him to the sisters. "How did you know it was me?"

Edana grinned. "Your sword makes a particular noise when it hits your shoe. We notice all sorts of things about people and yours was one of the hardest to hear. Who sent you, Neil or Slade?"

"Neil is worried you will not be safe enough."

Edana puffed her cheeks. "I am worried also. I always think I can do anything just as well as a lad, until I actually have to. Would you ride in the back then and see to our safety?"

"I will be honored. I will keep out of sight, but if you whistle I will come."

"I have a better idea," Slava said. "We will sing. Our singing has saved us before. Lads intending to harm us pause to listen when we sing, and it gives us time to decide how best to protect ourselves."

Aleen nodded. "'Tis why we stay together."

"Singing it is then." Geddes turned his horse and went back into the trees. He was pleased with Edana's honesty, and if he were not already so deeply in love with Taral, he would like a clever wife like Edana. Yet Taral was the woman in his heart and always would be. All he had to do was wait and after holding her that morning, he hoped his wait was nearing an end. The child was William's but it was also Taral's and loving her child would be easy.

"Did he hear all we said?" Laura wanted to know.

"Probably, but it does not matter. We will be in the land of the Kennedys soon." Edana urged her horse forward again.

CHAPTER IV

A little more than an hour later, the sisters stopped and dismounted to rest. Geddes did not join them and he hoped they knew why. He was not the only one following the women and he was outnumbered by at least eleven. If the sisters were perceptive enough to know he was behind them, perhaps they knew about the others as well. He hoped so.

Why the other men held back, he could not quite figure out and what they wore was even more curious. Soon a thirteenth man joined them and he had his answer. Geddes stayed in his hiding place and watched as the new man rode to the sisters and then dismounted.

Edana looked at the stranger and then looked at the pleased expression on Slava's face. It was not difficult to figure out who this man was. "You are Laird Kennedy?"

"I am. I am happy you have come back to us." He meant his smile for Slava, but did not take his eyes off of Edana.

Edana did not mean it as an insult, but she could not take her eyes off his kilt. "Sister, I believe there is something more you did not tell us." She turned to glare at her Slava.

Slava took a deep breath. "Would you believe I forgot?"

"Nay, I would not believe you forgot. This lad wears our same colors. Pray tell me we are not Kennedys." When Slava bowed her head, Edana closed her eyes.

Laird Kennedy was confused. "You did not know you were Kennedys?"

"We did not and we are not pleased." When Edana opened her eyes again, they were ablaze with anger. "How could you leave all nine of us at the mercy of a father who worked us like lads? Some laird you are."

Instead of being insulted, Laird Kennedy nodded. "I deserve your anger, but I did not know about you. I was in the process of rescuing you when you disappeared."

Edana was not so easily persuaded and stared into his eyes without blinking or looking away. He did not blink either, but he did finally look at Slava. If he was lying, Edana thought, he was very good at it. "We believed we were being forced into marriage."

He turned his attention back to Edana. "Is that what your father told you?"

Aleen usually let her sisters do the talking, but this time she could not hold back. "I am only eleven and I do not want a husband."

He quickly turned to her. "Of course not and I would not have allowed it. Your father lied."

Nessa rolled her eyes. "Again."

"Come, I will take you home."

Edana stood her ground. "Not until you promise we may leave if we are not happy with you. We have only come for a visit. That is all."

"But you are Kennedys," he said.

"Says you," Edana shot back.

Laird Kennedy knew she had a point. The color of a cloth was not proof, and from what he heard, the sisters were kept in seclusion all their lives. Why would they trust him? He took a moment to look at the faces of all nine sisters. Each had hair the color of night and eyes that could pierce a man's soul. Each would make some man happy and the clan was always short of eligible women.

For as long as he could remember, his parents hated each other and life was one long agony. It was for that reason he did not want to end up married to a woman who hated the sight of him. He intended to marry a woman who loved him and whom he could learn to love. Slava, he believed, was that woman.

Still, allowing the sisters to leave was not going to make the Kennedy men happy, and keeping warriors happy was a priority for a laird. He might actually suffer a revolt over such a thing and a revolt was not something he could afford. What he could do, however, was pretend to agree to their terms, and hope the sisters would decide to stay on their own accord. If not, there were other ways to persuade them -- there were always other ways to persuade a woman to do almost anything. He smiled finally. "Agreed."

Edana nodded. She knew the Kennedy guards were there and was not surprised when they rode into the meadow and surrounded them. However, they had not captured Geddes and she was relieved as well as impressed with his skill. She knelt down by the small stream of water, cupped her hands, drank and then walked to her horse.

The first thing she noticed was that none of the Kennedy men got down to help the women mount...not even their laird helped. She doubted Neil had ever let a woman mount without help -- it was the MacGreagor way and he was *The* MacGreagor.

Slava noticed too and was surprised by it. However, she was not surprised by the way being near Laird Kennedy made her feel. He was just as handsome as she remembered and just as strong. He was shorter than most MacGreagor men, but he stood up straight and did not slouch as the Kennedy brothers did. For that, she was greatly relieved.

*

Still hidden in the trees, Geddes needed to get back to Neil, but he was concerned. It did not appear the Kennedys meant to harm the women, but he did not like the look on Edana's face. He took a deep breath and let it out. Perhaps he should see what kind of reception the sisters were about to get from the Kennedy people before he went back to Neil.

*

Slava would have liked it if Laird Kennedy had chosen to ride beside her, but he had not. Instead, he rode at the head of the procession. He sat tall and proud in his saddle, but he was not beside her where she could see his wonderful eyes and feel them on her. Perhaps that was just how a laird was supposed to act. Perhaps later he would pay special attention to her...perhaps.

She also would have liked it if he, or one of his guards, relieved her aching back of the two bundles she carried. For a man, the bundles would not be heavy, but after several hours, they felt like a great burden to her. Yet the Kennedys had not offered.

For a brief moment, Slava wondered if she would be expected to shoe the horses and milk the cows once she got to the Kennedy hold. Such thoughts were not helpful and Slava tried not to compare any of her current circumstances to the way women were treated by the MacGreagor men. Not all clans were the same, she told herself.

However, when they entered the Kennedy village, the people were not smiling and certainly did not warmly greet them. If they bothered to look up from their boring lives at all, they did so with frowns or deep furrows in their brows. The women stirring large pots glared and Slava soon felt as though she had done something unforgivable. The worst thing she could think of was to show her ankles, so she quickly glanced down. That did not appear to be the problem, but just in case, she pushed her skirt down a bit more.

Occasionally one of the men smiled, but the sisters were clearly not as welcome here, as they had been when they first rode into the MacGreagor village. Slava's assessment was correct -- not all clans were the same and this one was downright unfriendly.

The cottage they were taken to was nice enough, but Laird Kennedy did not take them there himself, nor did anyone offer to help them down off their horses. Instead, one of his guards waited for them to dismount, opened the door, nodded for them to enter and then pulled the door closed behind them. No one helped them with their bundles either, but there were no cows to milk…at least not yet.

Cautiously, Aleen tried the handle to see if they had been

locked in. To her relief, it opened and she stepped out just in time to watch two of the guards take their horses away.

"I want to leave already," whispered Nessa.

"Where do you think Geddes is?" Alison wanted to know.

Edana found a candle and went outside, located a campfire and lit it. Shielding the small flame with her hand, she took it back inside and put the candle in the well-worn holder. The cottage was large, the floor was swept and in a few moments, men began to bring in two more beds. Then two women brought bedding and food for their noon meal.

"I am Slava." Slava was trying to be friendly, but neither woman acknowledged her introduction. Yet one woman seemed to be waiting for the other to leave. She did not introduce herself, but she did bite her lip as though she desperately wanted to say something. "What?" Slava carefully asked. The woman only shook her head, backed away until she was out the door and then turned and left.

"How very odd," Edana said.

Second from the youngest, Laura started to giggle, "Maybe they are all like the Kennedy brothers. They are witless."

Charlotte was thinking of something else. "All these years we thought the brothers were Kennedys, but we are the Kennedys and they wear different colors."

Alison couldn't help but roll her eyes. "The Kennedy brothers are not Kennedys? What a fine joke that would be."

Slava opened her bundle, found her brush and began to make herself look more presentable. "I wonder why the people are so unfriendly. Laird Kennedy did not appear to be unkind, but the people…"

"Perhaps we should ask them." Aleen went to the door and pulled it open again. "We should take a walk and see if any of them will talk to us."

CHAPTER V

From his hiding place at the edge of the Kennedy village, Geddes could see the women were neither fondly received nor pleased with the reception. Still, they were safe for now. He looked up at the sky to judge the amount of daylight he had left and then darted away.

*

The Kennedy village was old, the paths were well worn and some of the cottages were beginning to crumble. However, others were in good repair and the sisters speculated it was the same in all villages. They admired the flowers near some of the cottages, nodded to the people who seemed to be interested in the newcomers and continued to stroll up and down the different paths.

"Why do you think they are so glum?" Slava whispered to Charlotte. They followed behind the other sisters and looked so much alike it was sometimes hard to tell which was which.

Charlotte paused to peek through the open door of one of the older cottages. "I do not..."

"Because they prepare for war."

All nine sisters turned around to stare at Laird Kennedy, and each wondered how he managed to sneak up on them.

It was the beaten path that kept his movements so quiet, Edana decided. "With whom do you fight?"

"A clan that had something we wanted," Kennedy answered.

"What?"

"You."

He looked a little too smug for Edana's taste but she smiled anyway. "And now that we are here?"

"War will not be necessary. However, I am still missing a deerhound. You would not happen to know where he is, would you?"

"I do."

Laird Kennedy was pleased. He wondered if the sisters would lie to him and what he would do if they did. "Who?"

"The dog is with the MacGreagors."

"The new clan?"

Edana held her smile. "They said they left their home in the south of Scotland to avoid a war. They will be pleased to know they do not face another."

He narrowed his eyes a little and sneered, "Are they cowards?"

"I would not call them that. You will not either once you see them. They are very large lads."

"Bigger than I?"

Slava did not like the tone he was taking with her sister. "Much, much bigger than you," she answered and wondered if he would try to strike her for her insult. If he did, her mind would be permanently set against him. He did not even seem upset. Instead, when her eyes met his, she melted.

"Well, now we have no need to see if these very, very large

lads are cowards or not. My lasses are preparing a feast. I understand the nine of you sing very well and I will hear this singing."

Edana had to think fast. She could not be sure Geddes was not somewhere close, and she told him singing would be the signal that they needed help. "We do not sing for strangers."

"I am not a stranger, I am your laird and tonight you will sing for me." With that, he turned and walked away.

Slava waited for him to get far enough away before she touched Edana's arm. "What do we do now?"

Edana leaned closer. "We find Geddes and tell him…if we can."

*

Without the slow pace of the women, it did not take nearly as long to get home as Geddes thought. Even so, it was nearly dark when he arrived. As soon as he entered the MacGreagor courtyard, he slid down off his horse, handed his reins to a waiting boy, opened the door and hurried inside the great hall. Slade saw him coming and was right behind him.

"They went to the Kennedys." He paused just long enough to catch his breath. "The Kennedys are preparing for war."

Neil quickly stood up. "War against whom?"

"I do not know. Their village is less than half a day away. The sisters made it clear to Laird Kennedy that they had only come for a visit, but …"

"What?" Neil asked.

"The Kennedys wear the same colors."

Slade could not keep silent. "But the sisters believed they had no clan and said they had never seen the Kennedys."

"And I believe them. Slava knew somehow, but Edana was shocked and so were the others. The thing is, if Laird Kennedy does not keep his promise to let them leave, even the King of Scotland cannot help. They are, after all, Kennedys and their laird has a right to keep them."

Neil started to pace. "Could you tell how close the Kennedys are to going to war?"

"I could not. The people did not look happy and hardly welcomed the sisters. They are sharpening their weapons and making arrows, but I dared not stay long enough to see much more. The Kennedy laird has three deerhounds like the one Slade has, and I feared the dogs might give me away if I stayed longer."

Neil poured a goblet of wine for Geddes and watched him drink. "You will take three lads with you in the morning to watch them. Send one back each time you have something to report. You have done well, go to your rest."

"One more thing, the sisters noticed me. I thought they would send me away, but Edana was happy for the protection. She admitted she is not as brave as she wants others to think. Anyway, the sisters know I was watching and they promised to sing if ever they needed me."

"Do they know you have come back?"

"Nay, there was no way to tell them."

"Did the Kennedys see you?"

"Nay, of that I am certain."

Neil watched Geddes go and then turned to Slade. "How is the work going on your cottage?"

The message was clear and Slade hung his head. His laird wanted him to be nowhere near the Kennedys. For a warrior, it was the hardest of all commands to obey.

*

The sisters could not find Geddes, although they even wandered into the woods to look. No one said they couldn't, so they did. They therefore suspected he had gone back to the MacGreagors and most of them were relieved. Edana would have felt less alone if she could see him, but at least the MacGreagors knew where they were.

Something was not quite right in the world of the Kennedys and all nine sisters felt the same. There was little to do to fill the time but wander around and then go back to their cottage and wait. When it was time for the evening meal, two guards came to fetch them. By then, the people outside were far more friendly. Two of the women actually smiled as they walked by, and it eased their apprehensions.

The Kennedy great hall was much larger than the MacGreagor's. All sorts of weapons, both new and ancient, hung on the walls for decoration and thick animal furs covered the dirt floor. The table was considerably longer and could seat fifty people. It was adorned with bowls of apples, berries and grapes, along with goblets for water and wine.

As soon as they entered, the sisters came face to face with Laird Kennedy and eight other men. Colina, Laura and Aleen quickly moved to stand behind their older sisters.

"They will not hurt you," Laird Kennedy promised.

Edana was not pleased. "We are not inclined to take husbands. Send them away."

He looked disappointed. "How do you know you are not inclined, you have not yet met these lads."

"We are not inclined to meet them either. We did not come here to find husbands."

"Why did you come here then?"

Slava watched her sister, saw that she could not think of an answer and took it upon herself. "We are here to see you and you alone."

"I see." He was encouraged. It must mean she was interested in him and if she wished to see him alone, he could find wives for his men later. "Leave us." The Kennedy men began to grumble, but when he raised his hand, they quieted and left. "You will sit beside me, Slava."

She smiled, but it was not the kind of smile she might have turned to him just a few minutes earlier. Slava was not happy with his obvious attempt to marry off her sisters, but she decided to be pleasant, unless he gave her more reasons not to be. When he motioned to a chair near the head of the table, she sat down. As soon as he sat, Slava looked him right in the eye, "My father did not lie after all. He was indeed bringing us here to take husbands."

"Slava, that was not my doing, you must believe me."

"Then why did you have eight lads here when you know very well four of us are too young to marry? You even told Aleen this very afternoon, you would not allow a marriage for one so young."

"I meant only to give each of you someone to talk with during our evening meal and that is all. I thought that way you and I would have more time to ourselves."

It was a sensible answer...sort of, and she sort of believed it. She wanted to believe it. Otherwise, she was faced with the possibility that he was a very despicable man. Just in case, she let him know where the boundaries were. "Heretofore, you will have no lads for my sisters to talk with. They can talk to each other if they are lonely."

He smiled. He was not accustomed to a woman telling him what to do, but this woman was more beautiful than he remembered. There was something about her eyes and the way her hair hung around her shoulders. He was still gawking at her hair when he realized he was making her uncomfortable. He nodded finally and the servers began to fill their bowls with ham and cooked vegetables.

CHAPTER VI

The sisters said very little as they ate, but they didn't miss a word of Slava's conversation with Laird Kennedy. "How long have you known about us?"

Laird Kennedy swallowed his bite of food and took a drink before he answered. "Two MacDuffs came to tell me about you. They declared the nine of you sing like birds and I would want to hear you."

"Why did they not tell their own laird?" asked Charlotte.

"I suppose because you are Kennedys and not MacDuffs."

Edana was pretty sure they were talking about the two they always thought were Kennedy brothers. "What did they ask in return?"

"Their price for showing me where you were, was seven sheep and three cows."

Slava nearly dropped her spoon and stared at him in disbelief. "Did they mention a wife?"

"Nay, I recall nothing about a wife."

Slava was still staring at him. "Our father said he sold us for seven sheep, three cows and a wife. You are quite certain the Kennedy...MacDuff brothers did not also ask for a wife?"

"One wife for two brothers? I think I would remember if they had," he said.

Edana could tell her sister's rage was building as was her own. "Laird Kennedy, if you agreed to pay seven sheep and three cows to the brothers just for telling you where we were, how is it, do you think, our father came up with the same sum for actually delivering us to you?"

Laird Kennedy looked genuinely stunned. "I do hope you are not accusing me of something."

Edana was not about to back down. "Not yet. 'Tis just that I find the two matching sums curious. It would appear you offered that sum to the brothers who in turn offered the same sum to our father. But never have I known the brothers to forfeit a margin of profit."

He studied her searching eyes, "Obviously there is a liar among your acquaintances. The question is -- which acquaintance?"

Edana slowly smiled, "You are very good. Perhaps someday I shall challenge you."

Just as slowly, he returned her smile. "Perhaps someday I shall let you."

At only thirteen, Colina was thoroughly confused. "Challenge him over what?"

Edana lovingly touched Colina's arm to get her attention. "Laird Kennedy has managed to avoid answering my questions, not once but twice. That was very clever of him."

Colina nodded. "That *is* very clever. Most of us cannot outwit Edana."

Laura did not care about all that. "Seven sheep and three

cows? Is that all you think the nine of us are worth?"

He went from a swelled chest having thought he outwitted Edana to a near collapse over Laura's directness. "I did not buy you; I bought the directions to find you."

"Have you already paid?" Laura said. "If you have, you should demand it back. 'Tis we who came to you."

Laird Kennedy slowly let himself smile again. "I am just now reminded why I do not allow lasses to dine with me often. They have a way of turning things…"

It was Aleen who interrupted him this time. "I think we should kill father, our brothers and the Kennedy…MacDuff brothers."

"So do I," Nessa agreed.

He chuckled. "You do not really mean that." Yet when none of the women so much as smiled, he decided to more carefully consider their words. Yes, they were beautiful, but what did he really know about them? They were nine women who lived quite alone and might well be extremely dangerous. Perhaps Slava was not so beautiful after all.

The room was deadly still and none of the women remembered that the serving people were standing by the wall listening to every word. Then Edana noticed that one of the women looked terribly satisfied while the other was near a state of panic. For a moment, Edana paused, but it could not be helped. The sisters needed to know exactly what this man was about. "Laird Kennedy, would you really have gone to war to get us back? The MacGreagors did not snatch us away, you know."

"We were told they did?"

"By whom, the brothers or my father?"

"Your father."

There was no doubt in Edana's mind that he was not telling the truth. Laird Kennedy let them think his only involvement was with the brothers, but just now he admitted talking to their father. She felt bad for Slava's sake. "Then father is alive?"

"Why would he not be?"

"He had no brides to bring you and he believed you would kill him? Did you kill him?" Edana asked.

"I will say it again. I was not expecting brides and therefore I had no cause to kill him."

"But you did see him, otherwise he could not have told you the MacGreagors took us," Edana said.

"Perhaps I misspoke. I should have said your father sent word you were taken by the MacGreagors."

Slava sweetly smiled to put him off guard. "Oh I see. You were not expecting brides, so for no reason at all, father sent word that we were taken."

Laird Kennedy glared at the woman he hoped to fall in love with. "It would not be uncommon for a lad to report the kidnapping of nine daughters, now would it?" He next turned his glare on Charlotte, "I have not heard from him lately, did you kill him?"

The question surprised Charlotte, but she was quick to turn it to their advantage. "Nay, but we will if you like."

In spite of himself, Laird Kennedy liked her quick wit. "Should I ever require it, I will let you know. Perhaps when you talk to your father, you…"

"We will not be seeing him," Charlotte interrupted. "But I do have a question. Where does the King of Scots live?"

"In Glasgow this year, after that who knows?"

"That is what I thought. We shall see him next. How far is Glasgow?"

"Several days, I am afraid."

Charlotte hid her displeasure. Of all the sisters, she was the only one to see Glasgow and knew it was not that far at all. "We will need to ask for supplies in that case. My sisters are good hunters, but some barley would sustain us much better."

Laird Kennedy shoved his bowl away, folded his arms and turned to Edana. "Do you intend to take the younger sisters with you?"

Aleen grinned. "Of course she does, I want to marry the King."

Laird Kennedy laughed. "He will be pleased to hear it, but his wife might disapprove."

"I can wait, I am not old enough to marry yet anyway and maybe there will be a new king by then."

Charlotte pushed her bowl away also, "We shall leave in the morning."

"I would prefer you wait a day or two?" he said.

"Wait for what?" Edana asked.

"If you must know, I would like more time to win your sister."

"Which one?" asked Nessa.

Laird Kennedy turned to her, "Which one do you suggest?"

Nessa narrowed her eyes. "I do not like you, so I prefer you do not choose any of my sisters."

CHAPTER VII

Outwardly, he was pleasant, but on the inside, his blood was boiling. These women did not know their place and with one hand, he was tempted to show them. Still, he wondered how many had daggers hidden under their skirts and bet they all did. Nine of them could do some serious damage if they had a mind to. Just then, he remembered the two serving women, looked at them and wondered if either would help defend him. He doubted it.

He slowly got to his feet, and although he tried to hide it, his eyes betrayed his anger. "Nessa, you will not speak to me in that manner. I am your laird whether you like me or not. As for choosing a wife, we will leave that up to your sister."

Charlotte was suddenly alarmed by his manner and stood up as well. "It has been a long day, we should go now."

When they all rose, he put his hand up. "I wish to speak to Slava alone."

Slava shook her head. "'Tis not proper. Either I go with them or they stay with me."

He wanted to throw something but he withheld his ire and forced his smile. "As you wish. Good night then."

*

"At least we did not have to sing." Slava sat down on her bed in the cottage and folded her arms. "Did anyone see Geddes when we came back?" None of them answered.

"I do not like his dogs. They sat in the corner and watched us the whole time. I do not like them at all," said Colina.

Edana sat down on the bed next to Slava and folded her hands in her lap. "Are you very upset?"

"I am devastated. He hardly said a truthful word. Even we did not know Slade was a MacGreagor and father surely did not, therefore, he could not have sent the message. Laird Kennedy expected brides, killed our father and discovered where we were." Slava did not cry but she wanted to.

Said Sheena, "The Kennedy brothers must have found us, who else knew what we look like?"

"We are nine sisters who sing, how hard would we be to find?" Nessa began to undo her plaid and get ready for bed. "We should warn the MacGreagors somehow. Laird Kennedy said he no longer intended to attack them, but how can we believe him?"

Aleen sighed. "The people seemed happier. Perhaps he was not lying about that."

"You have a good heart, Slava," Charlotte said. "You try to see the best in all people, but there is something wrong with this lad. He wants something and he wants it bad enough to lie to get it."

"Aye," said Slava. "He wants me. He touched my hand and not in the way a friend might touch another friend's hand."

Edana tried to smile reassuringly, "Did it make you love him still?"

"Oh sister, what am I to do? I do prefer him above all other lads, but he is…"

"A liar," Charlotte said for her. "We are not more than two days ride from Glasgow at the most. He wants us to think 'tis a long journey so we will not go."

Sheena grinned at Charlotte, "Speaking of liars, since when are we going to see the King?"

"I could think of no other way to get us out of here. I meant to say the King is expecting us and we might well have to claim that, if Laird Kennedy does not let us go in the morning."

Alison raised her hand, "How many think we are trapped here?" All the sisters raised their hands. "We should make a plan. In the morning, we will tell him we have decided to stay another day. That way he will not try to limit our walks. Then we should look for the easiest way out. In fact, I should go now and see where the guards are posted."

Laura was still dressed and agreed. "I will go with you. Maybe we can find Geddes."

Edana watched the door close behind her sisters and then began to undress. "Mother said there was trouble when she and father married. Father's clan did not allow a marriage to someone from mother's clan. Father must have been cast off and that is why we never knew we were Kennedys."

Charlotte was shocked. "Why did you never tell us this before?"

"I never needed to before. We did not care which clan we belonged to as you might recall. Anyway, the brothers must be our mother's family, which explains why we were constantly feeding them."

"That is a frightening thought. I never imagined we were related to them."

"Mother said father was a handsome lad. She had only seen him twice and she did not know he was stupid."

"I am the most like him, am I stupid?" asked Aleen.

Edana grinned. "If you were I would have drowned you years ago."

Charlotte got into bed and covered herself. "Why did we always think the brothers were Kennedys instead of MacDuffs? I mean for what possible reason did father lie about that?"

Slava rolled her eyes. "Father never needed a reason to lie. He just said something without thinking and before he knew it, he was stuck covering his lie with more lies, so no one would guess he was lying."

"Aye and he fooled no one but himself."

"Do you think he is dead?" asked Aleen.

Edana leaned over and kissed her littlest sister on the forehead. "Do not fret. If he is, he will lie and say he is not." She started to go to a different bed when Aleen caught her hand. "What is it, little one?"

"I do not want a husband."

Edana decided it was her turn to sleep with Aleen and keep her warm. She crawled over her sister, got under the cover and drew Aleen into her arms. "You will not have a husband until you choose one, I promise. Now go to sleep."

All her life Aleen managed to fall asleep while her sisters

talked. With all the chores they did all day, the only time they could truly talk was at night, and the little ones were not about to lose sleep over it. Mostly the talk was about their dreams of having a husband and a home of their own someday, which bored the little sisters. Yet now it was the real thing and she tried desperately to stay awake. Even so, once her sister provided enough warmth, she closed her eyes and drifted off.

"…but could you forget him if we go back to the MacGreagors?" Edana asked Slava.

"Could you forget Slade if we stayed?"

Edana had to think about that for a while. She had been away from him for less than a day and already her heart was aching. How could she ask her sister to be strong if she was weak? "I could learn to live without Slade far more easily than I could learn to live without any of you. And if you married a lad like Laird Kennedy, and I was not here, I would fret constantly. I would find no comfort at all in loving a lad if it means losing a sister."

"I think I love Laird Kennedy, but I do not know. Did mother say how to know?"

"She said to see what a lad is before you accept him. And if there is any doubt, he should be refused."

Slava thought about that for a long time before she finally spoke again. "I must refuse him then, and I should be grateful I have seen what Laird Kennedy is. If you are able to turn away from love for our sakes, then so am I. Alison is right, we must make a plan of escape."

*

It was late at night and if anyone knew, he would be in big trouble. It was forbidden for an unmarried man to go to the cottage of an unmarried woman after dark, but Taral was already inside her cottage when he got back and he would be leaving again before she got up the next morning. So he took a chance and softly knocked. When Jessup answered, he was embarrassed and started to walk away.

"Wait," Jessup whispered.

Not completely dressed, Taral hurried to cover her long shirt and bare legs with a plaid, and quickly took Jessup's place in the doorway. "Are you hurt?"

"Nay, I came to say I am fine. I must go back early in the morning, but I wanted…"

"Thank you, I am pleased you did."

"Good night."

"Good night." She quickly touched his cheek with her fingertips and then closed the door so he would not get caught.

He meant to ask if she needed anything but she did not give him time, and once she touched him so tenderly, he couldn't think what he wanted to say anyway. It was just a touch and it might not mean what he hoped, but she was concerned for his safety and pleased he came to tell her he was all right. Maybe all those things together did mean something…maybe.

CHAPTER VIII

It was not quite sunrise when four MacGreagor warriors mounted their horses and headed to the Kennedy hold. They went first to see if the Kennedys prepared for war, and second to see if the sisters were safe. Not many months before, these same men spied on the MacDonalds and Gill was the one to report to Neil.

Just as the sisters suspected, when they opened their door the next morning, two guards were waiting to keep them from leaving. With a flirtatious grin, Edana approached the first. "Would you be so kind as to tell Laird Kennedy we wish to stay another day? The King is expecting us, but one more day will not alarm him." She waited for his nod, watched him walk away and then rejoined her sisters. The other guard seemed unsure of what to do, but when the sisters began to take a walk, he did not stop them.

The people seemed even more friendly, although some were still reserved. They talked to a few, liked some and did not like others quite so much. They looked up and down the paths, tried to see where their horses were, and judged the distance to the side of the forest that offered the thickest foliage and better places to hide.

Often they stopped to ask questions and it was on one of these occasions that the woman, who seemed reluctant to say something the night before, came to greet them. She was friendly when she took Charlotte's arm and guided her to a tree at the edge of the forest. Someone had carved a picture in the trunk of the tree and it was a very good likeness of a red deer. Soon the other sisters were standing close enough to hear.

"I must speak to you," she whispered.

"What is it?" asked Charlotte.

"'Tis the MacGreagor sword our laird wants and he will stop at nothing to get it."

Charlotte touched the etching with the tips of her fingers. "How do you know this?"

"I tend his children and I overheard him."

Charlotte was stunned. "He has children? Does he also have a wife?"

"He did, but he set her aside and sent her to be wife to a farmer."

Charlotte rolled her eyes. She could just guess who the farmer was. "Why do you warn us?"

"I wish to go with you. We hear the MacGreagors are good to their lasses. Is it true?"

"Aye, 'tis true." She paused when she realized one of the men was passing behind them. "I would love to be able to carve like this, but I am not talented." As soon as the man was out of hearing, she resumed her conversation. "We will be honored to take you with us, but I fear your laird wants to marry Slava. I am not certain we can get away."

"I…" the woman started.

Suddenly, Alison grabbed Charlotte's sleeve.

The guard Edana had spoken to earlier was fast approaching. "Laird Kennedy wants to speak to the four eldest."

Charlotte was neither intimidated nor impressed. "Laird Kennedy knows he speaks to us all or to none of us."

"You dare defy him?" the guard asked.

Slava quickly came to her sister's aid. "Do you dare defy me?"

As his possible future mistress, the guard realized Slava had the upper hand and backed off. "As you wish." He waited and then followed as all nine sisters walked up the path to the Keep.

Edana quickly glanced at Slava and knew her sister's state of mind was somewhere between hurt and furious. Of the nine of them, it was Slava who could be the most dangerous. She had never killed a man, but that was because she had a look that left no man in doubt of what she was thinking. Even Edana knew to stay clear when Slava was enraged.

This time, when the sisters were escorted into the great hall, they found three men waiting with Laird Kennedy. Slava guessed these three were why Kennedy wanted to see only four of them. She did not bother to smile. "You wish to speak to us?"

"You look upset."

"Do I? Perhaps it is because you are attempting to marry off my sisters again. Or do you need three lads to defend you against nine helpless lasses?"

She was fiery and there were occasions when Laird Kennedy found that exciting in a woman. If she wanted to spar, he would accommodate her. "I doubt any of you are helpless. Would you care for some wine or do you intend to stand there and glare at me all day?"

"I do not care for wine. For what reason did you send for us?"

"If this is your character, perhaps I do not want to marry you."

"Perhaps I do not want to marry you either. Tell me, would I be your second or third wife?"

"So you know. No matter, you would have learned it soon anyway. You would be my second wife…should I choose to have you."

"Allow me to save you the trouble. I do *not* choose you."

He glared at her for a very long time and then turned away. "I see." He walked to the table, poured himself a goblet of wine and drank it down.

The three other men were ogling the women and Edana's ire was beginning to surface. She slowly stepped away from her sisters and began to draw closer to the men. "Do you prefer us?" All three men nodded and smiled. "How many lads do you suppose we have killed?" Each looked at her in disbelief.

"Come now," Edana went on, "we are nine sisters raised by a lazy father and two stupid brothers, who had no notion of ever protecting us. You must know we quickly learned how to kill." She drew just a little bit closer and noticed that Charlotte was following her lead.

"You have killed a lad?" asked the first.

"Only one?" asked Charlotte, enjoying how the men were slowly backing up. "You think too little of us. Some lads say we are bonnie and some do not care to marry us before they…you know what I mean. Sadly, they did not live..."

"Enough of this foolishness!" shouted Laird Kennedy. His dogs abruptly came to attention and waited anxiously for his command, but he ignored them. He thought to approach Slava, grab her hair and force her to her knees, but he could not be sure she had no weapons, and thought better of it. She was not worth getting cut over. Still, he did draw close enough to try to intimidate her. "Tell me where they hide the MacGreagor Sword."

Slava rolled her eyes. "And I thought it was me you could not live without." She put her hands behind her back and accepted the dagger Nessa slipped into her grasp. "We do not know where they keep it. We have not seen it."

"But you do know it exists."

"Aye, it exists." Slava answered. "The people have seen it, but that was before we went to live with them. Laird MacGreagor has it somewhere, I suppose. Have I mentioned how big the MacGreagor lads are? If you attack them, you will die."

He narrowed his eyes and glared at her again. "I fear no lad."

Slava shrugged. "I am sure you do not. Is that all? We would like to go now. The King is expecting us and we must not keep him waiting."

At length he nodded. Then he watched all nine women leave and pounded his fist on the table. "See that none of them are let out, not now, and not ever!"

*

Geddes led the way to the village, showed them where to tie their horses, and took the MacGreagor men to the same place he hid and watched the sisters the day before. During the ride there, he tried to memorize the sound his sword made when it slapped against his shoe. Once they were well hidden in the forest, he duplicated that sound hoping at least one of the sisters would come close enough to hear him.

It worked. Aleen heard it, skipped off to gather her sisters, and then pretended to show them something in the dirt.

"Geddes?" Edana whispered.

"Aye."

"Tell Neil they want the sword."

"Do you know when they will attack?"

Edana giggled as though one of the others said something funny and shook her head.

Charlotte leaned against the tree and softly sang her words. "We will try to leave in the morning, but we do not think they will let us go."

"We will tell Neil," said Geddes.

Charlotte put her arm around Aleen and started back up the path. Soon the others followed, but Edana stared into the forest as though she wanted to say something more. At last, she decided against it and turned away.

As soon as the sisters were gone, the MacGreagor men spread out and crept from place to place until they were convinced war would most likely come the next morning.

Gill sent Mark back to warn Neil.

*

Neil, Walrick and Gelson were discussing the next day's work when the door to the MacGreagor keep opened. Considering the length of time they were gone, Neil was greatly surprised to see Mark back so soon. He listened intently to the younger man's report, sent him to find a meal and then sat on the edge of the table.

"So it begins." Neil thoughtfully ran his fingers through his dark, wavy hair and took a forgotten breath. "At least now we know who has been watching us. It was only a matter of time before one clan or another coveted the sword, especially now that it is the meat of so many rumors. This is precisely why my grandfather claimed it was lost."

Walrick nodded, "He was a very wise lad and so are you. No one will find it, but keeping it well hidden will not stop the attacks."

"Nay, but I know what will."

"What?" asked Gelson.

Neil took his seat. "First, we capture the Kennedys who are watching us, then we…"

CHAPTER IX

When the Kennedys were first spotted watching them days before, Neil wanted his men to just keep an eye on them. Yet once the order went out to capture the Kennedys, the MacGreagors showed their superior skills by stepping out from behind trees and bushes, so close as to greatly frighten the Kennedys. Soon all six Kennedys were rounded up, stripped of their weapons and seated on the ground where two MacGreagors could keep an eye on them.

*

With a clean plaid over her arm, the same woman who warned them of the attack, knocked on the door of the sister's cottage in the Kennedy village. She quickly glanced around, saw that no one was watching and as soon as the door opened, she stepped in. "I am Cathella, will you let me go with you?"

Colina took her hand and urged her to sit on the bed beside her. It was Edana who answered the question, "I do not think 'tis wise for you to go with us, but…" She saw the look of total despair in the eyes of their new friend. "We could send MacGreagor lads back for you."

Immediately, the woman's eyes lit up. "I would give anything."

Slava quickly took the seat on the opposite side of Cathella. "They are very big lads, but they will not hurt you. Where should they meet you when they come?"

Cathella did not have a ready answer and that pleased Edana. The last thing she wanted to do was set a trap for the MacGreagors. On the other hand, the last thing the MacGreagor men wanted to do was pass up a chance at having a wife. "Where are our horses, we have yet to find them."

"They are hidden but I can take you to them."

"In that case, we do need her," said Charlotte.

"Aye but the moon is not full and I am not convinced they will let us leave in the daylight."

"You are right; they will not let you leave. You must wait until there is a full moon," Cathella agreed.

Aleen gasped, "Another week? We will all be married by then and I do not want a husband."

"I must go," Cathella whispered. "I am in the cottage at the end of this path if you need my help. Please try to take me with you." She squeezed Edana's hand, got up, peeked out the door and then left.

"Do you trust her?" asked Slava.

Edana sighed. "I want to, but we have enough to do to get ourselves safely away. Perhaps one or two of us can come back for her."

"The MacGreagor lads might take her now if we ask them."

"Aye, but we dare not talk to them again so soon. Someone might notice."

Slava suddenly stood up. "Sister, we have to send the little ones away with the men tonight. Aleen is right, by morning we could all have husbands."

The panic in Slava's eyes alarmed Edana. "He cannot force us."

"Aye but he can. All he need do is threaten to kill one of us and we will agree to anything."

"I had not thought of that," Charlotte said.

Laura put her hands on her hips, "I will not go. If we are missing, they will punish the rest of you and you know it. I choose to stay with you."

"As do I," said Aleen. "We stay with you no matter what."

Said Nessa, "I have an idea. Suppose we challenge the Kennedys to a horse race? Our freedom would be our price."

"The Kennedys are not the wisest people, possibly, but they would never agree to give up nine women over a horse race. Even if we won, they would not honor their agreement." Edana's shoulders slumped. "We must think of another way."

Laird Kennedy knew he needed every able bodied man to fight the MacGreagors. According to his scouts, they were indeed very large men. Yet he was of the opinion that the bigger they were, the harder they would fall. As soon as the sun shed its first light, his men and his dogs fell in behind him, and he went off to war.

In the Kennedy village, women cried, children clung to their mothers and the elders shook their heads. All this for a golden sword? Nonsense. But then, what was the point in training warriors if they never went to war? Besides, the death of men was the best way to even out the numbers of men vs. women. To the old men, it made sense.

Halfway there, the Kennedys rode proud and hard across a meadow without ever realizing twenty MacGreagor warriors were watching them from the trees.

Befuddled, Gelson scratched his head. A boy of twelve sent to scout the area could have spotted so many MacGreagors, but the Kennedy laird didn't seem to think he needed scouts. For a moment, Gelson wished he had stayed behind to see what Neil would do with this foolish and overconfident man. Nevertheless, he waited for the last Kennedy to ride out of sight, turned the horses south and went off to rescue the sisters.

It was near time for the noon meal when the MacGreagors entered the Kennedy village. The women poured out of their cottages to watch. Some came out with swords in their hands determined to defend their children, but the intruders still had their swords in their sheaths. Instead of attempting to capture or harm the women, the men calmly walked their horses down the path toward the Keep. It was the oddest thing the Kennedys had ever seen.

Gelson looked from cottage to cottage trying to guess which one housed the sisters, until he finally spotted two men guarding a door. The two men were elders and as soon as he halted his horse, they ran away. He dismounted and was about to knock on the door when Edana opened it. "Are you ready to come home, lass?"

She threw herself into his arms. "We are so happy to see you. We tried to leave this morning but they would not let us."

Cathella ran up to Edana and grabbed her arm. "May I go with you?"

Edana looked at Gelson, saw his smile and then pointed to one of the warriors. He leaned over and put his arm down. Cathella ran to him, grabbed his arm and swung up behind him. In mere moments, six other women did the same and then Edana looked again at Gelson. "Is Slade very angry?"

"He builds a cottage for you."

She smiled and bowed her head. "I will be happy to see him. Can you help us find our horses?"

"I know where they are," said Cathella. When she pointed, the man she was riding with turned his mount. Soon all nine sisters had their bundles, were lifted into the arms of MacGreagor men and followed. As soon as they located their horses and the five eldest got settled, Gelson, Gill and all the MacGreagor men happily escorted them back toward the place they would call home from that day on.

*

Attacking the MacClurgs and the MacGreagors was no easy task. Their village was in the wide-open spaces where they could see an enemy coming from a considerable distance away. Even hiding in the woods would not conceal the Kennedys long enough to make a difference.

Before he decided to attack, Laird Kennedy had forgotten that, felt his spies should have reminded him, and made a mental note to see that they were better trained in the future. It occurred to him he had not heard from a spy all day, but he was on the move and they probably could not find him. He dismissed it as a trivial thing, just as he dismissed several other trivial things that day.

CHAPTER X

Kennedy halted his men at the edge of the forest to rest the horses and consider the situation. In the distance, thin plumes of smoke rose from chimneys, women appeared to be going about their chores as usual, and it did not look like the MacGreagors knew they were about to be attacked. He smiled a very smug smile. Surprise was indeed on his side.

He had been to this village before when Knox was laird, but even he did not like Knox and never came back. Now he was trying to remember how the inside of the Keep was set out, and where the MacGreagor might have hidden the sword. Killing the MacGreagors was one thing, finding a hidden sword was another, and if he had to, he was not above torturing people to learn where it was.

Of course, it was possible the MacGreagor laird wore the sword, but he doubted that. Laird Kennedy thought if he had it, he would not wear it except for special occasions...such as his wedding day. For a moment, he regretted losing Slava. He could always force her to marry him, but he could never trust her and he had already endured one unmanageable woman. Why ask for another?

Once he felt the horses were rested and himself ready, he decided it was time. If he wanted that sword, which he fervently did, he was willing to fight for it. He drew his weapon, waited for his men to draw theirs and put their shields forward. Then he let out his war cry and began the charge into the valley.

No MacGreagor warrior came out to fight him.

The women, he noticed, grabbed the children and were running into the woods, but without knowing where the men were, chasing after the women might draw them into a trap. After the battle was over, he planned to take the women, but first he had to fight the men. Still there were no men to fight and he began to fear a trap so much, he slowed his advance and called back his dogs. He was not yet half way there.

Then he spotted the man standing in the window of the third floor staring at him. It had to be Laird MacGreagor and Laird Kennedy thought he had the coward trapped. He wanted to smile his smug smile again, but where were the MacGreagor warriors?

By the time he neared the outside cottages with no battle to fight, he was spooked more than he could stand. He raised his hand to halt his men and reined in his steed. Nervous horses danced as the Kennedy warriors stopped and turned to look in every direction. Still, they were all alone in the wide glen.

It was a trap, it had to be! But what kind of trap and where was it? Assured they were not surrounded, Kennedy kept his eyes on the man in the window and so did his men. If it was a trap, Laird MacGreagor would nod his head to spring it, and then they would hopefully have plenty of time to react.

The minutes seemed like hours as Kennedy tried to decide what to do. Abruptly, the man left the window and in a little while, he and another man walked out of the Keep into the courtyard.

Laird MacGreagor's mount was an exquisite brown stallion with white markings, a white tail and mane, Kennedy noticed. Beside Laird MacGreagor, another man rode a very large dapple gray. Yet the two men rode out alone to face his bloodthirsty men and Kennedy became even more anxious. He repeatedly chewed his lip as the MacGreagor came closer and closer and thought to run, but that impulse passed quickly. Still he could not see the trap or figure out what to do.

Just close enough to talk, Laird MacGreagor stopped his horse. "You have come for the MacGreagor curse?"

The Kennedy blinked repeatedly and did not quickly answer. "Curse?"

"Once you have the golden sword, every other clan in the world will want to fight you for it. 'Tis indeed a curse. You will not sleep, you will fear everyone, even your wife, and you will surely die trying to keep it."

Neil paused to let his words fully register. "Perhaps I should give you the sword and rid myself of the curse. Of course, to save my clan I would have to tell the world you have it."

Kennedy saw his meaning and as of this moment, his only concern was leaving the glen alive. "Where are your lads?"

Neil smiled. "Right behind you."

Kennedy quickly turned in his seat. While he and his men were watching what Laird MacGreagor was doing, far more MacGreagor warriors than he knew existed, moved out of the trees and now surrounded them on three sides. The river, he knew, was straight ahead of him.

He was aghast. The MacGreagor men had not drawn their swords, did not carry shields and did not even look upset. He began to wonder exactly who these MacGreagors were. They had a golden sword they called a curse, the men were large enough to be giants, they could sneak up on a whole army without being heard, and if they wanted blood, he would be dead by now. "Who are you?"

"Some say we come from an ancient king of the Vikings. He and his wife sought a peaceful existence here in Scotland and so do we. Go home. A golden sword is not worth the deaths of all these lads." Neil turned his horse and headed back.

Walrick nodded to Laird Kennedy, turned and followed Neil. He waited until they were nearly back to the Keep before he looked at his laird, "Did you really come from a Viking?"

"Hell, I do not know. The lad looked terrified and I do not want him coming after the sisters later. So I gave him one more thing to consider. How many stories have we heard of the strange powers of the Vikings?"

"Too many to count."

"Then we might as well let them think we have such powers. Perhaps the next laird who wants to take the sword, or our lasses, from the giants will think better of it."

Walrick looked back. "He is leaving. I hope our lads got the sisters out."

Neil laughed. "Except for Gelson and Gill, I sent only unmarried lads. They got the sisters out."

*

Taral did not think she would miss Geddes so much, but when Neil sent the women and children to hide in the forest, she did miss him. She missed him a lot. He had not said as much but she suspected he loved her. He did not kiss her, but she did not know she wanted to be kissed. In fact, he had been more than patient with her, far more than most other men would have been.

She set her sewing in her lap and looked across the table at her friend. Jessup was happy now that Lucas admitted he loved her and asked her to marry him. Their wedding would be soon and then Taral would be alone in the cottage. A few weeks ago, she thought that was what she wanted, but now she might not like being alone. Now she wanted to be happily married.

Suddenly, Taral could not wait for Geddes to come home.

*

There was no need for a trumpet, or a golden sword, or even whistles to announce the arrival of the warriors bringing fifteen women from the Kennedy Clan to the MacGreagors. Instead, the people heard the voices of the singing sisters in the distance and gathered to listen. How they had missed the sound of their voices.

Leading the way, Connell lifted Aleen up and held on to her so she could stand on the horse and pretend to be the music conductor. Everyone found her antics delightful. Even Slade dared not interrupt their singing, as each step the horses took brought them closer and made their music grow louder and louder.

Taral waited patiently too, smiling to welcome home the man she hoped to marry and when they finally came to a stop in front of

Neil and Glenna, it was Slava who allowed one of the men to lift her down first.

Then she quickly went to stand before Neil. "'Tis my fault we left, but it will not happen again. We have seen how others live and we want to be MacGreagors."

"Then MacGreagors you shall be. Welcome home," said Neil.

Slava stood back and then began to slowly look at all the other men. They were far more handsome than she thought. Indeed, they were far, far more handsome than she thought.

-end-

Coming Soon – Book 3 in the Viking series.

MORE MARTI TALBOTT BOOKS

Marti Talbott's Highlander Series: books 1 – 5 are short stories that follow the MacGreagor clan through two generations. They are followed by:

Betrothed, Book 6

The Golden Sword, Book 7

Abducted, Book 8

A Time of Madness, Book 9

Triplets, Book 10

Secrets, Book 11

Choices, Book 12

Ill-Fated Love Book 13

The Other Side of the River, Book 14

The Viking Series:

The Viking, Book 1 explains how the clan came into being.

The Viking's Daughter, Book 2

Book 3 is coming soon.

Marblestone Mansion (Scandalous Duchess Series) follows the MacGreagor clan into Colorado's early 20th century. There are currently 10 books in this series.

The Jackie Harlan Mysteries

Seattle Quake 9.2, Book 1

Missing Heiress, Book 2

Greed and a Mistress, Book 3

The Carson Series

The Promise, Book 1

Broken Pledge, Book 2

Talk to Marti on Facebook at:

https://www.facebook.com/marti.talbott

Sign up to be notified when new books are published at:

http://www.martitalbott.com

CPSIA information can be obtained at www.ICGtesting.com
Printed in the USA
BVOW02s1850010415

394348BV00002B/134/P